I0563289

Ominous Visions, Grave Decisions

The Skylar Night Ghost Mysteries, Volume 1

K.D. Upton

Published by K.D. Upton, 2024.

OMINOUS VISIONS, GRAVE DECISIONS

First edition. February 2, 2024.

Copyright © 2024 K.D. Upton.

ISBN: 978-1956954067

Written by K.D. Upton.

Also by K.D. Upton

The Daisy Day Mysteries
Mystery of the Charred Bones
Murder in the Orkneys

The Kaitlynn Dahl Mysteries
The Kaitlynn Dahl Mysteries e-book Bundle
Snapshot to a Killer
Graded for Murder
Key to Murder

The Protectorate: A Supernatural Suspense
The Protectorate
The Guardians

The Skylar Night Ghost Mysteries
Ominous Visions, Grave Decisions

Watch for more at https://kduptonauthor.com.

Table of Contents

For the dreamers...

Chapter 1

I dragged my leaden limbs across the closet floor in an army crawl, each gasp harder than the last. The woolen cardigan hung a foot away. Stars floated in my vision, sweat stung my eyes, yet the heavy footsteps on my bedroom floors urged me on.

Sky. This was for Sky.

I pushed my damp palms against the cool wooden floor as I rose on wobbly legs. In a final act of desperation, I lunged and thrust the note into the sweater pocket, ending up as a heap of bones on the floor. Hopefully, she'd manage to find it in time to save herself and the town.

The measured steps stopped at my feet.

"I warned you."

I grunted when the boot kicked me in the ribcage. A hand roughly gripped my waist and flung me onto my back. Above me, angry eyes stared while my chest rattled with each breath. I clawed my throat and wheezed, clutching the ratty, tattered stuffed dog to my chest, unable to defend myself.

"You've lost, Hazel. This land is mine."

Struggling to stay awake, my body grew colder, losing all sensation, barely registering the punch in the gut.

"That's for your meddling. Oh, and don't worry. I'll say nice things at your funeral. I'm sure there won't be a dry eye in the house."

I shut my heavy eyelids. The gasps grew faint, while the lonely steps of my killer emerged triumphantly from the closet.

Despite my failure, there remained a glimmer of hope. I prayed that she would discover the note in time...

I sucked in a last thready wheeze. Focusing on the ground, I let my sweaty palm flop onto the floor.

"Pro...tect... her."

The heat scorched my body as my final ounce of energy flowed into the home.

"It... is... finished."

Chapter 2

Death followed me. It loomed like impending doom, and there was no shaking it. I can't explain it, but it's there, in my dreams, in the flicker of my periphery. Darkness surrounds me wherever I go. Yet, I never feared it. Not until this morning.

I dumped a spoonful of sugar in the ceramic mug and swirled it with a silver spoon, placing it in front of the most amazing person I've ever met. He had the most exquisite amber eyes, plump crimson lips, smooth brown skin, and perfectly straight purple hair. Nuri, also known as Anni Histamine, sat with a perfect pout while sipping his tea. He was the talk of the drag scene in Colorado, and couldn't go unnoticed due to his undeniable magnetism. He was blessed by the gods at birth and embraced his true self without hesitation.

The lavender slip dress highlighted his slim shoulders and long neck, and if I didn't know any better, I would have thought he was a cis female model. The heavens had gifted Nuri with a beautiful appearance and the sweetest soul. It was rare to see him so distressed.

I lifted my gaze from the Final Notice bill after the third dramatic sigh. Over the past few months, the stack had grown a foot high.

"What's troubling you?" I asked, glancing at the bills, questioning how I'd manage to pay them before they permanently shut off the electricity.

He propped his chin on his hand and absentmindedly swirled his herbal tea. "Nothing." No caffeine for him because it caused wrinkles. Supposedly.

"Nuri—"

"Anni. I'm in drag." His gaze flicked toward me for a second and he waved his delicate hand down his body for emphasis.

"Fine. Anni, what's troubling you? Don't say nothing because you haven't finished your cup or touched the scone."

The cardamom scones, made as a thank you for his investment in my herbal remedy store and cafe a year ago, were always his favorite and he never refused one. Not even when he ended his engagement with a wealthy French financier last month. We indulged in a whopping three scones for that occasion.

Nuri ceased swirling and frowned. "Sky, those bills..." He pointed a purple-painted fingernail at the stack I'd stuffed under the counter behind a locked door. "What aren't you telling me?"

My face heated up. I sprayed disinfectant spray on the countertop and roughly wiped it with a towel. "Everything's fine."

Nuri watched me for a few more seconds as I vigorously cleaned a persistent stain from the busy morning rush. The business was busier than ever, but it still fell short of covering the rent. Over the past two years, rent had been increasing rapidly, and although I managed to cover it initially with a steady customer flow, the latest rate hike had left me seriously struggling. If I couldn't find another revenue source and fast, I'd have to close, and that wasn't something I could stomach.

"If everything's fine, then why have you spent the last few minutes on the same spot?"

I blinked. The coffee stain was long gone. I tossed the towel in a tub under the counter and planted my palms on the counter. "I've got it covered."

Nuri reached over and patted my hand. "No, sweetheart, you don't. I'd have to be an idiot not to see the stack of bills you're hiding, and I wouldn't be the best investor if I didn't check up on you myself."

I froze. "Wait. You've called my bank?"

Nuri held up his hand. "Breathe, Sky. It's our business, remember? We're partners." He offered a sympathetic smile.

I snatched his mug and emptied the untouched tea into the sink.

"Hey! I wasn't done with that."

I turned my back and refilled his mug with hot water over a sieve of tea leaves.

"Sky, listen, if times are tough then let's talk about—"

I thrust his steeped mug in front of him so hard a few drops splashed onto the counter. "No," I replied curtly. "Everything is fine."

"Sky, it's not," he said, his voice soft.

I brushed away a few teardrops as the front door chimed. Saved by a customer. But this was no ordinary customer.

Her wavy brown hair bobbed around her shoulders and silver hoops swung in rhythm with her walk. A pair of skinny jeans accentuated her curvy hips, while a cashmere sweater embraced her ample chest. She casually ran her hand through her styled hair and plopped onto a chair next to Nuri, dropping her leather purse on the counter.

"The usual." She patted the counter and eyed Nuri. "Who pooped in your cornflakes?"

A look of distaste crossed Nuri's face. "Disgusting. And I don't eat cornflakes. Too many carbs."

Willow snorted. "Like that's a problem. How many times do you work out in a day? Three?"

Nuri raised two fingers. "What's wrong with taking care of my body? I don't hear any complaints." He smirked.

"How could you? You leave too fast."

Nuri's eyes widened in surprise. "I love openly, and as a result, I receive love in return. There are those who are destined to be with you forever, and others who are only meant to be there for a short time. But I live, Willow. I breathe it in and leave people happier than when I met them. If that's so awful, then I don't want what you have."

I looked at my dear friends in shock and disbelief. Despite both being stubborn, they had contrasting views of the world and cherished each other for it. But as with any strong personality, when their worlds collided, or rather their ideologies, as they frequently did, it was like a supernova explosion.

"Nuri, how many people have you loved and left? The French man only lasted a month. The woman before him lasted two weeks. You always follow this pattern. Wouldn't you prefer something more substantial?"

"Sure, but not at the sake of settling."

Willow Youngblood snorted. "No one is perfect. There's compromise, Nuri."

"That's where we agree. Perfection is unattainable, but that's not what I'm saying."

"Then what *are* you saying?"

Nuri twisted towards Willow, examining her weary features and tightly clasped hands on the counter. "I'll stop when you find the person who lifts your heart and sears your soul, making you unable to imagine life without them."

Willow shook her head. "That's in movies and fairytales. It doesn't exist." Her voice small and weak, she peered at her tightly wound hands.

"Not true. There's someone out there for you, Willow. Don't give up."

Willow flashed Nuri a brilliant grin. "We were talking about you. Not me." She smacked the counter, directing her attention at me. "How about it? Where's my usual?"

Everything shifted in an instant. A sense of calm filled the space between the three of us, tinged with a touch of sadness.

Startled by the feeling, I grabbed a mug and got busy making her nutmeg latte. It had been years since I last embraced my gift, and it unsettled me a bit.

During my early childhood, at the age of five, I had this uncanny sense for people's emotions. For the next fifteen plus years, I worked to suppress it. My maternal grandmother and school teachers made sure of it. My reputation remained intact thanks to my grandmother, who made sure I wasn't seen as a freak, but this time, the old sensation came effortlessly, unlike in my college days. It had solved a murder, but I stopped using it because of the renewed stares and losing my boyfriend. It invaded the personal feelings of others and was seen as a betrayal.

"All I've got are cardamom scones." I placed her plate onto the counter next to her steaming mug.

Willow sighed. "Not my favorite, but it'll do." She nibbled on the corner. "Has anyone seen Trixie?"

At the serving counter, a woman with brown hair and a pixie-like appearance sat to the left of Willow. We all gasped in surprise.

"Are you half fox?" Willow gawked, her hand on her heaving chest.

Trixie Diamond broke off a piece of Willow's scone and popped it into her mouth. "Yummy. May I have one please?" she directed toward me, ignoring Willow.

I set her up with a scone and chocolate milk.

"Lawd," Nuri drawled. "Are we grownups or children? Chocolate milk belongs to grade schoolers."

Trixie gulped down half of the glass and grinned, wiped her mouth with the back of her sleeve, and belched.

"Gross." Willow glared at her in disgust, as if she were a mysterious nocturnal creature. "You'll never attract a guy that way."

"That's where we're different, Willow."

"I hope it's not the only way we're different," Willow mumbled, at which Nuri chuckled.

"When the stars align, and it's meant to be, the right guy will come along. It's up to the ether."

We all shook our heads. It was useless to argue with Trixie. She believed in sprites, fairies, trolls, wizards, and witches, as well as destiny through the stars. Who was I to disagree? My gift made me an outsider, and I'd tried desperately to hide it, but not Trixie. I admired her for fully embracing her uniqueness.

Willow almost snorted her latte. Instead, she sprayed the newly cleaned counter. I grabbed the sanitizing spray and towel and started scrubbing.

"Whatever," Willow waved it off with a flick of her wrist. "Who is up for a night out on the town?"

Nuri became deeply engrossed in his scone as Trixie's eyes fixed on me, her face reflecting a curious and distant expression.

"Come on, guys," Willow pressed. "It can't all be work. Let's blow off some steam."

"What do you have in mind?" I asked, putting the cleaning supplies back. My phone dinged and I pulled it from behind my apron. I shot Nuri a glare, and he nonchalantly shrugged. It was from my bank app. He'd deposited another thousand dollars into the business account. Sadly, it wasn't enough, but I refused to tell him otherwise. Obviously, he hadn't realized the full extent of my financial obligations, and I couldn't find it in me to break the news. Yet.

"This will hurt," Trixie muttered, her eyes sad.

"What?" I stared at her.

"Something bad has happened."

Willow emitted a soft whistle. "Lay off the dope, Trix. You're creeping us out."

A hollow, vacant dread drained Trixie's face of color as she glanced between Willow and me. "I'm so sorry." Her voice cracked, and she stood, reaching for me, but my phone buzzed. An unknown number.

"Hello?" I whispered into the cell, still locked on Trixie's tortured face.

"*Skylar.*" The familiar raspy voice left me quaking. I hadn't heard it in over seven years, "*It's time to come home. Hazel's dead. I've booked your flight out of Denver tonight. Ophelia will pick you up once you've landed and drive you here.*"

"No," I croaked, my throat tight. I stood tall and rigid, my knees locked in place. I struggled to catch my breath as the room spun around like a whirlwind. "No, she can't be. We talked last night."

"*We'll talk when you arrive. Have a safe flight.*"

I hung up and stared at my phone. This was a bad dream. This wasn't real.

"Sky?" Willow glanced at Trixie, who stood by my side rubbing my arm. "What's wrong?"

I opened and closed my mouth several times before finally uttering, "I'm leaving to go home tonight."

I stashed my cleaning supplies under the counter and fumbled to take off my apron.

Trixie put her hand on top of my shaking fingers. "Let me help." She untied the apron and I rushed off toward the kitchen area, which doubled as my office. It was the size of a water closet, but it had room for a file cabinet and a compact desk for my laptop. I flung the drawer open and grabbed my purse, turned, and crashed into Willow.

"Sorry." I laid a trembling hand on her arm to prevent her fall.

"Sky, what's happening? Talk to us."

In the teeny hallway, Trixie and Nuri stood behind Willow. They all stared at me intently, blocking my exit and refusing to move.

I clutched the purse strap on my shoulder. "My Great Aunt Hazel died. I'm leaving. Tonight."

"Sky—"

"No." I raised my hand. "I can't." My lips trembled, remembering those soft brown eyes that I'd never see again. I cleared my throat and stood up straight. "I'll call later. Thanks for your concern, but I've gotta run."

I pushed past three of my closest friends and went to the front door, flipping the open sign to closed.

"Oh," I turned abruptly. "Nuri, would you please run the shop? I'll be gone for a week. Two tops."

"Already on it." He planted his hands on his curvy hips. "But it won't be me. Listen, we don't know much about your Great Aunt Hazel, but we *do* know she was more like a mother to you. You can't do this alone." He tilted his head and grinned.

I glanced from one person to the other, and each had their own grin.

Scratching my head, I glanced back at the door, itching to run. I wanted to flee from everything, but it wasn't feasible this time. "I can, and I must. Your lives are all busy. No, I can do this myself. Thank you for your concern, but—"

"Skylar Wren," Willow barked, "we are your friends, and friends don't leave each other in difficult times. You're not alone, girlie. We're all coming with you."

Tears welled up and I shook my head, unsuccessfully trying to blink them away. "You don't have to do this. I've got a flight out in a few hours, and there's only one ticket. I'm short on cash and..."

Nuri dangled the car keys from his fingertips. "Who's up for a road trip?"

Trixie and Willow simultaneously replied, "Me!"

"Good," Nuri nodded. "It's settled. Now," he eyed me curiously, "where are we going?"

I flicked the tears away and struggled to smile at each of them. "What about the shop?"

"Covered," said Nuri. "Kate's coming in as we speak. She's been bugging me for more hours, and she's more than happy to keep the shop afloat while we're away."

I exhaled a shaky breath. There were no other obstacles to overcome, and no reason to leave my friends behind. Where I was headed, I'd need all three. The past had caught up with me. The past I'd buried. I was ill prepared for the hornets' nest we were about to drive into. So, with a deep breath, I smiled. "We leave in two hours. I'll take the first shift driving." I turned, opened the door, and stepped through. "As to where we're going, any of you Huskies fans?"

Nuri rolled his amber eyes. "Lawdy, please tell me we're not headed for Alaska. It's too cold."

Willow punched his arm. "Too cold? Please." She snorted. "Colorado's cold, but no, it's not Alaska. The Huskies? Tell me you're not into basketball without telling me you're not into basketball."

Trixie giggled. "Connecticut, Nuri. We're headed for Connecticut."

"Better pack warmly," I suggested. "It's also cold there. We'll meet back here in two hours. Oh, and guys? Thanks."

Chapter 3

In the midst of a snow-covered Connecticut morning, my concentration was shattered by an early call while I was barreling down I-91, the slush from the road spraying sideways under my winter tires.

"Kaitlynn?" I whispered in shock. I dared not to wake my sleepy passengers. I glanced at the car's clock. 4:00 AM, which meant it was 1:00 AM Pacific time if my foggy mind was correct. I could see her wavy red hair now, and those blue eyes. Although it had been years since we last saw each other, the college bonds between us remained unbroken.

"Max," her voice wavered. *"He's... he's dead."*

Her choked sobs interrupted the initial shock.

"How?" I asked. "Was it an accident?"

No, it wasn't an accident. Kaitlynn, my best friend from college, relayed the gruesome details and her suspicions.

"Someone murdered him. And I won't rest until someone's held accountable, even if Detective Knight tells me to keep my nose out of it."

"Detective Knight? He's the new guy they hired, right?"

Kaitlynn went on about the newest detective and his obstinance while my thoughts lingered on the deceased. Max Stone was a detective in a small town nestled in the Cascade mountains close to Portland, Oregon. Kaitlynn had mentioned him shortly after she'd moved to Silverthorne. She'd gotten a job as a photographer and was in love with her career change even if it did irk her mother. I'd always thought there was more to Kaitlynn's and Max's relationship than just friends. The way she said his name and talked about him in our almost daily conversations made it clear that there was something more to their relationship. I could sense it, even from a thousand miles away, but now we'd never know for sure.

I spent the next half hour talking to Kaitlynn until she cried herself to sleep. A shiver ran down my spine. The steering wheel creaked under my sweaty grip, remembering those few short hours ago. Her sobbing had soured my stomach and sent my pulse racing.

Though I had been relieved it wasn't her, it might as well have been. Max Stone, the town detective and area hottie, had been murdered.

I yawned and squinted against the sunlight in the rose-colored sky. How odd. December mornings in Connecticut are typically overcast and dreary, but not this one. Unfortunately, I didn't have the time to mull it over. The moan-like grunt from my right made it certain.

"Are we there yet?" squawked the purple-haired, cat-eyed, crimson-lipped drag queen. Nuri sat up and inspected her reflection in the visor mirror. I couldn't imagine driving across the country all made up, but she'd insisted on making a splash in my tiny Connecticut hometown.

Like an omen, we sped past the Welcome to Raven's Hollow, Connecticut sign. Population 27,298. The word "death" was spray painted on "Raven's" in bright red, with streaks that looked like blood.

Slowing down to 30 mph, I murmured, "We're here." I glanced at the town I had left behind in a rush after my high school graduation. "None of it's changed."

Nuri's face twisted in disgust, as if he had just tasted something terrible. "Charming."

I chuckled. "It's not that bad. Not a fan of small towns?"

Nuri tsked. "I loved my small town upbringing, except for the nosy rosies. Oh, and the cheerleaders and jocks. That was awful. The adults in the town grow up to run it, reliving their glory days and living through their bratty children. I could do without that, but everything else is good."

"Wow. What a raving review of small town life." I chuckled.

"It's not bad. I miss the drive-ins, the parties after our basketball team won every Friday night. Oh, and the summer plays. Now *that's* something that I loved. Mr. Parker played a role in my 'coming out' as a transvestite. He's the reason I'm not just another corporate worker making millions."

I stared at him in the passenger seat, unsure if he was joking or not. "Okay, you say that like it's terrible."

"Making millions?" He stuck out his tongue. "It's alright, but it can't compare to living in your own skin. Fakeness kills. Don't get me wrong, I love small towns. But this one?" He shook himself. "Something's... off."

I dropped the topic and instead focused on the town I'd fled years back. Main Street was adorned with Georgian era homes built over two hundred years ago, and inherited by subsequent generations. Of course now, being December, every available light post, street sign, and door was decked with boughs of holly and twinkling lights. It was truly marvelous, and I felt a swell of pride inside me when I saw it. Raven's Hollow wasn't all that bad. Growing up, there were great times, but leaving felt like tearing off a bandaid from a festering wound. Colorado served as the healing air it needed.

"It's... cozy, I suppose," Anni said, forcing a smile on her meticulously made-up face, yet her eyes remained devoid of warmth.

I chuckled. "Wait until you see the house."

Navigating the narrow town, my neck muscles tightened as we headed towards the hill at the town's edge. The overnight snowfall draped the area in a white blanket, making the conifer trees sag and the tiny houses come alive for a busy morning of work, school, and errands.

We hooked a left past the local family-owned car repair shop and crept down the rocky dirt road. Bouncing every couple of feet, the other two passengers woke up

"Sorry!" I called out. "It's only for another couple of miles."

Trixie's emerald green eyes flashed defiantly at me in the rearview mirror. "You could have warned us." She elbowed her sleeping companion. "Willow, we've arrived."

Willow Youngblood sat up and rubbed her muddy brown eyes. In her sleep, she'd drifted to the side and used Trixie's shoulder as a pillow. "Wow, I didn't think the North Pole was real but this sure takes the cake, Skylar. Is Santa Claus next?"

"Funny," I said sarcastically.

I failed to mention her wit. Willow possessed not only a sharp tongue, but also an incredibly sharp mind. Nothing escaped her attention, and if someone seemed off, she detected it even before I did. My gift that is. Or rather my abilities. She didn't have them, not that I knew of, but she was incredibly perceptive. I, on the other hand, refused to believe everyone held some dark secret. My maternal grandmother complained that I saw the world through rose-colored glasses, but I saw it as believing in the best in people. Because of this, I ignored my gift. Sensing people's moods felt wrong. It was a glimpse too far. An invasion of privacy. It was also the reason I left this wondrous place a little over seven years ago.

"How's it feel to be back?" Trixie piped in. She ogled the pristine snow with tufts of green grass peeking through.

Willow bopped Trixie on the arm.

"Ow! That hurt." Trixie rubbed her shoulder while Willow glared in warning.

"It's alright, Willow. She didn't mean any harm."

Trixie grimaced. "Sorry, Skylar. I forgot—"

"Why we're here?" Willow snapped. "You're flightier than Skylar."

Here we go again.

Despite their quirks and strong personalities, my friends were the best in the world. I constantly wonder how I got so lucky. Their differences led to constant disagreements. Still, it was better to have them with me. Poor Kaitlynn didn't have anyone near her at the worst possible time. I sent a quiet, love-filled prayer to her as I continued down the road toward the clearing half a mile away.

Instead of the usual honeysuckle and witch hazel, the snow-covered scenery showcased overgrown weeds and branches. It looked more like a scene from a horror film than my cherished childhood sanctuary.

A layer of untouched snow, half a foot deep, covered the circular drive in front of the deteriorating home. Green shutters, barely hanging on, showcased the home's broken and battered windows. The cosmetic issues were minor, but the warped and drooping side porch was a different matter.

The silence inside the car was deafening when we came to a stop just feet from the front door.

Nuri whistled through her teeth. "Have mercy. This looks worse than a crime scene."

"Nuri Ari," Willow snapped, "hold your tongue if you have a lick of sense in you."

"It's Anni Histamine, darling." She gestured to her exquisite purple sequined gown and white fur coat. "And I call it like I see it. If you have a problem with honesty, then I suggest you invest in noise-canceling headphones."

"Let's not argue," Trixie piped in. "We're here to support Skylar. I think it's darling. With a little elbow grease, it'll shine like a new penny." Her plump pink lips gleamed in the rearview mirror.

At that, it erupted into a maelstrom of quips that roared within the confines of my SUV. I left them to argue among themselves while I exited the vehicle and made my way up the creaking front steps to the front door. Despite the smashed windows and worn exterior, the house radiated warmth.

I removed my gloves finger by finger, and laid my palm on the weathered oak door. My fingertips and palm were greeted by a wave of heat. How?

Flexing my fingers, I reached out and turned the warm handle. Crap. It was locked. I moved to the left, snow crunching with each footfall, and approached the sagging porch. No dice. I'd have to try the back.

I slipped on the ice, but managed to avoid doing a full split. Thank goodness I do yoga every day, otherwise I'd be feeling the consequences for a week. I brushed off the light snow from my coat and sleeves, then looked through the back door window. A flicker of movement caught my eye. I squinted into the dusty darkness of the kitchen. Puffs of my white breath fogged the window, and I wiped it off with my glove.

"What the...?"

I stumbled backward and almost fell onto a snow-covered flowerpot, now overrun with weeds. A man scowled at me from behind the window. His wavy chestnut hair was brushed back from his forehead, his strong jawline covered in stubble. His brown eyes locked with mine.

"Who... who are you? What are you doing in my great aunt's house?"

I scrambled to my feet, forcefully shoving the door open, and stormed inside, determined to unleash a tirade of questions, but I came to a standstill. I scoured the kitchen, searching left and right, but found nothing. I was alone.

"Hello?" I shouted, my hand on my racing heart.

Silence.

Great. I'm hallucinating now.

Hard raps echoed deeper in the home. I clipped through the house like no time had passed and made it to the front door. After a few rough tugs, it finally gave and my friends joined me, brushing off large flakes of fresh snow from their coats and hair.

Nuri, his purple wig askew, harrumphed, "Took you long enough." He yanked his wig into place and stood with hands on hips, a pout to his red lips. "We were arguing one minute about supporting you, and the next minute you disappeared."

"What he really means to say is thanks for opening the door." Willow grinned. "Where did you go? Don't you have a key for the front door?"

Trixie laid a hand on my shoulder and crinkled her brow. "Hey, what's wrong, Sky? You're pale. Are you feeling well?"

"What?" I had been scanning the foyer, parlor, and stairwell that thankfully remained in fairly good condition.

Trixie giggled. "You look like you've seen a ghost."

"Did you see him?" I blurted. "A man. He's about thirty and yea high," I gestured about six inches above my head of 5'5".

"Excuse me, did someone say man?" Nuri craned his neck into a pretzel, scanning the area.

"Anni, keep your wig on." Willow snorted. "Skylar, what man? Was there someone in the backyard?"

"The man," I insisted. "He was in the window."

Willow frowned. "What window?"

"The kitchen window. He was in the kitchen, but when I pushed the door open he had vanished."

"Alright, you're tired. Let's get out of here. I've checked us into a beautiful bed-and-breakfast about five miles from here. You need food, a shower, and some rest. This," Willow flicked her wrist, "can wait until tomorrow."

I shook my head. "No, I'm fine. I'm staying."

Willow gave me a bewildered look, as if I had magically grown antlers and a tail.

Trixie offered me a reassuring pat on the shoulder. "No one's taking you anywhere you don't want to go. It's your call. We'll stay if you want. Right, ladies?" She nodded at them to signal agreement, but both Willow and Anni just stared at her and then at me.

This was going south, and fast. I wasn't about to leave. We'd only arrived. Besides, I'd been to that B&B. It was cold and drafty, which wasn't any better than here. Plus, it was free to stay here, and since my herbal remedy store in Boulder wasn't exactly taking off like I'd hoped, I barely had enough gas money to get here. Of course, they were unaware, and I wasn't going to inform them just yet, but disregarding money, I wanted to stay. My Great Aunt Hazel was like a second mother, and this place was her sanctuary. She had valued me enough to leave it to me in her will, and it felt as if she were still present. Was it guilt from years of not coming to see her like I'd promised? Perhaps. The least I could do was stay.

I looked around for the light switch, then edged over to the wall beside the parlor and flipped the switch.

"It keeps getting better." Willow crossed her arms against her body and rubbed her hands up and down her arms for warmth. "No electricity. It's settled. We're leaving."

"Not so fast." I scurried around the rushing trio to bar their exit. "This is an old home, but Hazel kept a tight ship. Give me a second."

Great Aunt Hazel had mentioned the faulty wiring of this place. The lights were unreliable, despite several attempts by the electrician to fix them.

"Ah, yes. Now I remember," I mumbled. I formed a fist and slammed it against the wall next to the switch.

Speechless, my friends gazed at the dusty crystal chandelier, which was larger than my SUV.

"Let there be light!" I clapped my hands together and smiled. "Now, who wants to bunk with me in Great Aunt Hazel's room? It's the biggest and has a king-size bed. Plus, there's an ensuite bathroom to die for. Who wants a bubble bath?"

I was halfway up the stairwell before I realized no one had followed me. I turned to stare at them. "What?"

"Um, Skylar, are you sure it's safe to stay here? The wiring is faulty. How long before we go up in smoke? On top of that, does the heat work? The water? Listen, honey, this is a... will be a great home someday, but let's let practical heads prevail and stay the night at the B&B."

Trixie's pixie nose scrunched in disappointment, a flush spreading across her angular cheeks. "I'm sure the bubble bath would be fantastic, but maybe when there's heat."

A loud bang reverberated, accompanied by a puff of sooty smoke. Within seconds, the vents sprang to life.

I rushed down the stairwell and raised my hand towards the ceiling vents. A grin spread across my face. "Looks like we're staying. Heat's running. Who's up for that bath?"

Chapter 4

I rapped lightly on the bedroom door and pushed it open. Tears filled my eyes as I entered the room. The focal point of the room was the four-poster bed, which boasted a quilt made entirely of old t-shirts from different parts of the world. A potted fern, wilted, sat beneath the wide window to the right of the bed, alongside other scattered green plants. Great Aunt Hazel's reading glasses remained on the worn leather sofa chair, as if she would return soon to delve into the next murder mystery.

In whirled Willow. "Why not stay at the B&B? Only for a night."

She paused at the foot of the bed; I remained near the empty chair. Sunlight streamed through the window and cast a halo on the seat. Under the bright light, something sparkled.

"Skylar? Are you hearing me? It's not that I don't understand the sentiment of this place—you practically grew up here. But it's cold, dreary, and we're tired."

I bent down and carefully explored the space between the seat cushion and the chair, my eyes fixed on the object in my hand.

"Skylar?"

Elaborate decorations covered the circular object.

I showed it to Willow. "Is it a button?"

She looked at the object and then at me, her face showing a mix of confusion and surprise. She walked over, her boots clunking with each step, snatched the object, and studied it. After a pause, she handed it back. "It looks like a decorative button. Probably from one of your great aunt's fancy outfits."

"Hazel didn't wear fancy dresses, and this looks old. Like, really old."

Willow shrugged. "That's Nuri's department. If you want a root canal, I'm your gal."

I bit my lower lip to hold back a laugh, but a snicker still managed to escape. "Who would *want* a root canal?"

"You'd be surprised." Willow smirked.

"Right." I stopped trying to understand the male species. Undergoing a root canal was only one such trick men tried to snag Willow's phone number. A woman of means by her own measure and not someone else's was a catch indeed. What man wouldn't desire her? It didn't hurt she was an Elizabeth Taylor look alike, albeit a modern version. "About the B&B, how about you take the other two and go? I've only gotten here and I can't leave."

Willow held up a hand. "No need to explain." She headed for the door, then stopped abruptly and called over her shoulder. "If you change your mind, you know where to find us. I've already called an Uber."

I left Hazel's room, savoring the lingering scent of her signature rose perfume as I closed the door.

Downstairs, Nuri, Willow, and Trixie waited by the front door, concerned about me staying alone shortly after my great aunt's passing.

"We're five miles down the road." Trixie rose on her toes as she was wont to do when fretting.

"Ciao, bella." Nuri wiggled her fingers at me. "If the man shows up in the middle of the night, make sure he takes his shoes off in bed. Otherwise, have a little fun." She winked and whirled out the door, followed by Trixie and Willow, who eyeballed me.

The door closed with a click, leaving me in silence except for the furnace's chugging. I whirled around, admiring the photos, woodwork, and wallpaper, which had only been slightly retouched since it was first installed centuries ago. Hazel had droned on and on about the original owners, their acreage, which had sadly dwindled to only twenty present day. It was hard to believe the house ever stood on 100 acres. The idea of the manpower required for maintenance, especially during the colonial era when slavery was undoubtedly involved, made me nauseous.

I ran my fingers along the oak finial carved by the finest craftsman of his time when a soft knock rapped on the front door.

I sprinted to the door and opened it, chuckling. "I told you I'm fine on my ow—Oh!"

A man stood facing me, his expression guarded. He thrust a manila business-sized envelope toward me. "Skylar Night I presume?" His gray eyes flashed annoyance at me. "This seals the deal. It's the deed to the house. There are taxes you'll need to pay, but you can do that at the town hall."

I glanced at the envelope, then back at him. "Who are you?"

His eyes widened in surprise. "I'm Ryan Irwin."

I waited for him to continue, but he did not. I mused if even a scantily clad female model on horseback would manage to get him to utter a single word. His anger was so intense that it took my breath away.

"Have we met?" I stuck my hand out to shake his, hoping to disarm him, but I needn't have bothered. "I grew up in this town, but I don't recall seeing you around."

He looked briefly at my hand. "I moved back five years ago."

"Moved back?"

"My family left when I was a toddler. If you have any questions, I'm sure your grandmother can answer them." He turned to leave. "Good luck, Ms. Night. You'll need it."

"Wait." I hustled out the door and touched his shoulder.

I gasped in surprise when he jerked away with a disgusted expression.

"I am sorry, Mr. Irwin. I meant no harm." Leave it to me to offend the first person I met once home. This wasn't going the way I'd planned.

His gaze softened slightly, yet his body remained tense. White puffs of breath floated in front of him in the freezing cold. I held the envelope close, watching snowflakes settle on his inky black hair.

"What did you mean? Good luck about what?"

He hesitated, appearing uncertain of what to say. "The home. It's in need of repair." The crinkling of his forehead lasted a mere second, but I'd caught it. While it wasn't usual to perform what Kaitlynn called my "voodoo" on people, let alone strange men, I mentally reached out almost instinctively. He was hiding something, and at the mention of my grandmother, an ounce of preparation was key to whatever scheme she had in mind. My struggle was my inability, or rather inexperience, with performing on demand, but time wasn't on my side. At present, Ryan was marching through wet slogs of snow toward his Jeep, trying for a hasty exit.

"Uh, Ryan?" I jogged forward. Muttering curses to myself for not having a coat on, I accidentally stepped on something solid and fell forward, crashing into him. He lost his balance and lunged forward, hitting the driver's door with a thud. I instinctively reached out and grabbed his chunky wool sweater, holding on as if my life depended on it. Legs in a split, face against his derrière, I clamped my lids shut and wished the ground would swallow me whole.

"Ms. Night?" he snapped.

What I intended to say was "yes?" but it came out as a squawk.

"Kindly remove your face from my backside."

I struggled to find traction, slipping multiple times. I pushed against him in dire need of support.

Ryan, still braced against his car, angled his head to gaze down at me. Did I see a hint of amusement in his eyes?

"Ms. Night, your grip is impressive, but I'd rather avoid being frisked at the moment."

I flushed hot red and jerked. Yet again, I lost my balance and ended up in a mound on the wet snow. He pried himself off the Jeep door and offered me a hand.

I planted my booted heels firmly in the ground and stood up. Huffing from the exertion, I opened my mouth for a hot retort when I was interrupted.

"Skylar Freya Night. Stop fawning after the man and apologize for pity's sake."

As if the below freezing temperature wasn't cold enough, the woman's words sliced through me like an icicle on steroids.

"Hello, Grandmother." I rose to my fullest height, awaiting the inevitable admonishments, while Ryan Irwin observed with curiosity.

"I see you've met my granddaughter," she addressed him. "Trust me, she's flightier than she looks. Have you met my Ophelia?"

Ryan shook his head.

"What a pity." My grandmother unabashedly sized him up, which made the tips of his ears grow redder. "She's a doctor. You'd make beautiful babies."

I smacked my palm against my forehead and inhaled deeply. "Grandmother," I snipped, "why are you here?"

Despite a few wrinkles around her eyes and mouth, her smooth complexion and glossy black hair made her look much younger. While many in town gossiped about her love for boxed hair dyes, only Ophelia and I knew the truth. She didn't need it. For some reason, Grandmother Wren had barely aged. It annoyed me to no end when people constantly mistook her for my mother.

Her mouth twitched at the corners. "Is that any way to greet your grandmother, dear?" She waved me over. "Come give me a hug. It's been nearly a decade. And for heaven's sake, stop accosting this poor young man."

Surprisingly, Ryan failed to smile at her or even take much notice, which was rare in these parts. Grandmother Wren was like royalty here, and virtually everyone catered to her every whim. Not him though. He had already hopped into his Jeep and started the engine.

Ryan Irwin bid a brief farewell, calling, "It's been a pleasure, Ms. Night. Oh, and the handyman comes every Saturday. He'll fix whatever you need."

With the engine roaring, tires spinning, and snow flying, he sped down the long, curvy drive and vanished.

The handyman? Was that who I saw in the house earlier?

"I'm waiting." Grandmother Wren tapped her foot impatiently. The snow never touched her. It was like the snowflakes feared provoking her temper.

I stomped over and hugged her, taking in the familiar scents of honeysuckle and alcohol. Probably from one of her concoctions. She was the reason for my interest in all things herbal. Begrudgingly, mind you. Oh, I loved my grandmother. Aside from my sister Ophelia and a few distant cousins, she was practically all I had left in the world. However, Great Aunt Hazel was the only one who kept me rooted in life. She was the only one who truly understood me and offered encouragement, even when my maternal grandmother was unkind. Hazel reminded me of my mom in that aspect. Poor Mom. I wished she was here now. She'd know what to say. Up until this point, she stood alone as the only woman willing to defy Grandmother Wren.

Grandmother Wren smiled tightly. "How about some tea?"

We meandered towards the warmth of the home.

I shut the door and shook off the bone-chilling cold.

"Let me change into some dry clothes." I trudged up the stairs feeling my limbs creak with each step up.

"I'll get the kettle going. Hazel left you in good supply I imagine." She sighed bitterly. "Hurry up, Sky," she said when I reached the broad landing.

I turned and looked down at her petite form. She remained in the same spot, a smug grin on her face. "There are some things you should know about the house. It requires some whiskey."

Oh bother.

I stomped into Hazel's bedroom, now mine, and stripped clear of the wet clothing, donning an emerald green sweater, slim jeans, and woolen socks. I ambled down the steps, nibbling on my lip. Whenever whiskey came into play, either someone died or she had a trick up her sleeve, which usually didn't benefit me. Since Great Aunt Hazel had already died that left the other option. May the gods help me.

Chapter 5

The kettle made a piercing sound on the old stove, and I filled two cups, adding milk and sugar to one. Tea was something Grandmother Wren was especially particular about in life. She preferred it the British way, and any other way would be tossed aside for a fresh cup.

We sat at the round Formica table from the 1960s, covered with a simple white cloth. The well-maintained Easter egg blue seats with white piping looked almost brand new. The only downside was how they clung to your skin during summer.

Leaning my elbows on the table, I blew on the scalding liquid while waiting for my grandmother to speak. She mirrored my actions as we sat across from each other, in no rush to start. It was pointless to prod her. I'd learned that in my teens. My body tightened when she placed the untouched cup on the table and leaned back in her seat.

"Skylar, this house," she tapped her purple-painted nail on the table, "was gifted to you by your Great Aunt Hazel."

I coughed and spat out my tea, prompting my grandmother to give me a few smacks on the back.

"Get it together, Sky. It shouldn't come as a surprise. You were her favorite."

"But the house? I assumed it would be yours to inherit."

"It's rude of my sister, but she's never been a fan of mine. Leave it to her to stab me in the back posthumously."

It was clear that Grandma Wren was just beginning her pitch. I stayed quiet, expecting the inevitable punch. It always came.

"Everything you see belongs to you. The furniture, the boxes of crap she hoarded in the attic, all of it." She eyed me curiously and her voice dropped to barely above a whisper. "Have you any plans for Honeysuckle House?"

Selling the property quickly, as painful as it was, would solve my money problems. The herbal shop I opened in Boulder after college wasn't thriving as I had expected in the few years since, and I needed the money from this sale to keep it running. However, the idea of selling this home had its own share of difficulties. This place had been in our family for eons. I have a vivid memory of Hazel proudly stating that we were among the original founders in this area, and this house was constructed by our ancestors many generations ago. Among the twenty acres that remained, there was a designated area that served as a family cemetery, where the Wrens, Nights, and other family members were buried. My mother, and now Hazel, rested there. Selling it felt like parting with a piece of my soul, yet with overwhelming debt and creditors closing in, I had no choice. I was committed to not letting Great Aunt Hazel down. She gave me money to start the business despite her own financial difficulties. I couldn't let the shop fold.

I placed my palms flat on either side of the tea cup and met my grandmother's gaze. In times like these, it was best to rip the bandaid off. "I'm selling it."

The slam of her fist on the table sent me jerking backward. Tea from our cups sloshed onto the white linen tablecloth.

"I knew it!" Her lips pursed and her skin became as red as a ripe cherry. I watched in awe as she hopped up faster than any seventy-five-year-old woman I had ever seen, and angrily paced the room, gesturing with her finger in anger. Grandma Wren mumbled and then gave me a piercing stare with her red-rimmed eyes before resuming her restless pacing. It was like she was possessed. All we lacked was a spinning head, and I would have fled from the house, never to return.

"A money grabber," she snapped. She halted in front of me and I sat frozen in the chair, too scared to even twitch. "How could you? These are our ancestral lands. Our ancestral home was never meant to be sold. Not then, not now, and not ever. Do you have no shame?"

"I... you see... my business—"

"Your business," she hissed. "That ridiculous shop will fold. I've seen it. You are best here with your people." She clamped her mouth shut as soon as the words escaped.

"The store will not fold," I replied hotly. Back ramrod straight I rushed on. "What do you mean 'I've seen it?'" I air quoted. "You haven't visited me once in Colorado, not even for my graduation. At least Hazel showed up. Heaven forbid you give a crap about me."

A sharp smack from her palm made my head jerk.

"Watch your tone with me, child."

I rubbed my stinging, hot cheek. We stared each other down. Any warmth for this woman vanished and memories of my youth rushed back.

"I prepared for this sort of action." She bobbed her head for emphasis.

A prickle of warning tensed my muscles and a slight throbbing worked at my temples.

"This house should have been mine. I'm the oldest, not Hazel." She started pacing again. "If you are intent on selling, then I'm left with no choice." She paused in front of me. "Skylar, it's time for you to come back home and reclaim your rightful place in this house, and in this town."

I sat there open-mouthed, unable to utter a single word.

"Hazel coddled you. She enabled your whimsical fantasies, and it stops now. I own the rights to the land, and I absolutely refuse to sell them. Without my approval, you're stuck. It's for your own good. One day, you'll understand that."

I jumped to my feet. With my fists clenched, I fought to hold my tongue in check. "You're mad. Who do you think you are, barging in and lecturing me about my life choices? Hazel loved me. She truly *saw* me, and I loved her for it. Think, Grandmother. Remember the last time you put your foot down? Look how that turned out."

I wanted to scream. Typically, life was something to be enjoyed. I believed in live and let live, but my grandmother's presence always ruined it. Peace vanished, chaos ensued, and my life was turned upside down.

"Your mother was a disappointment. Instead of making the most of her opportunities, she wasted them on your father. She could have been—" She clamped her mouth shut.

"What?" I searched her heated stare but only saw a guarded woman. It was like talking to a statue. I threw my hands up in exasperation and made a beeline for the front door. Her heeled boots echoed behind me. When I reached the door I flung it open and rounded on her. "Please leave, Grandmother."

She retrieved her black coat from the banister, donned it, keeping her focus on me the entire time. Taking her time, she strolled towards the door. "You'll come to your senses before long."

I rolled my eyes in frustration. "Are you leaving? Or do I need to call the police?"

She flinched like I'd slapped her. "That is unnecessary. I'm leaving, but before I go—"

I groaned.

"Before I go, make friends with the house." She tapped her nose and winked. "Better to be friends than foes."

"You're talking nonsense."

"One last thing." She turned and faced me, flicking her straight black hair over her shoulder. Marisa Tomei could have been her doppelganger. "I've purchased your business as an additional insurance measure. Apparently your co-owner wants out. As you're unable to pay the bills and I did, I currently hold over fifty percent ownership of the business. I'm closing the shop. Right now, the store is being cleared out. What doesn't sell will be shipped here. Welcome back, Granddaughter. Time to unpack. You're expected at the funeral tomorrow morning at nine sharp. It's a pity it takes place the same day as the gala. Never mind. We'll attend both. The gala starts at 6:30 PM. Wear that sapphire cocktail dress you brought. And put on some makeup for pity's sake. We have a reputation to uphold, and you need to use that sense of yours. We're out to catch Hazel's killer. See you soon."

With that, she made her way to her car, climbed in, and departed, leaving me fixated on the brown slush she had left in her wake.

Chapter 6

I stood at my great aunt's doorstep, staring into space until I started to shiver from the cold. I closed the door and hurried to the kitchen, slumping into the chair. I clung to the delicate teacup, even though the tea was cold, replaying the scene with my grandmother.

"Great Aunt Hazel was killed?" The teacup slipped from my fingers and crashed to the table, shattering. I could only stare as the tea splattered onto the pristine white tablecloth, the stain expanding into a Rorschach-like shape. A few seconds later, it shifted. Initially, I thought I was hallucinating, then the stain moved and I jumped up, knocking over the chair. I cowered against the white wainscoting as it clanged onto the floor. The 1960s-style refrigerator hummed to my left.

I couldn't believe my eyes as the blob morphed into a perfect EB.

With my legs trembling and on the brink of giving way, I urgently dialed the first person that came to my mind.

"Beauty sleep, child," Nuri slurred. *"This had better be good. I don't wake up looking like a goddess. It takes work."*

"N-N-Nuri," I wagged my finger at the offending letters like an idiot. "Letters... letters on my table."

"Letters? Okay. Um, honey, are you drunk?"

I stomped my foot. "There are letters on my tablecloth," I whispered, scanning the kitchen every which way but Sunday. In my fear-filled mind, it made sense, but all he heard was a babbling idiot.

Get it together, Sky!

I breathed in for a count of three and let out a noisy exhale. "I spilled the tea, and it formed letters."

"Beer? Have you found a six-pack of beer? No." He tapped his finger against something. *"Wine! Oh, honey, what kind? Cabernet? Pinot?"*

"Forget the alcohol," I hissed, clutching the phone to my ear. "Get over here and see for yourself. There are actual letters on my tablecloth."

"Right, and I'm the Pope."

A loud bang erupted.

"What was that?"

"Someone's in the house," I whispered, my throat tight. I visually swept the room, the hair on my arms bristling.

BANG!

I clamped my hand over my mouth to muffle a squeal.

"We're coming, honey. Cops are on the way." Nuri's silky smooth voice jostled over the line like he was in a dead sprint. The image would have made me laugh if not for the grim reality of someone being in the house. I resisted the temptation to stay frozen against the wall and ventured into the hallway towards the front door. I took tentative steps, on my tippy toes, wincing at every creak from the wooden floors.

BAM!

The parlor now. The person who was with me showed no intention of staying quiet. It was as if they wanted to be found.

I crept, heart pounding, sweat streaming down my face. With one final, shaky breath, I gathered my courage and took the leap.

"HA!"

Ready to defend my sanctuary, I landed in a crouched position, hands in fighting mode, prepared to kick, swat, or tackle the intruder. To my horror, a tall, broad-shouldered man with dark reddish hair sticking out at his temples stood in front of me, facing the ancient fireplace. It occupied more than half of the wall space, which was impressive given the 11-foot ceilings.

A plume of sweet cigar smoke circled in the air as the man leaned back and exhaled.

"Excuse me," I squeaked, not sounding the least bit fierce like I'd intended. "What are you doing here? Who are you?"

The man's body tensed before he twisted his head to the right. His profile belied a man of some significance if it was the 1600 or 1700s. He sported a wig. An honest to goodness wig with tight white curls and a blue bow in the back. I estimated his age to be in his late twenties to early thirties. While in usual circumstances, he'd strike anyone as attractive, I was less than thrilled by his appearance in my home uninvited.

"Might I ask the same of you?"

He pivoted to face me. With a hand on his hip, he eyed me curiously through another puff of his fat cigar. I ogled him much more out of surprise than anything else. He sported a purple patterned silk waistcoat, a fitted white shirt underneath, tight orange pants with knee-fastenings, and white silk stockings. His shoes resembled the black pumps my great grandmother would have worn, complete with purple silk straps tied in a bow.

Anger simmered beneath his intense stare, but he made no move toward me. I kept crouched and ready to flee if necessary.

"Me? This is my great aunt's home." I cocked my head and regarded his clothing. It was like he'd stepped out of a time warp.

His snort caught me off guard. I stopped gaping at his clothes and straightened, determining he'd have attacked by now if he'd been so inclined.

"The police are on the way. Any minute now." I added the last bit for my own benefit. I kept looking at the front door, praying someone would come barging in.

"Police?" The man frowned. He squinted, as if struggling to remember but couldn't.

"Yes. They're coming any second." I turned to look at the door, willing it to open.

"Not on this property. Sarah?" He called out, stalking toward the back of the home, distancing himself from me. "Sarah?" he repeated with more irritation. "Call the constable."

Constable? What was going on? Was this another of Nuri's pranks? Gosh, I'd wallop him for this one. Although, truth be told, it was a good one. The best so far.

The tension drained from me and I chuckled. Of course this was a prank. Who else would dress in this garb?

The man had walked out of sight by the time two loud raps announced my wily companions. The door swung open and they entered one by one, all wearing stern expressions.

"Are the cops here? Are you okay?"

They were all talking at once until I raised my arms. "One at a time!" I grinned. "First, I'm safe."

While Nuri and Trixie breathed a sigh of relief, Willow stayed on high alert, poised to attack. When the other two embraced me, she quickly scanned the home.

Gasping for air in their tight embrace, I choked, "I can't breathe."

They released their hold and took a step back, yet continued to keep a hand on each shoulder, keeping me at arm's length.

"Tell us everything," said Nuri.

"Start from the beginning," Trixie seconded.

I decided to show them instead of saying anything more because it all seemed crazy. Seeing was believing. "Follow me."

Motioning for them to follow I hurried to the kitchen along the same path the man had just taken. I walked through the parlor, which was once a grand dining room with a beautiful fireplace, and pushed open the swinging door. Striding over to the kitchen table, I turned towards my companions and jabbed my finger at the table.

"There."

I stood in triumph, anticipating their gasps of surprise. However, after one awkward moment of peering at the table and then back at me, their concerned stares left me confused.

I turned my head and looked down at the tablecloth stained by the tea just a quarter of an hour earlier.

Nuri patted my shoulder. "Honey, it's been a long trip. Maybe you need some rest. Willow, Trixie, and I will order some food and we'll stay here tonight."

Willow groaned. "I don't think we need to go that far. Why don't you stay with us, Skylar? We've got two double beds, and I'm sure Trixie won't mind sharing."

I rubbed a hand over my face and sighed. The white tablecloth was pristine, no signs of any stain.

"It was right there."

Their sad eyes and furrowed brows made me want to scream. "I'm telling you. I spilled some tea and letters formed out this... blob-like stain."

It was pointless. Without the evidence, I appeared crazy, and there was no point in pressing it further.

"The bang! Nuri, you heard it. There was a man in the parlor."

"A man?" Nuri's brown eyes crinkled with worry.

"He was dressed weird."

Willow snorted. "I promise you Nuri was with us the whole time, Sky."

"No, it wasn't Nuri. There was a thirty-something man dressed in period costume in the parlor."

I eyed my friends. They looked confused and alarmed.

"Did he leave?" Trixie rubbed her thin arms. She was only wearing her turtleneck.

The furnace chugged on, but it was still only sixty degrees in the house. It took some time for these old homes to warm up to a comfortable temperature.

"No, he mentioned something about having Sarah call the constable—"

"Hold up." Willow raised her hand. "Constable?" With an exhale, she pursed her lips. "Are you sure that weren't sleeping?"

"No." I stalked closer to the table. "There was a tea stain here." I jabbed at the exact spot. "Then there was a loud bang that came from somewhere in the front of the house. Nuri heard it too. After the second bang, Nuri told me you all were coming and that you'd call the police for me. When I went to investigate—"

Nuri whistled through his teeth. "I told you to stay put. You could have been killed. White people. They've always got to 'investigate,'" he said, air quoting the last word. He rolled his eyes. He jabbed his pink-painted fingernail into his sternum. "I'd have bolted out the back door and probably crossed the state border by now."

"He was standing in front of the fireplace smoking a cigar," I insisted. Nuri crossed his arms, looking askance at me. "When he turned, I noticed his outfit. Straight from the 1600s if I'm not mistaken. He was wearing a white wig—"

Nuri clacked his steel-toed boot against the floor. "A wig? My kind of man. Was he cute? Tall? Because I can't have a short man."

I groaned and clenched my teeth. Staying composed around this crowd was difficult.

"What did he say?" Trixie chimed in, sending Nuri a gentle look of warning to shut him up.

"Nothing. He wanted to know why I was here. Although I think he called me Clea."

"I'm not a fan of this. He sounds a little scrambled in the head if you get my drift." Willow dialed a number on her cellphone and brought it to her ear. She paced to the table and sat in the chair.

Trixie rubbed my arm. "There's an explanation. I'm sure of it. When the police arrive, we'll figure this out." She offered a reassuring smile.

"How long?" Willow demanded more than asked. She slammed her phone onto the table. "Fifteen minutes they say. There's some gala going on tomorrow night, and apparently this town can't spare help any sooner." She stared at me. "Where did he go? Is he still here?"

"I don't know. After he walked into the kitchen, you all arrived."

Willow drummed her fingers on the table. "We'll split up in pairs. Trixie and Nuri, you've got the bottom floor. Sky, you're with me upstairs. If you find anyone, use the bear spray I gave you before we started this trip. That should neutralize him until the police get here."

"Bear spray?" Nuri stared at her dubiously. "Why not wait for the police in here? We're safer in numbers."

"He's right," said Trixie. "This is a huge mansion. There could be any number of hiding spots, and that leaves us prone to attack. Staying together is the best option."

"Haven't you seen those horror shows, Willow?" Nuri stared at her. "It's divide and conquer. We'd be falling right into his trap."

I thought Willow would give in, but she defiantly walked through the kitchen. Pausing, she turned right before reaching the back door. "We'll take the back stairwell, Sky. Let's go before I lose my nerve. Oh, and Nuri, keep your hands off the man. Out of all of us you're the weakest link."

"Pardon?" He huffed. "Why am *I* the weakest link? I may wear dresses, but there're tons of muscle under this carefully quaffed appearance." He snapped his fingers and pouted.

Willow grinned. "I'm sure you can take any man on and tell the tale, Nuri. It's the way you cave to any good-looking man that leaves me wanting. You're like a moth to flame, pal. Sorry," she raised her hands, "but it's the truth. All he'd need to do is wink at you, and you'd be mush."

Nuri smirked. "I *am* a sucker for a good-looking man. Yummy."

Willow chuckled. "Watch your backs. We'll meet back here in ten minutes."

Trixie followed Nuri out of the kitchen and I traipsed over to Willow, who had a foot on the first step, gripping the stairwell railing.

"What is it?" I asked when she didn't move. "Change your mind?"

Willow bit onto her lower lip. "Ghosts."

My eyebrows shot up to my hairline in astonishment. "What about them?"

"Do you believe in them?"

Over the years, I had thought about it, but strange encounters since childhood left me uncertain about how to answer that question. "I haven't ruled them out. Why?"

"No reason. Stay close. Let's find that intruder. He's got some explaining to do."

Chapter 7

By the time we had searched a couple of rooms upstairs, the police showed up. Or more accurately, the agitated detective was now in the foyer, looking around. He reminded me of a hawk, able to spot even the smallest details within seconds of arriving. He had successfully irritated my companions with his questions and grunts since he got here. While Willow started recounting the events, intentionally leaving out the parts that made me sound crazy, I focused my thoughts, took a deep breath, and extended my mental reach, hoping to sense his personality, regretting it right away.

I almost fell to my knees from a mix of nausea and overwhelming emotions. I swayed and thrust a hand against the banister. The voices, including angry ones, grew louder until it reached a frenzied level, causing me to tremble. Trixie's pale gray eyes appeared suddenly, as if emerging from a fog. Wrinkles crinkled her forehead as her words blasted through the loud voices blaring within my head.

"Skylar? Are you sick? Quick, get her some water."

Trixie motioned for the chair closest to us in the parlor, and Nuri raced to get it. I sat, holding a glass of cool water courtesy of Willow, sipping in quiet shock over what I had just experienced.

"Skylar Night, I presume." The detective furiously scribbled on his little notepad. "The current owner." He snapped his notebook shut and stared at me, lingering on my hot cheeks. "I've heard from these three what happened. Now I want to know what you saw."

"I... I was in the kitchen."

"Alone?"

"Yes. I spilled some tea."

Willow coughed into her hand with a slight shake of her head.

I redirected my focus to the detective, who maintained a poker face in his unremarkable black suit. The contrast between his bronzed skin and the bright white collar of his shirt caught my attention, just like the black stubble on his jawline. A muscle twitched at my close inspection.

"There was a loud noise."

"In the kitchen?"

"No, it came from around here. I called Anni and—"

"Anni?" He flipped open his notepad.

"Sorry." I chuckled awkwardly, sounding like a raspy duck. "Nuri is Anni."

The detective glanced at Nuri. The confusion was understandable considering my friend looked very male today except for his purple nails. Nuri modeled in his heyday and hadn't lost any of his charm. We'd laugh at how he passed for a cis male and lamented over all the ladies' hearts he'd broken. That was Nuri; gallant gentleman and gorgeous broad. Nuri and Anni were individuals who were beautiful in both their masculinity and femininity.

The detective scratched the back of his neck and stared between Nuri and me.

"Nuri is Anni," I stated again. "Anni is his stage name."

Nuri tsked. "That makes me sound grander than I am. Hello, detective." Nuri stuck out his hand. "I'm Nuri Ari, aka Anni Histamine."

Surprise crossed the detective's sculpted face. "You're a drag queen?" His demeanor changed instantly, even though it was more of a statement than a question. He pumped Nuri's hand, eyes lit up. "Have you performed anywhere around here? Boston? New York maybe?"

Nuri, for once, remained speechless, looking to Willow for help.

"He's a huge deal in Colorado," said Willow, "but I'm afraid his talents lie westward."

Nuri reluctantly dropped the detective's hand. "I can perform here if I wanted," he sniped. "Give me time."

The detective stared in fascination at his full, pouting lips.

"Detective?" I prompted, waiting for him to acknowledge me. When he did, I couldn't help the teensiest of grins. Anyone who liked drag queens was A-okay with me. Judging from his interest, he was either a wannabe queen or he cared for someone who was. "After the first bang, another followed, and Nuri—"

Nuri cleared his throat.

"I mean Anni, told me to stay put. He had Willow call the police. While searching the house, I stumbled upon a man in historical clothing near the fireplace."

The detective gestured to the parlor. "In there?"

"Yes. He asked why I was here, which I thought was crazy, and then he called to a woman named Sarah, asking her to call the constable."

The moment I uttered the word "constable" I grimaced.

He arched a brow. "Constable?"

"It's bizarre, but the whole thing is. Why was he in my great aunt's home, and why would he wear those clothes?"

"The first question I can't answer," the detective said. "The second, however, I might be able to shed some light. Raven's Hollow puts on a gala each year in honor of our town's founding. It's a fancy affair with a catered meal, champagne, and a fireworks display to round out the night. Anyone worth anything attends, but it's by invite only. Although the whole affair bores me, I'm in charge of security, so..." His gaze fell to his shoes.

"This has what to do with my intruder?" I asked.

He blinked at me for a second. "Each attendee must dress in period costume."

"What year was Raven's Hollow founded?" Willow asked.

"1622," the detective replied.

"That explains the getup," I mumbled.

The detective stalked for the door and opened it, pausing at the threshold. "I'll be in touch, Ms. Night. Until then, keep your doors locked. If you have any other intruders give us a call. It's probably a teenage prank. The kids are out of school, and we always have issues this time of year. Idle hands and all that. Anyway, have a good night."

He bid us goodbye and left. While my friends launched into another diatribe about me not being safe alone in the house, I thought back on the man I'd seen. He wasn't a teenager. Something didn't feel quite right about the whole prank thing either, but I hadn't the time to consider it further. The detective was right. There was a gala event tomorrow night, and I'd been ordered to attend.

I glanced at my watch. It was late. If I was to be anything other than zombielike at Hazel's funeral, then I'd better sleep, but the thought of a gala the night of the funeral twisted my britches. I dared not give Grandmother the final say in all of this.

I tugged at a strand of my hair. "Ladies, I hope you brought your best dress."

Willow wrinkled her button nose. "Why?"

"Because we have a gala to attend tomorrow night, and I'm not going alone."

"But we need an invitation," Trixie protested.

"Don't worry about that. Just make sure you've got something to wear. This house is filled with Great Aunt Hazel's jewelry and gowns. Surely we can find *something* to wear."

"I don't know," Trixie said. "There's security, and if they're all like that detective, we don't stand of chance of getting in. He's grouchy."

"A tincture of chamomile would do him well," I mumbled and made a mental note of it. A drop or two in his beverage would calm him down a bit. Anything to get past that exterior, and those angry voices I heard when reaching out to him. They weren't his. It was like several people yelling at him simultaneously, vying for his attention. There were deep secrets with that one, and something told me I'd find out soon enough.

Right now, I needed to focus on the funeral and gala whether I wanted to or not.

"My grandmother invited us," I said.

Their faces lit up with surprise.

"Grandmother?" Willow crossed her arms, the stubborn wiliness of her activated. "You forgot to mention a grandmother. Why are we here? Wouldn't the house belong to her?"

I shook my head. "Hazel willed it to me. It's a long story. The house is mine no matter how much my grandmother wants it."

"Wait," Nuri held up his hand, "she wants the house?"

"Yes, but she can't have it."

Trixie reached out and grabbed my hand. "Which grandmother?"

"What?" I stared at her confused.

Trixie's pale cheeks flushed as she shyly smiled. "Maternal or fraternal?"

"Oh, she's my maternal grandmother."

A hush fell. With the mention of my mother, I tensed. Kaitlynn was the only person I confided in about her. It was best left in the past, but here the past and present collided. Still, I wanted to avoid talk about my mother.

"Grandmother Wren invited us to the gala."

Trixie beamed. "How lovely! That's kind of her. She's welcoming you back."

"You could say that." I pressed my lips together, hoping they didn't pick up on the tension.

"What are we waiting on?" Nuri clapped his hands together. "Let's go fishing. I get dibs on the feather boas!" He bounded up the stairwell. How could anyone be so smooth and fluid in their movements?

Willow snorted. "Come on. We'd better get a move on or he'll have picked all the good stuff."

Trixie grinned. "Who's telling him that they didn't wear boas in the 1620s?"

"Let's not rain on his parade... yet." I chuckled.

When Trixie and Willow hit the landing and turned into my Great Aunt Hazel's room, I halted. I turned, directing my gaze towards the parlor opening. A wave of purple shimmered and disappeared.

I stifled a shriek and hurriedly stepped into the room, happy to be surrounded by my friends, but something cautioned me to keep quiet. No need to set their alarm bells blaring. They'd think I'd lost my marbles and would never agree to attend the gala, which wasn't an option. On top of that, I'd need an army to confront my grandmother. That and a little stash of whiskey!

"Ladies, take a look at this!" Nuri held out a magnificent sapphire blue gown.

Willow and Trixie oohed and awed at its extravagance while I fingered the delicate fabric.

Nuri whispered, "It's silk," and squealed like a child let loose in Disney World.

"Oh, look at the corset," Trixie squeaked, her mouth hanging open. "I think it's bone."

"The shoes!" Willow darted behind Nuri and pulled out pumps from a cardboard box in the same shade as the dress. "This one's mine." She swirled the heels high overhead and spun in a circle.

"Wrong." Nuri carefully laid the gown on the bed and snatched the shoes from her.

Willow bounded toward him and swiped, but Nuri stood a good four inches higher. She jumped for them but missed each time.

"No," Nuri tsked. "These are for Skylar."

"Me?" I laid a hand against my chest. "No, I'm not getting in Willow's way. Remember the Tattered Peony?"

Willow blew a wisp of curly brown hair out of her eyes. "As I recall, I negotiated that dress. It looked better on me anyway."

"Not what I remembered," Nuri harrumphed. "That gown was made for these hips." He patted his cushioned derriere, swinging his hips left and right.

"She tore it off you." I stared at them both, remembering that night. It was the prettiest gown, and surprisingly they both fit into it. Don't ask me how, it just happened, and each of them, of course, wanted it for themselves. We had an event at the Tattered Peony, which hosted tea events to showcase local shops and businesses. It brought in our first returning customers, but that event nearly ruined our fledgling group of friends. Over a dress.

"Yes, and she won't do that tonight." Nuri heaved a hefty glare of warning at Willow as she longingly eyed the gown. "Right, Willow?"

"Fine, but you better have another kick-ass dress in there. Preferably blue." She lingered on the gown a moment longer and then strolled into the huge walk-in closet with Nuri rubbing her shoulders and cheering her on.

Trixie's angst-filled gaze met mine as she sat on the edge of Hazel's four poster bed. I didn't need to scan her because she usually wore her emotions, and today was no different. Her angular features and pixie hair cut made me wonder if she was fairy born, but I resisted exploring that possibility. Witches, wizards, trolls, and dragons were child's play, not for mature adults. Ghosts too. When I was six years old, Grandma Wren punished me by cracking my knuckles until I tearfully apologized and admitted that my mom, Lark, couldn't have spoken to me because she had died when I was four.

"Out with it." Trixie patted the bed beside her and I obligingly sat down. "This grandmother of yours. She's..." She tilted her head and squeezed her eyes shut, struggling to find the perfect word, "...she's difficult."

Trixie hardly ever spoke ill of anyone. Describing someone as difficult might as well be her swearing.

Her pale ivory skin flushed pink. "What did she do?"

"Grandma Wren, we've never seen eye to eye. Ever since I was born, there was friction. At least that's what my mom used to say."

"Your mother." Trixie patted my knee. "When did she pass?"

I sucked in a breath and smiled wistfully. "I was eight. She went to buy supplies for my birthday party."

Trixie gasped. "She died on your birthday? Oh, Sky. That's horrid."

I shrugged, used to it now. The pain in my heart would surface whenever thoughts of her crossed my mind or someone brought up her name, but those instances were infrequent after I left Raven's Hollow. Too many memories of Raven's Hollow, most of them dreadful. After my mom died, Grandma Wren got custody of me, and the rest was history. I was done. Finished. A cooked goose, so to speak. Locked in my room during long nights, I sought refuge in imaginary friends or cherished memories of my mother's auburn hair and radiant smile. It would lull me to sleep until the morning rays poked through the curtains and a new day of torture began.

"It's in the past. Grandma Wren took custody of me, and I stayed with her until my high school graduation."

"Is she always grumpy?"

I snorted. "No. Sometimes she's downright mean."

Trixie wrinkled her nose in disgust. "But you're her granddaughter. Why treat you so poorly?"

I balled my fists and tapped my thighs. The mere thought of everything brought out a side of me I'd prefer to leave alone. "I'm not Ophelia."

It was true. I wasn't her, and I'd never wanted to be, but in Grandma Wren's eyes, Ophelia was the fair-haired child.

"Who's Ophelia? A cousin?"

"Nope, Ophelia is my twin sister."

"You have a twin?" Willow and Nuri's heads popped out of the closet, eyes wide in surprise.

My friends huddled in front of me expectantly. They were used to me spilling my guts to them because I couldn't keep anything a secret. Not anything major. I was a firm believer that secrets were the root of all evil. If Grandmother Wren hadn't kept my father's letters from my mom all those years ago, maybe she'd be alive today. Now, I'll never know.

"Who's older?" Nuri pressed. "Are you identical?"

"I am, and no, we're fraternal. She's two inches taller, has brown eyes and black hair. We've both got pale skin though."

"Where is she? Does she live here?" Willow asked, a navy blue satin gown draped over her forearm. She had on two satin heels of varying heights, which made her hip jut out.

"Ophelia lives in Boston. She's an emergency room doctor, saving lives. She left soon after I did, but with Grandma Wren's blessing."

Willow blinked. "Meaning?"

"Meaning I left in the middle of the night after high school graduation with the shirt on my back, a few protein bars stuffed in my pockets, and a couple hundred dollars to my name. I drove to Colorado and entered college when I ran out of money. Grants are a wonderful thing."

Willow kicked off the shoes and knelt before me, and Nuri followed suit. It was like I was the queen of the court. These ladies were my world. They'd been there through breakups, the herbal startup, the debt, and were here now. Nuri funneled money into the business so much that he became my co-owner.

"Wow. That bad, huh?" Nuri asked.

"It wasn't all bad. There was Hazel. She rushed in to kiss my scrapes and bruises, and if I needed the doctor, she always drove. For all intents and purposes, she became my mom. Funny how they looked a lot alike too. Down to the one dimple, except Mom's was on the left and Hazel's was on the right. Oh, and Mom didn't need glasses."

"Did you keep in contact with Hazel after you left?" Trixie asked.

"We texted and called all the time. One time I flew out when she needed surgery. Instead of going to Boston, she went to New York City to stay clear of Ophelia's watchful eye. She'd have called Grandma Wren the moment she found out about Hazel's operation."

"Why is that bad?" Trixie asked. "You were there to see Hazel."

"Because Grandma Wren would have refused me access."

"What?" they all said in unison.

"Technically, Hazel's power of attorney was Grandma Wren. Hazel never had any children. So if Grandma Wren found out, she'd have refused me access to my aunt. One time, she found Hazel's second phone with all our secret texts. Three hammer strikes, then the blender, and it was toast. It took me a month to gather enough money to purchase Hazel a new phone and send it to her."

"Whoa." Nuri grunted. "That's intense. Did she ever physically hurt you?"

"Careful, Skylar Night."

Our attention immediately shifted to the door. The blood drained from my face.

"Grandmother Wren. To what do we owe the pleasure?" I blankly stared at her, wishing she'd disappear.

"We need to talk. In private."

Chapter 8

Willow hopped to her feet and raised her chin defiantly. "Whatever you need to say to Sky, you can say in front of us."

Nuri stood, arms crossed against his sculpted chest, half naked from the waist up. Even Trixie popped up, her jaw set. I marveled at them, my friends.

I stood up from the bed, holding back tears, to confront my grandmother.

She peered at each of them through her red spectacles. She narrowed her eyes and motioned me closer with a curled finger. "I see you've found a coven of friends, young lady. But we need to talk." She held up her palms in surrender. "I promise not to lay a finger on her."

Willow tapped her foot, dress still over one arm. "You've got five minutes."

Leave it to the lawyer to limit discussion. Yeah, she's a lawyer *and* a dentist. Some people love misery.

I flashed her a thankful grin before making my way to my grandmother, who I then trailed into the hallway. Portraits of generations past hung from the wire strung across the top of the wall. For some reason, Hazel hadn't changed this with any subsequent renovations. Females on one side, males on the other, facing each other. The clothing and hairstyles may have changed, but the slim builds and attractive features were consistently passed on. Everyone but me had black hair and either brown or gray eyes. I was the sole heir with blonde hair and hazel-green eyes. These, of course, were one reason Grandmother Wren treated me poorly. Oh how she'd rage on and on about them. Why couldn't it have been Ophelia? Why waste it on me? I had no idea who she was talking to as she ranted, but she would swing her arms and wander aimlessly in the library until the early hours. In our rooms, Hazel huddled with us as we listened to the sound of glasses shattering against the walls and floors, knowing she would have to clean up the mess the following day. Ophelia would be asleep in bed soon after Grandmother Wren drank herself into a stupor, and Hazel would slip out, blowing me a kiss goodnight.

Grandmother Wren stood in front of her mother's stern and unsmiling portrait. It felt like her eyes followed me whenever I'd walk these halls.

"I see you've found the sapphire dress. Good. Wear it tonight, along with the shoes. Hazel packed them specifically for this occasion."

"What?"

She hurried along, paying no attention to my question. "Your hair is best kept down, in waves." She touched the ends of my hair and nodded. "That should do fine. Detective Hill will be there tomorrow night, and we must pump him for all the information we can get on Hazel."

"About that—"

She snapped her fingers directly in front of my face. "Focus. You'll wow the detective in this dress, and I'll woo the chief."

"Woo?" I giggled. "No one uses that word anymore, Grandmother."

She frowned. "Whatever. Get the detective to open up. Use your womanly charms and find out what the autopsy report says about Hazel. She was murdered or my name isn't Morgana Wren. We'll need to be on our toes, Sky. No distractions." She wagged her finger an inch from my nose. "Do you understand?"

"Why do you think Hazel was murdered? Clearly, there was no bullet wound or knifing or else they'd have called it that from the start. Is it poisoning?"

A smirk played on Grandma Wren's lips. "Now you're thinking like a Wren."

I inhaled deeply. "I'll *never* be a Wren. *I* don't treat people like they're garbage."

Her smirk vanished and turned into a sneer. "You listen and listen good," she growled. "If Hazel meant anything to you, then you'll help. I always said she was wasting her time on you. I told her that you'd let her down."

"You're talking in riddles, Grandma. What are you on about?"

"It's not the time," she snapped.

"Fine." I couldn't outwit my grandmother, and the motivation to argue vanished.

"That's a good girl. Now, go back to your friends. I'll send Pedro to pick you up at 8:30AM sharp. Sharp, you hear?"

She stalked over to the stairwell and descended. Halfway down she turned toward me and called out, "One last thing. Ely Collins is presenting at the gala. Try not to make a fool of yourself. He's single, by the way. Lord knows what he ever saw in you. 8:30 sharp, young lady!"

With that she stormed out, slamming the door shut.

In like a hurricane, and out like a bomb. That's my maternal grandmother.

I skulked into Hazel's bedroom. My group of friends met my gaze and they moved closer, forming a tight circle around me.

"She's a horrible woman, Sky," Willow snapped. "We heard everything from the door." She swiped a few tears from my cheek with her thumb. "Your aunt was murdered?" She wrapped her arms around me and I sank my head onto her shoulder while Nuri and Trixie rubbed my back.

"How long have you known?" Trixie asked.

"Since Grandma Wren stopped by unannounced this morning after you left. She's wrong though. I haven't any womanly ways, and even if I did, I wouldn't use them to gather information. It's wrong."

I took a step back and observed the worried expressions of my loved ones. The only one missing was Kaitlynn. Gosh, how I wanted to call her right now. She'd know what to do.

Nuri clucked. "Who's this Ely Collins? Tell me he's tall, dark, and handsome." He wiggled his shoulders like a grooming peacock. "He sounds delicious."

Willow huffed. "It's just a name, Nuri. How can a name sound delicious?"

Nuri jutted his hip out and crossed his arms. "Did you not hear the meaning Grandma put behind that name? It's like she sugared it up and rolled it in molasses. Please," he flicked his wrist, "it's all in how you say it. *Ely* sounds like buttered shrimp over fettuccine good."

"Enough with the food," snapped Willow. "You're making me hungry."

I chuckled. "Relax. Shrimp and lobster rolls are bound to be at the gala. It's Grandmother's favorites. As for Ely, ugh." I rubbed my throbbing temples. "He's the past."

"Does this past have a picture?" Nuri leaned in closer like I'd conjure a photo out of thin air.

"Nuri," Trixie admonished. "It's none of our business."

Nuri swung his eagle-eyed attention to Trixie, wagging a finger. "Honey, if it's male and good looking, then it's all my business."

"But not attractive, right?" Willow's lips twitched upward. "Attractive is fish fodder."

"Wait." Nuri looked at me. "Is he attractive?"

"He's—" I started.

"Because I don't do attractive."

Trixie's eyes widened. "What's the difference?"

"Please!" Nuri rolled his eyes. "Attractive is needy. It's insecure with a dash of drama. Lawd," he groaned, "the drama. Attractive men whine about everything, and the second your attention drifts, it's cheater this and cheater that. All that drama carves wrinkles a mile long. Nobody's got time for that."

Nuri patted his shiny scalp.

"Careful, Nuri." Willow tapped the corner of her eye. "I think the fuss has etched a line."

Nuri shrieked and ran for the bathroom, sticking his face close to the mirror, inspecting for any wrinkles while Willow belly laughed.

"You really shouldn't needle him," I said, though Nuri's frantic search and squeals did bring out a giggle or two and relieved some tension in my shoulders.

The other two focused their attention on me, their eyes questioning.

"Ely was a high school sweetheart. Grandma Wren believed we'd get married eventually. When I left..."

"You didn't tell him, did you?" Willow asked.

I shook my head.

Trixie's mouth hung open. "Ever?"

"I haven't spoken to Ely since graduation. He tried calling, emailing, and texting, but I ignored it all. It had to be a clean break. Grandma Wren would've found me and dragged my butt back to Raven's Hollow." I shuddered at the thought. "That wasn't happening."

Nuri sauntered in, a smug smile on his flawless face. "False alarm. It was only a wig hair. Phew! What a relief."

He stood between Willow and Trixie as they stared in silence at me. "What did I miss?"

"Nothing." I was determined to steer the conversation to something else. Anything else. "Gowns, ladies. We've got," I checked my watch and cursed, "forty minutes until I'm a pumpkin and in bed asleep. It's an early morning."

Willow, Nuri, and Trixie shrieked into action, racing for the closet while I remained at the foot of the bed and took in the beautiful 1600s dress and shoes laid out on it.

I stripped out of my clothes and carefully stepped into the satin bodice and petticoat. By the time my companions had returned, I was tugging at the bodice and scratching my head as to how it closed.

Nuri lunged forward with a swat at my hands. "No! You'll ruin it."

I held my hands up while he worked feverishly at putting me together.

He held up a blue satin-looking torture device. "This is the stomacher you forgot. The bodice doesn't wrap fully around. See?"

He wrangled me this way and that until I was cinched into the ancient garments, gasping for air.

I massaged my sore ribs. "I can't breathe. Loosen it a bit."

Nuri frowned. "That's the style."

I pulled at the square neckline, only to be struck by the puffed sleeve that narrowed at the forearm. The lace collar on my shoulders and cuffs alone could fund an entire army. Although the empire waist was flattering, the stomacher practically choked the life out of me. No wonder women fainted all the time back then.

"What's this made of anyway?" I tugged against the stomacher to no use and watched the others dress.

"Whalebone."

Trixie grew a pale shade of green. "Whalebone? That's awful."

"It's 1630s fashion, Trix," Nuri said matter-of-factly. "It's satin, and lace, and sparkly spangles, and it's all hand sewn. These are the finest of craftsmanship, and I should know, being in the fashion industry. You all look marvelous." He beheld us with a gleam, swiping away a tear. "Take a spin. Go on."

As instructed, Trixie created a swirling cloud of powder pink. Willow followed in her pale green gown, and then Nuri couldn't help himself.

Somehow he'd found a lavender gown. We were all quite glamorous and awkward in our historic dresses, struggling to breathe and walk properly. After tomorrow night, I would look into loaning Great Aunt Hazel's gowns to a museum. That was where these all belonged, not kept in a closet for some yearly gala. These were a part of history, and everyone had a right to see them.

We swept our hair up and dabbed on makeup. Once we were all satisfied with our outfits, we carefully hung them up and put on our street clothes. Except me. I slipped into my flannel pajamas and fuzzy slippers, looking longingly at the comfy bed.

With the garments and tiaras carefully draped over their arms in their bags, my friends headed for the bedroom door.

"Alright, ladies." Nuri snapped his ebony fingers. "You're in this until after the ball, Cinderellas. Let's not ruin them. Stay away from red wine, cocktail sauce, heck, don't eat, and only water passes those lips. Got it?" Turning for the door, he said, "The chariot turns into a pumpkin at midnight tomorrow. But first there's the funeral. Black attire for all."

We descended the stairwell carefully so as not to trip over the voluminous bags, and I escorted them out to the car Nuri had rented. They climbed in one by one, and I watched them drive off until only the exhaust remained. Once the house was locked up tighter than a drum, I snuggled into the bed and tucked the comforter under my chin, staring up into the faded pink and green canopy until my lids grew heavy.

"Goodnight, Hazel," I murmured, feeling silly. Could the dead hear us?

I rolled over onto my side and stared at the clock. 2:00 AM. Less than five hours from now, I needed to be up and dressed, prepared to meet the nosy locals. And if not? Lord only knows what wrath I'd pay. On that, I prayed a Hail Mary and fell soundly asleep.

Chapter 9

I slammed my fist on the bedside table, knocking the alarm to the floor. With a grunt, I rolled onto my back and squinted at the pink canopy, glad that the loud noise had come to an end. The morning light wasn't due for another couple of hours, and as much as I wanted to linger in bed, snuggling in the warm blankets, the dreaded day had arrived.

I sat up and stretched, wiggling my fingers, trying in vain to pump warmth into them. These Connecticut winters were brutal. For as long as I could remember, I'd suffered from poor circulation, but unlike teddy bears and tutus, I hadn't outgrown the dreaded cold.

My phone buzzed. I tapped the buttons with my icy fingers to read the message. I smiled at Nuri's words of encouragement and replied with a note of thanks, reminding them I'd meet everyone at the funeral. Against my feeble objections, they'd insisted on attending to provide moral support. Deep down, I was forever grateful. While coping with the passing of my dear great aunt was already terrible, dealing with my maternal grandmother was beyond the power of alcohol to ease the pain.

I flung back the warm blankets, stuffed my feet into fuzzy pink slippers, and shuffled off to the bathroom. Since I'd laid out my clothing for the day, I was showered and dressed in no time. Little did I know I would spend another hour waiting for the Uber. Luckily, Great Aunt Hazel had a supply of good books to read, and I found myself perusing the pages of the last one she had bookmarked. I fingered the pages. Holding it up to my nose, I inhaled deeply and closed my eyes, drinking in her lingering smell. It felt as if she was still here as long as I kept my eyes closed tightly.

My phone beeped, letting me know the driver was here.

I set the book down on the end table and tugged on my coat when I noticed a piece of paper underneath the end table. I picked it up and flipped it over.

"You've been warned" was scrawled in pigeon scratch.

I tucked the scrap of paper in my coat pocket upon hearing a honk, then headed outside to the car. The driver, a young woman, chewed her gum, blowing a huge bubble and popping it the second I was buckled in.

"Where to?" she asked while turning the car around and down the long drive, sliding a bit in the process.

"Chamberlain Funeral Parlor."

With her pert nod, we were off. I pulled out the piece of paper and studied the script. The handwriting wasn't familiar.

The snow covered trees blurred by, and on any ordinary day, I'd have clung to the seat, not daring to caution the driver about car safety, but the funeral had dampened any give a cares, and this note had left me stumped.

The driver pulled up in front of the funeral home. "Here you go. Don't forget to leave a good review," she said without even looking at me.

As soon as I shut the car door, she zoomed off, no doubt to another waiting client.

The cloudy sky gave way to the first rays of sunlight as I made my way to the entrance. The funeral home had a simple brick exterior with a canopied drive-up and a few green bushes. The choking scent of asphalt filled my nostrils. I stepped inside. The muted beige carpets and white walls of the lobby were littered with yellow and white floral arrangements, which helped create the peaceful environment welcome to all backgrounds. The sign for Great Aunt Hazel's funeral stood in the lobby, and I dutifully followed the carefully constructed signs to the chapel. A staff member greeted me at the threshold to the sanctuary, a cordial, but respectful smile at the ready.

"You have arrived earlier than expected," the woman said, her bright eyes shining at me.

"Oh, I'm sorry." I hesitated. "Should I leave? I can come back later."

She gently touched my arm. "No need." She handed me a program. "Please, come in. Are you part of the family?"

The middle-aged woman smelled of athletic ointment. Her stomach growled while she studied my face.

I nodded and gripped the program tightly to my chest.

"With eyes like that, I'd say so."

"Pardon?" I walked behind her onto the red-carpeted aisle into the chapel. Neat rows of pews, each decorated with honeysuckle and white lilies, lined up before us.

"Sorry. I speak before thinking." The woman grinned. "Your eyes remind me of Hazel's."

"You knew Great Aunt Hazel?" I scrutinized her face, but no kindling of recognition popped up.

"We were schoolmates. I've recently moved into town, right about the time you left. I'm afraid we were never introduced. Hazel was a good woman. Your mother too."

"My mother?" I whispered, wide-eyed.

She had a warm and welcoming chuckle. "She was quite the rebel. We, my mom and I, spent many nights drinking tea and calling the gossip tree, trying to locate Lark. As usual, Lark was found when she was good and ready. Tell me, Skylar, did you inherit her spunk and tenacity for life?" Her eyes twinkled with fondness.

"Uh, I don't really remember my mother."

The woman tucked a strand of hair behind my ear. "Well, from what Hazel said, you've got her spunk."

We'd come to the end of the aisle, closest to the casket. I took a quick look at it and felt a lump in my throat. "What did you say your name was?"

"Twyla Griffins." She held out her hand. "If you need anything else, please find me. I'll be in the lobby directing guests. If you'd like more privacy, we have the family room over there." Twyla turned on her navy pump heel and walked back down the aisle, calling out, "I look forward to getting to know you, Skylar Night. Let's have coffee when you're ready. My number is easy to find."

Without looking back, she wiggled her fingers in my direction. Soon, I was alone again.

ALTHOUGH THE FUNERAL went off without a hitch, I wasn't out of the woods yet. The reception was held in a different area of the funeral home, and I was all too grateful to end this and climb into Hazel's bed to remember her in my own way. I'd sent my companions home as this was too much to ask and promised them we'd get together later. Pizza, hot wings, and boxed wine awaited me. I would get through this. First, though, was the greeting line, then the reception. I'd estimated it to take two hours maximum. When I walked into the reception room, however, my hopes deflated like a hot-air balloon. The line was, like, a mile long, and Morgana herself was at the front of it. And what was worse, it wasn't Ophelia she demanded by her side.

"Skylar," Morgana barked, a stern look of warning directed squarely at me. "Stand beside me. Ophelia, darling, please stand on her left. Let's make Hazel proud, ladies."

She patted each of our hands, squared her shoulders, took a deep breath, and smiled at the first mourner among hundreds.

Over the next hour, we shook so many hands and consoled so many people my facial muscles twitched. Moreover, my hands were so swollen that my rings constricted circulation in my fingers.

I cracked my neck. "Only a few left," I mumbled to my twin.

Ophelia snorted. "Have you forgotten the gala?"

The gala? No one would have blamed me for forgetting it except for Morgana. She'd have skewered me alive because the Chamberlains' Christmas Gala was the bee's knees of events. Everyone craved an invitation, but only a select few, or rather a select couple of hundred, residents graced their ancestral halls. Those uninvited wept privately while simultaneously binging video reels of attendees and stuffing their faces with popcorn, ice cream, and pizza waiting for this year's scandal to unveil itself. Because if there was one constant in life, there was *always* a scandal at the annual Christmas gala, and the Chamberlains always paid a videographer to film it.

"Crap. I forgot."

Ophelia raised a black eyebrow at me. "Better be on your toes, Sky. Morgana's out for blood, and you're a part of her plan."

I briefly glanced at my sister before the next mourner approached, extending their hand and offering a similar condolence of "So sorry for your loss" or "She's in a better place." They meant well, so I pasted on a smile and grit my teeth through it.

"Great. Can't you do it? Why me?"

Ophelia grinned sheepishly. "There's a lot to learn, little sis, but not now."

Ophelia shook her black hair about her shoulder, a mega-watt grin on her face. "Hello, Dr. Moore. Thank you for coming. Hazel raved about you."

I cast a suspicious glance at my sister. As far as I was aware, she hadn't been to town in years either, and she wasn't a fan of Hazel's, which meant no contact.

The man warmly gripped my sister's hand in his. "She was a fine woman. The town will sorely miss her."

"Didn't you sign her autopsy report?"

The doctor did a double take. "I, uh, yes. Yes, I did." He dropped Ophelia's hand like stink on a junebug.

"Forgive me, but I have forgotten the cause of death."

I looked at my sister in shock and noticed the doctor's stiffness. "I'm not at liberty to say. Sorry for your loss."

He stepped up and offered his hand. When I reached to take it, Ophelia muttered under her breath, "Can't or won't, doc?"

The doctor ignored Ophelia, simply saying, "So sorry for your loss, Ms. Night. Hazel was a remarkable woman. Strong as an ox. She will be missed."

Ophelia, having ruffled the good doctor's feathers, moved on to the next in line. Some older lady with bright orange hair and smeared lipstick pulled her into a bear hug and slapped her on the butt.

"Ms. Night?"

I returned my attention to the doctor and blinked. "What?"

He grinned. "I asked how your herbal shop is doing. It's in Colorado, right?"

"It's fine, thank you. Have you been there?"

"In college, yes. I skied a lot, but never in Boulder."

"I should think not. There's no skiing in Boulder."

"What?" He tugged at his collar, and bead of sweat clung to his brow.

I tilted my head and studied the man further. Mid-thirties, he looked dapper in a navy suit. His short brown hair gave off a military vibe, and his eyes were warm but weary. He kept looking over my shoulder.

Instinctively, I used my gift and reached out. His soul practically yelled, "Danger!" I took a sharp breath when it hit me. Morgana looked at me from the corner of her eye and then to Dr. Moore's pale face before turning her attention back to her current mourner.

"Boulder," I repeated. "There's no skiing there." I offered a weak smile, but he'd failed to see it.

"Sorry," he said. "I meant I'd never visited Boulder. That's where your shop is, correct?"

"Hazel's pet project." She'd been my biggest supporter. I wish she could have seen it in person.

"She bragged about you." His jaw twitched and then he pointedly stared at me. "May I be frank?" He leaned in close. His breath tickled my ear. "Hazel was..."

I waited. "Was what?" I prompted.

I searched his eyes, but found only fear. His gaze moved away from me towards something behind me. I slowly turned. A group of people stood ten feet behind us. They were familiar faces. Some friendly, others not. There was the man from yesterday, the one I'd accidentally groped. He stood by a striking brunette who could have been his twin, and she stood by Mr. Thane Chamberlain, his wife, and their son. Drake Chamberlain wasn't someone I cared to see, much less talk with, and fortunately, they'd skipped the line, offering a wave in greeting. Morgana simply stared at them, a mere nod as acknowledgment. The Chamberlains weren't to be trifled with. They owned over ninety percent of the town, from the funeral parlor to the bridal store. From birth to death, they had you covered. It had always been that way. With the money came the attitude, and Drake was no different. Years ago, he entered kindergarten with a football signed by a renowned quarterback, and class couldn't begin until he shared the story. The teacher stumbled over her words, trying to rush him, but she was powerless as Drake Senior waited by the door until his son was done. Only after he'd left, football in hand, did our teacher visibly relax. Senior made everyone quake in their boots. If you blinked the wrong way, he'd fire you. Thankfully, he hadn't fired our kindergarten teacher, but many *had* been fired, and it was all because of his arrogant offspring. Unfortunately, right now, he was staring at us. That wasn't the worst of it though. Morgana had apparently abandoned Ophelia and me and was now leaning towards him, whispering in his ear.

Ah, the Collinses. Never did I expect to see them again. Fate had a funny way of messing with you. If they were here, then...

I gulped down dread and returned my attention to the doctor. "Dr. Moore—"

"Joshua." He placed a sweaty hand on top of mine.

I looked down at our hands. "Joshua, are you unwell?"

He retracted his hand and rubbed it on his jacket. "Never better. Take care, Ms. Night." With that, he stepped into the crowd.

"Awkward in four, three, two..." Ophelia mumbled, but I was too intrigued by our town doctor that I failed to register Ophelia's warning.

"Skylar Night," called out the silkiest voice north of the Mason Dixon line. "Look what the cat dragged in."

Chapter 10

I swiftly snapped to attention. For a long time, I was haunted by that voice in my dreams, but therapy helped me forget after several years. Except this wasn't a dream and my therapist couldn't help me now.

The mischievous grin on the doe-eyed brunette's face was directed at me. She hung on the arm of a broad shouldered, blond-haired, brown-eyed man that looked fixedly at me. The man's jaw twitched in annoyance as the woman clung to him. She ran her fingers along his arm.

"Did you miss me?" She teasingly pouted her full red lips. "Look who it is, babe. Your old trash." The man stiffened.

"Myra, enough," he barked, his tone laced with deadly steel.

"Oh, pooh." She batted her eyes up at him as he towered over her 5'2" frame. "I'm only having fun."

"At a funeral?" I snorted. "Classy as always, Myra."

"Don't be jealous. I can't help the heat between us." She ran her finger over his lips.

The way she was throwing herself at him was certifiably embarrassing. His stone-like expression and rigid stance were clear signs that he was at his philandering ways again, and I wouldn't allow myself to be entangled in the drama ever again. The last time was the final straw.

"Careful, Myra. The drool smudges your makeup." I motioned to her cheek to indicate imaginary drool. I was rewarded for my efforts with her middle finger.

Her husky chuckle drained all the pleasure out of it though.

Myra Humphreys, my arch nemesis since grade school. Not much had changed. She had been chasing after Ely Collins since puberty, the same guy who enjoyed pranking me with worms in my sandwiches and flattening my bicycle tires. To my reddened, puffy face, Grandmother Morgana always insisted his incessant teasing meant he liked me. I disagreed. Love should never cause pain or make someone feel inferior. I suppressed those shaded memories deep within my mind as soon as high school started. The swim team's star performer, who used to tease me, began showering me with gummy worms, honeysuckle flowers, and picnics by the cemetery. Most felt the cemetery picnics were too creepy, but it melted my heart. Ely recognized the irreplaceable love I had for my mom and made a sincere effort to include her. He had turned into a lovable goof. It would have been better if he hadn't changed from the person he was in middle school. It could have spared us all a great deal of pain.

"Come on, Ely. The company stinks." Tossing her head back, Myra sashayed off, hips swaying seductively. The alluring exit would have worked if not for one tiny detail.

"Whoa!"

Myra's seductive wink morphed into dread when she awkwardly stepped wrong on her freakishly tall heels, causing her ankle to twist. Arms flailing, she slammed into my grandmother.

Ely was staring pointedly at me, sadness blanketing his face.

"I'm sorry," he mouthed.

Myra shrieked again and he attempted to pick her up, but she put up a fight, kicking and flailing, not wanting his help. Her spandex dress rose higher with each movement, and she stopped a few times to tug her hemline, which barely covered her plump butt.

"Show's over," Ely called out. His gaze fixed on me for a moment, but Myra saw it, hopped up, and jerked his arm.

"Get me a drink. Now."

She stormed off to a corner, nursing her wounds, accompanied by her high school clique. I turned back to the line, which had apparently come to an end.

Ophelia scowled. "Only you could make a scene at a funeral."

Tears stung my eyes and the lump in my throat expanded. "Not now."

"Sky—"Ophelia pleaded.

I disregarded her, darting past all the whispers. I stumbled upon the first exit and escaped through it, not stopping until I was positive I was alone. In the middle of a fairly large garden was a memorial bench. Even though it was winter I spotted patches of green. Luckily, the sidewalks were cleared, but not the benches. I cleared off half a foot of snow and perched on the edge, rubbing my arms against the frigid chill that penetrated my skin. Why do I always forget the essential items? Although I needed a coat, I wasn't willing to walk back into that chaos.

Inhaling the icy air, I counted to four and then exhaled. In the harsh winter cold, there was a sense of freedom. Colorado was breathtaking and wild, though nothing compared to home.

I sat up when I heard the scuffling of shoes on pavement.

"You'll catch your death in this cold. Here."

I shivered, my hands clenched under my frozen chin. "Ely, no. Myra will skin us both."

He chuckled, and a white puff of air floated between us. There was always a lingering feeling between us, no matter how hard I tried to forget. I even tried a gut cleanse to rid him from my system. Trixie had promised it would work, but instead, I'd ended up on the toilet all night, bent over in pain, still yearning for the blue-eyed bandit, as I called him. Ely had captured my heart from the moment I laid eyes on him in high school, and resistance was futile.

Ignoring my meager protestations, he draped his jacket across my shoulders. I greedily pulled the edges closed and relished in the warmth.

Ely cleared a space beside me and sat. He brought his hands together in his lap and looked down at them. "I wanted to apologize, Sky."

"Stop. It's ancient history. You're with Myra now."

He snorted. "No. No, I'm not."

I studied him carefully. Everything about him remained the same, from the inch long scar above his temple to his adorable dimples.

Ely rubbed his palms together. "Myra and I—"

"It's none of my business."

"Yes, it is. When you left town, that note..."

I felt the sting of longing and pain of seven years past come flooding back.

"That note," he began more assuredly, "was brutal. It hurt, Sky. We had plans. You and me, remember? We were taking on the world. It didn't change after graduation."

"Ely—"

"Let me finish. I was angry, and I took it out on you. It was unfair, and I'm sorry."

My lips quivered, but I dared not look at him. I jumped up and bolted for the first door I saw. I aimlessly walked through the hallways, barely feeling the warmth as I opened door after door, but couldn't locate the reception. Dang. How many rooms did this place have? How many contained corpses?

The heavy thud of Ely's footsteps propelled me on down the hallway, but he had already rounded the corner.

Blast this tight dress and heels. Whoever invented them needed to be shot.

"Sky—"

"No." I shook my head vehemently. "Not today."

Ely jogged around me, spreading his arms wide. "I won't let you leave. Not this time."

Clenching my fists, I struggled to stand on wobbly knees. My heart pounded like a drum in my chest as sadness overwhelmed me. His tortured face stared back at me. I did that. I hurt him, and I'll have to carry that guilt forever, but now wasn't the right time settle it.

A low voice came from behind Ely. "Is there a problem?"

I glanced at him, then looked away. "Is there?"

Jaw set, he took a half-step to the side, bowed, and waved his hand in dramatic fashion. "No problem."

I tipped my head back for a moment and closed my eyes.

"Your grandmother sent me to find you."

Ryan stood between Ely and me, and stretched out his hand. Ely's jaw clenched with anger, hands tucked in pockets, eyes locked on Ryan's outstretched hand.

"I don't need someone to rescue me." I pushed past both of them, feeling Ely's hot stare burn into me.

Once at the corner, I stepped, hearing heavy footfalls close behind.

"Left," Ryan called out.

I pushed the door open, mumbled a silent thanks, and scurried over to the refreshment table. Fortunately, no one at the reception had noticed our entrance.

I tried pouring red punch into a plastic cup but ended up decorating the white linens instead. After tossing two more cups into the trash and rounding for a third, someone dangled one in front of me.

"How about some liquid courage?"

I noticed a gold signet ring on his pinky finger with an "F" engraved on it.

"It helps. Trust me." Ryan wiggled the cup.

I gingerly took it and gulped down a drink. Eyes stinging, I spluttered and coughed.

"You okay?"

His smile warmed his brown eyes. He felt familiar somehow.

"You're no damsel," he said, his eyes lingering on my lips.

I glanced down, my cheeks on fire.

"Hazel talked about you. A lot." His chuckle quickened my pulse.

"Ryan," a model thin brunette strode toward us, "where did you go off to?" She was arm-in-arm with Drake Chamberlain, who stifled a yawn. "Hey, Drake had the best idea about our wedding. What about getting married at the Chamberlains' stables? It'll be perfect."

"Horse stables?" Ryan sounded unsure. "What about the smell?"

"No worse than you." She punched his shoulder and grinned.

"It's up to you, Brook. Whatever you want."

The brunette squealed with delight.

"Oh, Brooklyn, this is Skylar Night. She's Hazel's great niece. Skylar, this is my younger sister, Brooklyn. Do you know Drake?"

I nodded but kept staring at Brooklyn, who was scanning me from head to toe, her lips turned down at the edges.

Brooklyn laid a protective hand on Drake's chest. A brilliant emerald on her ring finger sparkled underneath the lights, a princess cut diamond surrounded by mini sapphires. "How do you know Drake?" she asked dryly.

"We were schoolmates," I replied while Drake scrolled through his phone, answering texts. "I've known him since we were knee high."

"Schoolmates?" She eyed Drake, who only glanced at us. "Drake," she patted his chest, "don't be rude. Say hi to Skylar."

I shifted on my feet, suddenly feeling small. Ryan narrowed his eyes at her, but she ignored him.

"Hi," Drake said, glancing up from his phone for a split second. "Sorry about your aunt."

"Great Aunt," Brooklyn corrected. "Men." Although she chuckled, it held a hint of unease. "They don't know family like we women. Am I right?"

"Great Aunt Hazel looked younger than most women her age. Great or not, she was my aunt, and I appreciate the sentiment, Drake."

"Right." Brooklyn placed her slim hand on her hip, chin thrust forward. "Didn't you leave in a hurry years back? Where I come from, family sticks together." Anger flashed behind her guarded brown eyes for a second.

"I didn't abandon my great aunt."

"Sure you did. Leaving for seven years and not returning is the very definition, but your family is quite adept at that, aren't they?"

"Brooklyn," Ryan barked, but she was already backing away, tugging a bewildered Drake with her. He'd finally pulled his nose out of his texts long enough to notice the change in tone.

Drake halted, drawing a stern glare from Brooklyn. "Skylar, what are your plans for Honeysuckle House? I bet it would be worth a pretty penny." Drake glanced at Ryan, who shook his head so slightly I almost thought I'd imagined it.

"I hadn't really thought about it." It wasn't true, but this was neither the time nor the place to get into any of it. Besides, why did Drake even care?

Drake's phone beeped for the hundredth time. His brow wrinkled as he swiped the message off screen, sticking his phone into his jacket pocket. "Good luck with whatever it is you do. Hey, Brook, I need to run." Drake kissed her on the cheek.

"What?" Brooklyn dropped his arm. "We've got wedding plans to go over. You promised."

He waved at her, backing away. "We will. It's a business thing. I'll be back in no time flat, promise."

Drake jogged off toward the door. He wrapped his arms around the shoulders of two black-suited men at the door and escorted them out of the room, though not before he gave a brief nod to his father, Mr. Thane Chamberlain.

"Ryan," Brooklyn tapped her designer shoe with impatience, "are you coming? If Drake isn't helping, then you will." She stalked off toward another group of young business professionals close to the door. From the looks of it, they are well off.

"Sorry about that." Ryan motioned toward his sister, who was avidly arguing with a stout, thirtysomething blonde woman with braces and tightly curled ringlets. "She's usually not like that."

"Really?" I was doubtful.

"She's, well, she's Brooklyn. Whatever she wants—"

"She gets." I'd seen the type all too often, especially in my high-end herbal shop. "You don't owe me an apology. She does, but I won't hold my breath. It doesn't matter."

Ryan rubbed the back of his neck. "I'll see you around." He turned to walk away but paused. "I liked Hazel. She was very dogged when she put her mind to something. She loved you. She was always bragging about you and the herbal shop. I can see why."

His eyes held mine for a minute more before he turned and walked across the room. When he joined Brooklyn's group, the blonde woman had left. In her place, there was a young woman with tanned skin and jet black hair, who rose up on her toes and kissed him, casting me a curious stare.

My stomach burned with jealousy. Why were all the good guys taken? I scanned the crowd and spotted Ophelia's jet black hair. She was cozied up to Morgana, who was whispering something into her ear. Ophelia kept her gaze on me as I made my way over.

Morgana leaned close and murmured, "It's now or never. Keep Ryan Irwin on a short leash. He likes you." She gave him an approving nod.

"Why?" I crossed my arms. "Are you planning an arranged marriage?"

Morgana's wine glass stopped midway to her lips. "No, Sky. Your marriage is a topic for future conversation. Right now, focus on Ryan. He's the key to all of this."

"How so?"

"Because if he didn't kill Hazel, then his sister did."

My jaw dropped open.

"Sky, close your mouth. It's unbecoming of a Wren," Ophelia chided.

I pushed on. "What evidence? Why accuse Ryan of murder?"

Morgana clucked. "All in due time. First off, corner Dr. Moore. He's hiding something about the autopsy. Ophelia's tried, but—"

I laughed and mockingly put a hand to my chest. "Dear Barbra, fair-haired Ophelia couldn't *do* something?"

The scathing glare Morgana hurled at me was enough to curl my toes and make me a believer in death stares. "Find out what caused Hazel's death," she snapped. "We'll regroup in fifteen."

Ophelia and Morgana walked away, leaving me staring after both of them.

Chapter 11

" Surprise!"

Nuri, Trixie, and Willow wrapped their arms around me, jostling me up and down. We were a burrito of differences when it came to hair color, eye color, and personalities, but these were my friends, and friends don't abandon those in need even if you beg them to. It's an unspoken truth, and I was forever grateful for them.

I eyed Nuri. "I thought you were at the B&B resting for tonight's gala."

Nuri batted his false eyelashes. "Rest is overrated, especially when it comes to friends in need."

We stood in a circle, holding onto one another. Their shiny faces were a beacon of strength. Nothing encompassed the love I felt for these people. My people. Morgana was right after all. I'd found my coven. The name was odd, but we *were* a coven, and I'd protect it with all my might. Hazel taught me that.

"Speaking of need, who's up for some sleuthing? It's all hush hush, but Morgana has given me an assignment, and I need to come up with something in," I checked my watch and groaned, "ten minutes."

Trixie whispered, "What can we do? I brought my incense, pins, and voodoo dolls."

"No hexing. We need to coax Hazel's cause of death from that man." I nodded toward Dr. Joshua Moore, who was by the refreshments about fifteen feet away, mingling amongst the forty-odd people there.

Willow whistled. "Dang. I'd look good on him." She smirked. Willow was always catching and releasing, so much so that the men of Boulder she hadn't toyed with were few and far in between.

"Down, girl. He's not a piece of meat." I patted her arm.

Willow pulled out her compact and puckered her lips. She snapped the compact closed and smacked her lips together. "Ladies, leave this to me."

Dressed in a low cut V-neck slip dress, Willow pushed up her ample bosom and weaved through the crowd while the rest of us watched. If anyone was capable of bringing a man to his knees, it was her.

"Girls, it's like a lamb to slaughter." Nuri fanned his face. He'd changed into a classic suit and tie topped with a black fedora and giant green peacock feather that bounced every time he moved. "The poor man doesn't stand a chance."

Trixie cocked her head. "I don't know. His body language doesn't match hers. Has she finally met her match?" She raised a blonde eyebrow in surprise as Willow retreated, coming toward us. She sidled up into the circle we'd created and rolled a strand of her silken hair around her index finger.

"I don't get it. It normally works. Are the men in Connecticut defective?"

I bit my lip to fight the giggle, but I needn't have bothered. Trixie and Nuri's cackles turned more than one person's head.

Seeing Morgana's stern frown I shushed them.

"What did he say?" Nuri asked.

We expectantly looked at Willow, who stared down at her ring. "Uh, nothing. It didn't work." Without warning, Willow grabbed Nuri's forearm and squeezed so hard he yelped. Eyes wide, she said, "Maybe he's gay."

Nuri glanced over at Joshua, sipping from a clear plastic cup. It wasn't red like the fruit punch I'd spilled earlier. Instead, his held a brown liquid.

"Nah, he's straight. Sorry, girls."

"What?" Willow visibly deflated. "That's not possible. He resisted all my charms."

Nuri tsked. "Maybe you're losing your touch."

Willow glared at Nuri. "Take that back."

"Stop it, you two." Trixie looked like Tinker Bell in her tiny green dress. "He's not gay, and it's got nothing to do with Willow."

I strained to see above the good doctor above my companions' heads. Willow and Nuri blocked my view with their bickering.

"What are you saying, Trixie?"

Trixie stepped between them, placing a hand on each of their chests. "You two need a room. There's enough electricity between you to charge New York City."

"Don't be ridiculous," snapped Willow, crossing her arms. "He's not my type. Plus, he's gay."

"I'm not gay. I'm bisexual." Nuri jutted his hip out and scanned Willow from head to toe. "Nah, she's too skinny."

"Skinny?" Willow scoffed, jamming her arms down by her sides, face bright red. "Why I oughta—"

"Enough," I hissed, seeing we were drawing the crowd's attention. "This isn't about the attraction between the two of you."

"There's no attraction." Willow opened her makeup compact and dabbed at her nose, preening in the tiny mirror. She was great at most things, but acting wasn't one of them. From her furrowed brow to her rigid shoulders, Willow was riled up. Nuri and she always nitpicked each other, and up until this point, I'd thought them friends, but perhaps Willow wanted more.

"This is about Hazel. Trixie, if he's into women, then we're screwed. Willow's our ace."

Trixie grinned. "Everybody has a weakness, be it male or female. But Willow's not his type."

"No need to rub it in," Willow sulked.

Trixie looked directly at me, a gleam in her eye. "This is all you, lady."

I blinked. "Uh, me?" I held a finger to my chest. "No. You're mistaken."

Trixie shook her head. Brown curls framed her slim face, bobbing with each movement. "The man's been staring at you all night."

She wasn't wrong. I had been aware of him watching me for the last hour, and I couldn't help but wonder what he wanted to tell me in the receiving line. That jolt of danger I'd sensed from him wasn't something I could ignore, and if Trixie believed I was the key to opening the man up, then I'd better belly up to the bar.

I straightened my shoulders like I'd seen Willow do on multiple occasions in bars, cafes, and even the zoo. No ground was off limits for her pursuits.

"That's it." Willow rubbed her hands together. "Get in the zone, chica. You've got this."

I rubbed my sweaty hands. "All I've got are nerves."

Willow rushed over, touching my arm as Nuri stood behind me, massaging my shoulders. His velvety smooth voice hovered near my ear.

"You are a goddess. Men weaken in your presence. Be bold. Be brave. You are beautiful."

The hairs on my neck and arms stood on end. I gathered myself and proceeded confidently. The crowd disappeared, leaving just the two of us. Like magnets, we were pulled towards each other. I glided to a stop in front of him. His cup touched his lips, but he paused, instead lowering it to the table, and then reached for a lock of my hair. He twirled it around his finger and gave me a piercing gaze.

My heart surged into overdrive.

"Uh, so there's this question I've been meaning to ask. Well, actually, it's not me. My grandmother—" I chuckled nervously.

Joshua dropped my hair and ran his finger along my collarbone, fingering my pendant. "Is this a family heirloom?"

I scratched my forehead and adjusted my stance. "Um, yeah. It's been handed down for the last, uh, several generations. Gosh, is it hot in here?"

I fanned my face as his gaze lifted to mine. "Was it Hazel's?"

The light above flickered, highlighting the amber specks in his irises.

"N-no." I gulped. Goosebumps sprouted like wildflowers on my skin. "It was my mom's. My grandmother's before her."

Joshua let his hand fall to his side and inched closer. He lowered his face, his lips hovered above mine. Even if I wished to, I couldn't tear my eyes away.

"About this question." His lip curled into a boyish grin. "Does it involve dinner and a movie?"

I pawed at my neck. "I, uh, I have to go." I stepped backward, but his arm was around my waist, pulling me to him.

"You are stunning," he whispered, nuzzling my cheek.

"Skylar."

I froze and broke contact with Joshua. All of a sudden, I was clueless about where to position my hands. In front of me, then behind, I finally locked them together and stared at my disgruntled grandmother.

"It's time to leave. You've got the gala tonight." Morgana directed her attention to Joshua, a look of displeasure on her smooth face. "I've heard you'll be in attendance. Breaking hearts all over town, doctor. Isn't your job to repair them?"

A smile played on Joshua's lips. "I'm no surgeon, Mrs. Wren."

"*Ms.* Wren. I haven't met a man worth marrying."

"How could that be possible?" Joshua raised his cup to his mouth, eyeing her over the rim.

"It's a Wren trait. Now, off you go, Skylar. The driver will pick the lot of you up at Honeysuckle House."

Morgana stormed off, her thick heels echoing on the tiled floor.

"She's quite the remarkable woman." Joshua set his cup down again and stepped toward me. "About that date..."

I skirted past him and hotfooted it to my friends, who seemed miles away amidst a mountainous terrain. On the second step, my ankle twisted, and I careened forward.

Joshua swooped in and scooped me up. "Careful. You owe me a dance tonight." He winked, set me on my feet, and walked off into the crowd.

As soon as I returned to my friends, they erupted in cheers.

"Alright. You've had your fun. We've gotten orders to leave by the grand dame herself. Everyone set on their gala wear? Meet me at Honeysuckle House no later than 6:30 tonight and we'll touch up our makeup."

"Wait," Willow tugged my arm. "Did you find out the cause of death? Or were you just playing?"

I sighed. "I was unsuccessful, but maybe tonight—"

"Tonight?" Willow squealed. "You have a hot date! Way to go, Sky."

"It's the gala," I protested.

Willow placed her hand on her hip. "Will he be there?"

"Yes."

"Then it's a date."

"Willow," Trixie piped in, "leave her alone."

"Yes, let her be." Like a bouncer, Nuri took me by the elbow and skillfully guided me through the crowd of onlookers. "But you'll be spilling the beans sooner than later," he whispered into my ear.

Chapter 12

The moment I got in the car, I mentally checked out. The bumps and nudges on the snow-packed roads lulled me into a peaceful state, and it wasn't until I heard the honk that I noticed we were parked in front of Honeysuckle House.

I thanked the driver, stepped out, and the car drove off. Once it was no longer visible, I pivoted and observed a yellow light while making my way to the front door. Even though it was peculiar, I assumed the handyman was behind it and continued to the front steps to open the door. The abrupt sound of metal hitting something hard made me freeze. As I extended my trembling hand to unlock the door, it creaked open.

My heart racing, I retrieved my cell from my purse. I moved cautiously, cringing at the sound of my boots on the wooden floors, finger poised over the emergency button.

"Hello?" It came out like a croak.

The silence sent shivers down my spine.

I crept up the stairwell, hesitating when I reached the landing. Maybe the handyman was the one who did it, right? I remember Ryan talking about a person who would check on the house weekly.

The memory came rushing back.

Yes, he *did* mention a handyman. He likely forgot to lock the door when he left. That would explain the eerie silence.

A sense of relief washed over me just as a loud, metallic clang reverberated like metal hitting concrete.

Eyes wide, I gripped my cell until my fingers ached. "Who's there? I'm calling 911."

The front door suddenly swung open. Like a statue, I stood rooted to my spot. My eyes were the only part of me that functioned. I looked down into the foyer, attempting to peer into the parlor. Nothing. The surrounding temperature plummeted. I extended a trembling hand and felt warmth just a foot away. This was freaking nuts. Was I crazy?

I swung my arms in different directions, but it was the same. It was icy cold where I was and warm only a foot away.

I was either mad or this was some freakish nightmare I'd wake up from any second now. What do people always say when it comes to dreams? Right, physical pain was a rare occurrence. Or was it smell? Crap! Why couldn't I remember that paranormal psychology class I took with Kaitlynn?

This isn't helping, Sky. Pull it together.

Inhaling deeply, I closed my eyes to concentrate, standing tall and trying to ignore the tingly sensations along my arms and hands. If this was a dream, smell would likely be absent. Opening one eye, then the other, I blew out the breath. Nothing. Okay, let's try pain. I'd pinch something. If I was awake, then it would hurt.

I gazed down at the front door, wide open and motionless. Licking my lips, I closed my eyes and turned my head away. Taking skin in between my fingers on my belly, I silently counted to three, then pinched hard.

"Ow!!!" I yelped and clamped a hand over my mouth.

I exhaled when I saw no movement. So, this wasn't a dream. Great. Now what?

With my finger on the emergency button, I held up my cell when the floorboards creaked behind me. My hair stood up on the back of my neck and I immediately bolted. In my haste to descend the stairwell, I lost my footing when my heel slipped on the edge of a step. I stumbled forward but managed to catch myself just in time and continued my descent.

Legs pumping hard, air burning my lungs, I landed in the foyer and ran through the front door, skidding to a halt in the freshly fallen snow. I craned my neck and glanced up at my family home. On the right side of the house, there was a flickering yellow light and tracks in the freshly fallen snow.

Human tracks.

I swallowed the bile that shot into my mouth and trudged through the snow toward the light. Wasn't this like a horror movie where the female character foolishly ran towards danger?

A cellar door halfway down the side of the house was open, emitting a gentle glow of yellow light. I remembered the cellar from years ago when

Grandma Wren would lock us inside if we hadn't finished our chores. Ophelia experienced that punishment only once, whereas I was locked in a dungeon for hours, too many times to count. Ophelia learned to shift blame onto me to escape trouble, and our twin bond was forever damaged.

CLANG!

I jumped sideways, crouching in a defensive posture. The area was completely blanketed in snow. The trees swayed against a strong breeze, and a branch banged twice more against an old swing set my sister and I used to climb in our youth. Now rusted, it contrasted sharply against the white backdrop and brown tree bark.

It was only a tree branch. Nothing to worry about. Still, why was the cellar door open? I hadn't been around this side of the house since my return, but Hazel hadn't used the cellar in years.

I dialed the police. No since risking my life.

"*911. What's your emergency?*"

"Hello, I'm Skylar Night at Honeysuckle House. There appears to be an intruder." I kept my voice low and repeatedly scanned the horizon for movement, ready to flee at a moment's notice. Momma didn't raise a fool.

"*Can you see anyone?*"

"No. I'm outside, but my front door was open when I returned from—" My throat closed up and tears prickled at the thought of Hazel's funeral. The thought of never seeing her curious, kind eyes again made me dizzy.

"*Miss? Are you there? Are you hurt?*"

"Sorry. No, I'm fine. I've returned from a funeral and the door was unlocked. I heard a loud bang outside, and then saw my cellar door open."

"*Miss, stay where you are. I'll send someone right away. Please stay on the line with me until the officer arrives.*"

It only took five minutes before blue lights flashed from the drive.

"They've arrived. Thank you!" I ended the call and trudged through the snow, feeling sweat forming on my neck.

I waved at the police car as it rolled to a stop on the circular drive near me. When the car door opened, I moved forward but quickly closed my mouth before speaking.

I could recognize those eyes anywhere. They were difficult to forget.

"Hello, Skylar."

Ely effortlessly navigated through the snow, closing the short gap between us, and stood there, his gaze fixed on me.

"There's been a report of a break-in. When I heard it was Honeysuckle House, I jumped."

His voice resonated with a deep, low timbre. It had always made my knees weak and belly flop, and this time was no different.

I cast my eyes towards the passenger seat, scanning around him. "No Myra?"

Rocking back on my feet, I forgot about the cold, the intruder, and the cellar door. Everything disappeared when he was around.

"Myra's not a police officer." His lips twitched. The softness of those lips, so wonderfully velvety.

Ely placed a hand on my shoulder. "Sky? Are you okay?"

My head snapped backwards. "Yes. Why?"

He grinned. "Because I've asked you a question twice."

My jaw dropped in a surprised "o" expression. Did I mention that time stopped with Ely? Yeah, I needed a life. One that didn't rise and set on Ely. Just when I thought Colorado was the solution, being with him brought back all the emotions I had suppressed, and my world was thrown into turmoil again.

"Sorry." I shook my head. "What did you ask?"

"Did you go inside?"

I gestured towards the cellar. "No. I figured I'd let the professionals handle it."

Ely glanced at the cellar door. "I meant the house." He walked over, feet crunching over the snow, until he came within a foot of the door. He pulled out a flashlight, shone it into the cellar, and cautiously went down.

"Anything down there?" I anxiously waited, rubbing my hands together and stepping side to side, anticipating his return. "Well?"

"Hang on," he called out, voice muffled.

I paced back and forth to the old swing set at least ten times before I called out to him again. "Ely? What's taking so long?"

Silence.

"Ely?" My voice rose an octave.

I stood next to the cellar door, my body trembling with cold, and stared at the yellowish light coming from inside. Cobwebs clung to the doors and hung from the threshold. The cold should have scared away the spiders, but I still shivered at the thought of them. When I was younger, my mom would read me *Charlotte's Web* repeatedly until I was no longer afraid of spiders. I was terrified of them for as long as I can remember, but my mom eased my fears with that story, and I eventually grew to tolerate, then even enjoy them. They were friends of sorts. I didn't mind even when my mom died and my grandmother locked me in the cellar filled with spiders, thinking I'd beg for forgiveness. It reminded me that sometimes the spookiest things aren't as terrible as they appear.

I brushed my hair out of my eyes and descended the short stairs into the cellar.

Dust particles floated in the yellowish light. In front of me, a wooden chair stood waist high, two feet away. The cold, damp air swirled around my ankles and up my dress. I stomped my feet on the dirt floor and used my cellphone's app flashlight to illuminate the area. Old wooden shelves, five levels tall, clung to the wooden walls surrounding the desk. There was another door off to the right corner of the ten by ten-foot room.

How strange. I'd never seen it before. Hazel must have built it within the last seven years, but why?

I made my way towards the doorway, my shuffled footsteps stirring up dust on the dirt floor. Along the way, I took a closer look at the shelves, running my fingers over the icy glass jars. To my astonishment, I came across row upon row of mason jars brimming with blueberry, raspberry, and strawberry preserves. The other containers had olives, herring, and cod, each with a delicate label tied to them with a hemp cord and written in my Great Aunt Hazel's familiar script. On a separate set of shelves, there were smaller, circular green jars that were the same size as face lotion. I opened one and sniffed. Hints of pine, berry, and musk tickled my nose. I twisted the cap on again and pocketed it for later perusal. On the table, there was an old ink well, some papers, and a few herbs that caught my attention. I picked up the paper. It was an old newspaper clipping about a rich heir, missing for two days. I stuffed it in my bra for later reading and kept moving. It shouldn't have taken Ely this long to speak up or come back. Stepping forward, I illuminated the doorway and gasped.

Lunging forward, I fell to my knees. "Ely! Ely, answer me!" His eyes were closed and a trickle of blood seeped from his forehead near his hairline.

He moaned, moving his head back and forth. I set the cellphone on a shelf, directing its light onto Ely as I cupped his face with both hands, patting his cool cheeks.

"Open your eyes."

Ely's eyelids cracked open a bit and he raised his hand to his head. "What happened?" he asked groggily.

"You tell me." I dropped my hands from his face and rocked onto my heels.

"I was near the table when I heard a scuffle. It sounded like two people arguing. When I got closer, the sounds ceased and bam. Lights out."

I touched his neck, checking his pulse. Strong and steady. "You probably have a concussion."

He grinned. "Since when did you become a doctor?" He clasped my wrist and rubbed his thumb over the sensitive side of it.

I stuck out my tongue. "When did you become a cop? I bet your dad had a field day with it."

Ely's mirth faded, replaced with frustration. "Not at first. He eventually came around to the idea."

I narrowed my gaze at him. No way did Mr. Collins *come around* to his only son being a cop. Head of the FBI or CIA? That's more like it. "Only a cop?"

He grinned wryly. "There's pressure to rise the ranks. An FBI brochure found its way on my desk at home the other day."

The gentle rub of his thumb across my skin muddied my thoughts. I pulled back and grabbed my phone. Peering into the other room, I shined it over his head. The room was about the same size, but there were no shelves or tables. A lone row of moving boxes was stacked against the far wall.

"There's no other egress."

He chuckled. "Egress? You've gotten all grown up on me."

I barely glanced at him, only long enough to catch my breath. The fire in his eyes threatened to consume me entirely. "Focus, Ely," I scolded. "Someone hit you, no one climbed the stairwell out of the cellar, and there's no exit in this room either. So who hit you?"

Ely glanced into the adjacent room. "Huh. Is there a false wall or hidden door?" He lifted himself onto his knees.

"Careful," I warned. "Let me call an ambulance. You're injured."

With a grunt, Ely stood up. He swayed to the right but thrust out an arm against the doorway. "I'm fine."

He entered the room. Fingertips on the walls, he nudged, pushed, then shoved.

"There's no egress." He placed one hand on a hip and the other on his sidearm. "No one came out of the cellar? You're sure?"

"Positive."

"Then who—"

The slam of the cellar door echoed through the two rooms, stirring up dust. I sprinted towards the cellar door and pushed. It didn't budge. Ely and I both leaned in, putting our shoulders against it, and pushed with all our strength against the solid oak door. We persisted until it became difficult to breathe and Ely began to cough.

"It won't work. We're trapped," he said through another coughing fit. He slumped to the stair beneath him and laid his head against the wall. "Use your cell."

I pressed the emergency button for the second time today when the light went out on the phone. "Uh, Ely?" I dangled the phone in front of him. "My phone's dead."

"What?"

"You wouldn't happen to have one on you?"

Ely keyed his radio. "This is Officer Collins. We need assistance at Honeysuckle House. We're presently trapped in the cellar. Over."

Ely's face had a waxen, pale complexion. His clothes were coated in sweat and dust, and his hair was covered in cobwebs from pushing against the cellar door.

He keyed his radio again. "Officer Collins requesting backup at Honeysuckle House. We are trapped in the cellar. Over."

We waited another few minutes, but there was no response.

"Sky?" His voice sound thready and weak.

I sat in front of him, gently moving his hair away from his forehead. His skin had a cool and clammy texture. I slid closer, nose to nose, examining his eyes in the faint light cast by the solitary bulb hanging above the wooden worktable. His eyelids sagged and his pupils expanded.

"Sky? I-I don't f-feel right."

His eyes rolled back and his head dropped forward.

"Ely?" I gripped his shoulder. "Ely!"

I banged against the cellar door and yelled until my throat was raw. Tears flowed down my flushed cheeks. I tugged and pulled his heavy frame toward me and leaned against the wall with Ely's head resting on my shoulder while my legs were wrapped around him and ran my fingers through his thick hair.

"Everything will be fine, Ely," I whispered into his ear. "Someone will come looking for us."

I rocked his weighty frame, desperately hoping for it to be true. With Ely unconscious, no doubt in serious condition and no way of communicating with anyone, his chances were slim.

"It'll be okay." I kissed his clammy cheek. "It'll be okay."

The overhead light flickered and then turned off. There was only darkness.

Chapter 13

Whereupon Morgana used to lock me in the cellar, she'd turn off the light and tell me to "think about what you've done," which was funny because I generally hadn't done anything terribly wrong. Did I cram clothes into my chest of drawers, causing them to pile high and the drawers to stick out? Yes. Did I forget to thoroughly clean the dirty dishes before putting them in the dishwasher? Sure. Was it necessary to confine me in a dark cellar with no food, water, toilet, or light for hours? No. So, while my current situation would have scared the pants off many and sent them hyperventilating and hysterical, I was fine. If it hadn't been for Ely's condition, I wouldn't be too scared. Ely's breathing, steady as it was, grew fainter. If I were a betting person, I'd say he had internal bleeding.

I spent the next ten minutes banging my fist on the door, but all I got was scraped knuckles and a splinter in my palm. Luckily, the cellar door had cracks, letting in a trickle of light for my eyes to adjust.

Think. What would any rational person do?

I slid out from behind Ely and rested his head on the wooden step. He was too heavy for me to move. Since he'd assumed there was a secret door or hidden passage in the adjacent room, I shuffled my way there, arm outstretched, feeling the racks along the way until I reached the other room. Inch by inch, I felt along the walls, up and down I squatted. When I reached the back wall, I stubbed my toe on a box and yelped. Once we were out of there, my top priority was to install ten lights in every room.

I turned to the third wall. A wave of panic churned in my stomach, ready to overflow. Sweat beads dotted my brow as I meticulously scanned the wall, searching for any irregularities that might indicate an escape route. Then I felt a dip in the wall around waist level. It wasn't big, perhaps an inch in diameter, and it was circular.

I swallowed hard, held my breath, and pushed my finger into the divot. *Click!*

The wall shook from a series of bangs and clangs. I kept my palm against it as the vibrations grew stronger and the clanging louder. Without warning, the wall collapsed. Warm air rushed against my face and a blinding light made me shield my face.

I squinted into the space, eyes tearing from the light. It was a heated crawl space. Eureka!

Hope gave way to frustration as reality took hold. Ely's weight made it impossible for me to drag him through the tunnel while unconscious. What now?

Maybe if I crawled in, it could lead me into the house and I could call someone there. It was a risk I had to take.

I put my hands against the opening and lifted myself into the shaft, hurting my knee on the rough metal edge. It went back roughly five feet and hooked right. The overhead lights were positioned two feet apart on the upper right corners of the ventilation-looking shaft. I rubbed my bloody knee and set off on all fours. A rumbling sound grew within the tunnel. It was as if a bull were dancing and bouncing off metal walls. I scurried back and was about to hop out when a head peeked around the corner of the tunnel. Bright green eyes locked onto mine.

"Hurry. This way."

In shock, I watched his head disappear around the bend. He came back in less than thirty seconds.

"Are you hurt?"

I pointed a finger at him. "You're the man in the parlor. How... why..."

He muttered and scurried around the bend towards me, lamenting that women would be the end of him. He dropped onto his stomach and stretched out his hand towards me. He noticed the blood, and his brow creased.

"Where are you injured?"

"What?"

He lifted my bloody fingers. "You're injured. Where?"

"Oh. I cut my knee. I'm fine." I licked my lips, glancing behind me. "There's a man—"

"A man?" A frown crossed his face and his eyes narrowed.

"A friend," I hurried on. "He's hurt. Something hit him on the head and he's unconscious."

With a grunt, the man signaled for me to exit the tunnel. I reluctantly complied.

I clung to the wall as he exited the tunnel. I had to maintain my sense of direction since the light diminished halfway into the room.

Standing tall, the man dusted off his trousers and white stockings. "Lead the way."

I cautiously traced the wall and jumped when he grabbed my elbow. He was as cold as ice.

"Sorry," he said, his voice low. "To ensure your safety, I must have physical contact with you."

I swiftly glanced in his direction. "So there is an intruder?"

"You were wise to leave the house when you did. I've bound them for the time being, but they won't be restrained for long."

We reached Ely's motionless body in seconds. I reached out and touched his neck. "His pulse is slow but strong. Can you help me?"

The man picked Ely up like a bag of sugar and tossed him over his shoulder. "Go. I'll follow."

I traversed the room again and moved into the one next to it. In order to better maneuver Ely, the man insisted I enter the tunnel first.

"How long is the tunnel?"

"Twenty feet. Grip his shoulders and pull. I'll push his feet. He'll slide on this surface. It turns right and then it's a straightaway."

I grabbed Ely by the armpits and pulled. He barely moved a few inches. Scooting backward, I heaved again. Tugging and pulling, we continued on for about ten minutes until we finally reached the end.

"Is this a mini elevator?" I asked, eyes wide. It was the size of a standalone freezer.

"Get in," he said gruffly.

I crawled into the back left corner, sat on my bottom, hiked my dress up to my hips, and brought my knees up to my chest. "Slide him over," I said.

The man flushed red and looked away. "Miss, what in the devil's name are you doing? Pull your dress down."

"We don't have time for modesty. Hand him over."

The man forcefully shoved Ely across the space. I took Ely between my legs, letting his body rest against my chest, and sat crammed up against the metal wall.

"When you're ready, pull that lever over your left shoulder." He wagged his finger to a red handle hovering above my head.

I gripped it and yanked down. The floor shifted, throwing me off balance. I clung to Ely, startled by the sudden movement. Gears cranked and squealed while we slowly turned in a circle. A sliver of light grew above the man's head until we were in full view of my Great Aunt Hazel's parlor. I sat in disbelief, unable to utter a sound.

"Hurry," the man whispered as he scurried out of the opening and into the parlor, sliding Ely out and flinging him up on his shoulder again.

I scooted out and tugged my dress down. "What now?" I whispered.

The man motioned for the front door.

We tiptoed across the parlor and into the foyer. Once outside, he lowered Ely onto the hood of the police car.

"Wait here. I'll check it out and see if they've left."

The man darted off before I could say anything. I kicked the snow, pacing back and forth. Ely's chest rose and fell. What was taking so long?

Shivering in the frigid cold, I rubbed my arms and waited.

Five minutes passed. Ten.

I marched over to Ely and snatched his comms. "This is Skylar Night of Honeysuckle House. Officer down. I repeat. Officer down. "

Chapter 14

A squad of police cars junked up my circular drive. Red lights flashed and sirens blared. An ambulance slid to a halt behind them. The medics rushed to put Ely on a gurney. They checked his pulse, wrapped a blood pressure cuff around his bicep, stuck an oxygen cannula to his nose, and lifted him to the ambulance. I jogged behind them. When I went to step into the ambulance, a firm hand on my shoulder halted me.

"Miss, we need to ask you a few questions."

A pock-marked face, squatty-framed man stood inches from me, staring through bottle-thick glasses. The police-issued uniform strained at the seams, displaying his ample girth. He chomped on gum like a kid at a baseball game, his breath reeking to high heaven.

"Can't I answer them later?" I glanced back at Ely's pale face.

"No. Come with me." The police officer roughly jerked my arm.

I stumbled, yanking free. I followed him without thinking, rubbing my sore arm. After all, the law was the law.

He came to an abrupt stop just shy of a man in an inconspicuous black suit stationed by the front door. The man held a notepad in one hand while chewing on the end of his pen. Opposite him stood a young police woman. She spouted what I had told her when they arrived.

"Officer Collins was struck by an unknown object and found unresponsive upon our arrival," the woman officer recited.

"Dust for fingerprints and search for a blunt object. The forensic anthropologist is already in the cellar. Follow her lead."

The female officer nodded and jogged off, disappearing around the side of the house. A constant flow of cops entered and exited the house, while others in white outfits meticulously searched and documented the crime scene.

The contemplative man faced me, tapping his pen on his notepad. "Miss Skylar Night, I presume?"

"Yes."

"I'm Detective Perry. Would you please tell me what happened?"

I carefully reviewed the events, eager to return to Ely as soon as possible.

"You saw no intruder? Only the door open?"

"It was unlocked and slid open. Is this going to take much longer? I want to accompany my injured friend to the hospital."

"One more question, Miss Night. Who has keys to your home?"

I paused. It was really just Morgana, Hazel, and me. And oh yeah, Ryan Irwin mentioned a handyman. "Three, maybe four. Detective, I really need to leave."

I turned and headed for the ambulance as soon as the detective said, "We'll be in touch, Miss Night."

As I reached the ambulance, the sound of tires on snow came to a halt.

"Where do you think you're going, missy?" an older man shouted at me. "Haven't you done enough to my son?"

A salt and peppered haired man in black-rimmed glasses bore down on me. He wore a navy suit, blue silk tie, and wing-tipped shoes, his tie flailing in the brisk breeze. I begrudgingly stepped back from the ambulance. The boxed jawline, sleek nose, and wavy blond hair were all too familiar. This was what Ely would look like in thirty years.

"Mr. Collins, it's always a pleasure." I rubbed at the sore knots on my neck, readying for battle. Ely's father never approved of me, and it had caused many arguments between Ely and me.

"This is all your fault. Stay away from him. Bad things happen when you're around."

He pushed past me to the medic, who took one look at the furious glare barreling toward him and hopped into the ambulance.

Mr. Collins pushed his hand against the ambulance door, preventing the medic from closing it.

"Mr. Collins," said the medic, his voice firm, "please remove your hand."

"Not until you tell me what happened. How's my son?"

The balding medic pushed his glasses up the bridge of his nose. "In need of care. Please step away and let me do my job."

"Your *job*," Mr. Collins spat, "is to tell me the condition of my son."

The medic let out a weary sigh. "He's unconscious. There appears to be a head injury, but for further answers, he needs a hospital. You can ride with us. Hop in if you want, but if not, back off. I've got a job to do."

Mr. Collins hesitated.

"Or I can yank this door shut and cut off your hand. Your choice."

At last, Mr. Collins retreated. He turned a vicious glare at me, jabbing a finger into my sternum. "If he dies, I will ruin you. Stay away from him."

He stalked back to his car then sped away.

"He's an arrogant prick," said the medic. "Don't listen to him. The guy may be a millionaire, but that doesn't mean he owns you or anyone else."

I mustered a weak smile. "Thanks."

The medic checked Ely's blood pressure. "We've got to go. Are you coming? Normally, we only permit family, but I'll make an exception this time. Back in the day, you two were practically engaged."

I cocked my head. "Do I know you?"

The medic shook his head. He bit onto a syringe cap and exposed the needle. After injecting it into the IV line, he recapped it and dropped it into the hazards box. "No, but I knew your mother. The Wrens are legends around these parts."

I stepped up into the ambulance and sat by Ely while the medic slammed the back door shut and pounded a fist on the wall separating us from the cab. The van started moving, bumping over potholes in our driveway, causing the IV bags to sway, and sending us pitching forward and sideways.

The medic gripped onto a cabinet behind him, unfazed. "The name's Fergus. I graduated with your mom."

I thought I knew everyone in my mother's life. I spent years combing through her yearbooks, relentlessly questioning anyone who had penned a message for her. Fergus's name was unfamiliar.

"How well did you know her?" I asked.

"Not well." He cracked a grin. "She was popular. Too good for the likes of me."

"Popular?" Grandmother Wren had painted a different picture of my mom in high school. Morgana used the words rebellious, defiant, and stubborn to describe my mother, whom she claimed was an outcast.

Fergus chuckled. "You sound surprised."

"I heard she was an outcast."

Fergus grew pensive. "Is that what Morgana called her? How sad. Your mom was the most popular girl in school."

"Are you sure we're talking about Lark Wren?"

"Lark ruled the school. She was the lead cheerleader and—"

"A cheerleader?" I squeaked in surprise.

He nodded. "She was in charge of dances, fundraisers, and decorating lockers. She didn't just do the jocks' lockers either. Lark also decorated the lockers of the math league when they went to State. She was an all-around great person. Everybody loved her, including Mr. Collins."

My jaw dropped open.

"Oh yeah. Thane pined after her for years, but she never liked him. Thought he was a smug jerk, and she was right. She had an uncanny ability to judge someone's character. Weird."

Fergus checked Ely's pulse again, and I could only stare.

How did I not know any of this? The yearbooks only showed her class picture. A head shot with hopeful gray eyes against a blue background with neon blue and pink streaks. Shoulder-length wavy brown hair framed an oval face with high cheekbones and ivory skin. To men she was model beautiful, but I'd never heard how kind she'd been. Morgana's conversations revolved around her intense fights and defiance, including dying her hair purple and getting a belly ring.

"Mr. Collins... what was he like in high school?"

"Just like he is now, except back then he was the star quarterback with a flock of girls around him. Now he's a successful businessman with a wife and kid. Respect and wealth are his mistresses."

"Was he ever nice?"

"Only to your mom. Lark had that effect on people. She brought out the good in most. Ely's grandfather was a real son of a—ah, he wasn't a good person. Drove his son to the brink. Football was everything, and Yale was the only option. It made sense because that's where all the Collins' sons went after high school. That family is full of doctors and lawyers, but Ely's dad wasn't smart enough. He went finance, and a good thing he did because he's brilliant at it. He has an instinct for it. His dad, though, was brutal. Lark spotted his father smacking him upside the head after a hard loss one game.

She boldly strode up to him and deflected his punch, warning him to stop harassing his son or she'd return the favor."

"My mom did that?"

"Yep. Lark was scary when she got mad. Interestingly, Ely's grandfather never touched his son again."

"Wow."

The ambulance hit a pothole, causing us to momentarily hover off our seats before slamming back down.

"We're almost there. Hang on. This last turn is a doozy."

I grasped the nearest handhold I could find while Fergus braced Ely's gurney. Soon, the back door flew open and multiple hands reached up and grabbed the gurney. Blue and green scrub-wearing men and women stood off to the side in the distance, anticipating Ely's descent. Fergus hopped out and greeted the woman inputting data into a tablet.

"White male, twenty-five years of age. He's sustained head trauma of unknown origin. His pulse is 170 over 100. No known allergies."

"Alright, Fergus. We'll take it from here," said a petite brunette. Her hair was pulled back into a severe bun. She jogged behind Ely's gurney as the others wheeled him into the ER.

I jumped down from the ambulance and followed the wake of people into the emergency department, stopping short of the double doors leading into the patient care area.

The brunette jogged over from the triage area. With a hint of suspicion, her brown eyes locked onto mine. "Only family. Mr. Collins already called, Skylar. He won't allow you entry."

I rubbed the back of my aching neck and nodded. "Of course."

The woman's name tag read Beatrice.

"Beatrice Strong?" I asked in disbelief. When I last saw her, she had braces, a back brace, and pimples. "You look..." I struggled to find the right words that weren't offensive.

Beatrice shrugged. "Things change."

"Betty! Come on," called a voice from behind her.

"I've gotta go. Sorry, Sky."

Beatrice offered a sad smile. She turned and went straight into the heart of the ER. When the doors closed behind her, I stood for a few minutes.

Time was a funny beast. Everything for me had stood still in regard to Raven's Hollow. From Beatrice's pimpled face and Ely's youthful arrogance, it had all frozen in place. It was like seven plus years hadn't passed, and yet the moment I crossed town lines, that all vanished. While our bodies grew, including our minds, our feelings were forever stunted. High school was dreary at best, but it wasn't because of the mean girls, jocks, geeks, and nerd drama that abounded in most. It was because high school scarred us in ways no one could repair or heal. Doubly so in my case. I'd never gotten over my mother's passing, and my grandmother saw fit to remind me of what a loser I'd become ever since. All those insecurities resurfaced the second I drove into town. I feared it always would.

"Stay away from him."

I slowly turned. "Mr. Collins. I'd say good evening, but that's not appropriate."

"Nothing about you is appropriate, Ms. Night. Please leave, or I'll have you physically thrown out."

Within a blink of an eye, I closed the distance between us. I stared into those eyes filled with anger and I held my ground. "Lay a hand on me," I hissed as the whole ER lobby looked on, "and you'll deal with Morgana."

He flinched, hesitating a second before stepping out of my way.

"Ms. Night, I'd be careful in who you place your trust in. Morgana Night bites both ways."

My back stiffened, but I kept walking out into the frigid afternoon air. I had no idea where I was going, but I didn't want the man to see how he affected me until I was out of sight.

I leaned against the outside wall, next to a wooden bench, and pulled out my cell.

"Nuri? Can you pick me up at the hospital? It's a long story."

In just ten minutes, Nuri showed up, giving me the chance to think clearly and come up with a plan.

"Drive me home. We've got a gala to attend."

Nuri looked at me sideways but stayed silent.

As we approached town, the business shifted from fast-food restaurants to older, well-established boutiques, restaurants, and bars, and I retrieved the newspaper clippings I had hidden in my bra from the cellar. The columnist wrote of a town founder's mysterious disappearance.

Ebenezer White, Founding Town Member, Inherited a Fortune.

I shuffled to another one. *Founding Member Fathered a Love Child?*

Then there was the final title. *Ebenezer White, Murdered.*

I swallowed hard, tracing a finger over the hand-drawn picture. His square jaw and blond hair were distinctly familiar.

"Nuri?" My voice cracked in shock. "Um, do you... are there such things as ghosts?"

Nuri's eyes briefly met mine before refocusing on the road. "Ghosts?"

I showed the artistic rendering in the old newspaper clipping from the late 1980s.

"Ebenezer White," I said.

"Yes?"

"I've seen him."

"Who's Ebenezer White, honey?"

I dropped the photo onto my lap and stared at it. "He's one of Raven's Hollow's Founding Fathers."

Nuri tightened his grip on the steering wheel.

"I've seen him, Nuri. He's been in my house."

Nuri shook out his lovely purple wig. He'd been getting ready for the gala event tonight. "Ebenezer White is haunting your house? Why?"

"I don't know yet." I leaned back into the seat, closing my eyes. The day had grown long and twisted, and the last thing I wanted was to attend a gala event. However, the gala was the perfect event to figure everything out. "Hope you're ready, Nuri. Because tonight, we're on the hunt."

"The hunt for what, sugar?"

He pulled onto Honeysuckle House's long drive. The crowded, bumpy path with overgrown branches flitting in the breeze felt more like a haunted house than the serene sanctuary I once knew.

"A killer."

"Girl," Nuri clucked. He pulled in behind the lone police car left behind. "You're scaring me. First your great aunt and now this?" He gestured towards the newspaper clippings on my lap with a flick of his wrist.

"They're connected. I don't know how or why yet. But I'm going to find out."

Chapter 15

Nuri spun the car tires on the drive, splattering dirty snow on my black pumps. I waited until he disappeared from view before approaching the lone deputy by the front door.

With a mischievous gleam in his eye, he stood with his hand resting on his gun. "Hello, stranger." His clean-shaven face broke into a wry smile.

"Xander?" I asked.

I raced across the distance, launching into his waiting embrace as he opened his arms wide. He wrapped his arms around me and spun me in a circle. Grounded once more, I stepped back, a hand to my dizzy head, and beamed at him.

"Look at you! How? Why?"

Xander grasped my hands and squeezed. "Too much to tell. We'll have to catch up sometime. For now, the chief wants me back at the station. The house is yours."

He released my hands, delved into his thick police jacket, and pulled out a key. "Lock up behind you. It's not Mayberry, Sky."

Walking towards his police car, Xander called out, "Trouble has a way of finding you, love. Tell Ophelia I expect a call now that she's back in town. Talk later."

He mockingly saluted me and slid into his car.

"Ophelia left you a mess, Xander. Why open that Pandora's box?"

Xander grinned slyly. "Everyone's a sucker for a man in uniform."

I chuckled and waved, realizing arguing would be pointless. Ophelia and Xander had dated all four years of high school. They were inseparable, but after graduation, she went to Harvard, and Xander became a distant memory.

Xander waved goodbye and left. I watched until he was out of sight before heading into the warmth of the house.

I shut the door and turned the lock, surrounded by the smell of cleaner, rubber, and aged leather.

The sound of Darth Vader's death march blared from my phone.

Ugh. Not now.

"Hello, Morgana." I said into my cell, scanning the foyer, parlor, and sitting rooms still on edge.

"What have you done to Ely? His father's been reading me the riot act for the past ten minutes. I always knew that boy was trouble."

I silently counted to three, twisting my head left and right against the knots forming in my neck and shoulders. "Ely came in an official capacity."

"Say that again?" she snapped.

"The front door was open and I called the police."

"What does that have to do with Ely?"

I suppressed the sigh on the verge of escaping. "He's a police officer."

Morgana whistled. *"Since when?"*

"I don't know. You tell me. You're the one who's lived here for ages."

"Watch your tone, young lady."

"He came to check out the house and cellar."

"The cellar is locked."

"It wasn't. Ely entered the cellar to investigate, but he never came out. When I walked in, I found him on the floor bleeding. About that. Since when did Hazel build an additional room in the cellar?"

"There's always been two rooms in the cellar, Sky. Now, speaking of Ely, did you actually lose it and whack him over the head?"

My nails bit into my palms as I fought the urge to hang up. It was ultimately pointless. We'd do this dance all over again when she showed up on my doorstep fifteen minutes later.

"No, I did not. My main focus was finding a way out of the cellar."

"Why not go out the way you came? Skylar, sometimes I honestly wonder if your mother dropped you on your head."

"Leave Mom out of this."

"Now, now, don't get testy. ˆ

My cell creaked in protest under my tight grip. "Morgana, someone closed and locked the cellar doors. My mobile phone lost power and Ely's was in his car. He tried his comms, but received no response."

Morgana's usual curt tone became softer. *"How did you get out?"*

"There's a tunnel from the cellar's add-on room. I crawled through it, pulling Ely with me, until it dead-ended into a metal box. I pulled a lever, and we found ourselves facing the parlor."

"Wonders never cease," Morgana whispered, almost to herself.

"Grandmother, what aren't you telling me?"

"Focus on the gala, Sky. Tonight, you must bring your A game. Remember, the driver arrives at 6:30 PM. Don't keep him waiting."

She hung up before I could respond.

I stomped up the steps to Hazel's room, opened the door, and froze.

"What the...?"

The room was in complete disarray. The lamp was on the floor, the sheets were strewn, and the mattress had been moved. Someone was looking for something, but what exactly?

Chapter 16

The driver arrived promptly, just as grandmother said, and we set off towards the grand homes of Raven's Hollow. Most had been built in the seventeenth to eighteenth centuries. Positioned away from the main road, the grand estates exuded a Victorian charm, complete with winding graveled drives, immaculate lawns, and stone fences. The wealth that flowed through these homes and their gardens for centuries made me feel slightly sick. The greed and arrogance that resided in these homes had ruined countless lives.

"Wow." Through the shaded limo window, Willow marveled at the sparkling lights that adorned the trees lining the Collins' drive. She was as gorgeous as ever. Her hair was elegantly gathered in a messy bun while her cat's eye makeup was flawless. Willow was runway ready. "How loaded are these people? Does Ely have a brother? Younger, older, it doesn't matter."

"Willow," Trixie admonished, tugging at her fitted apple-green bodice. She never complained, but from her pulling and tugging, the bone corset was more than a nuisance.

I chuckled. "He has an older brother, but Felix left years ago. I think he's in New York."

Willow's lashes, decorated with fake crystals, shimmered as she narrowed her gaze at me. "Tell me he's a lawyer."

"He works in finance and is extremely wealthy."

Willow grinned. "Please, for the love of all that's worthy, tell me he's single."

"He is."

Willow leaned her head on the headrest, being careful not to mess up her bun, and closed her eyes.

"Great," Trixie rolled her eyes. "She's preparing for battle. Poor man doesn't stand a chance."

Willow peeked out one eye at Trixie. "I thought you swore off men."

"No, I'm not on the prowl. There's a difference. Why can't you let fate happen?"

Willow re-closed her eyes. "I don't believe in fate. I make my own way."

Nuri tried smoothing down his fluffy skirt. No matter what we did, the skirt continuously snapped back into place. The poor ladies of bygone days had to endure the atrocious combination of an itchy hoop skirt and no undergarments. They were torture devices. How did they ever go to the bathroom or stay clean? It's miraculous that any of them made it to adulthood.

"Fate or not," Nuri said, straightening his lavender wig, "tonight's about Hazel."

"Right," Trixie tried leaning forward, hand extended in an attempt to grasp my hand, but she gave up, yanking at the corset under her gown. "What's the game plan? How can we help?"

I thought of what Morgana wanted... Scratch that... what she *demanded* of me, and her theory that Hazel had been murdered. Without an autopsy, there was no real way to definitively determine what happened to her.

I looked at Willow, whose eyes were still closed. "Willow, as someone skilled in bringing out people's inner demons, why not tackle Drake Chamberlain? He's a pompous jerk, but his family owns three-quarters of this town, and if anyone knows anything, it's him. Be warned, he's already engaged to Brooklyn Irwin. She's less than friendly. I doubt she'd appreciate you flirting with her man."

Willow raised her head off the headrest, peering out the window as we stopped and started for the umpteenth time behind a multitude of cars. "No worries. I've dealt with the like before, but if Trixie could intercept Brooklyn and keep her busy for a time, I'll pump that man until his brains pop out."

Nuri laughed throatily. "I bet you will, sugar. Pumping is your favorite action." She raised a brow at Willow's sour expression. "Darling, don't harm the bearer of truth. Men turn into sheep around you. It's your curse."

Willow relaxed against the headrest, snorting. "It's a *gift*."

Though Nuri wore an amused expression, to his credit he kept quiet. No sense in rattling the tiger's cage. Get Willow riled up, and we'd never get to the gala. Surviving Willow's storm would require a bottle of champagne, three shots of whiskey, and a night of singing karaoke.

"Brooklyn's troubled," Trixie stated.

We all stared at her.

Trixie shrugged. "She's carrying a secret. Her brother isn't aware either. It's like a dark cloud follows her."

"Does that mean you won't help with Brooklyn?" Willow asked.

"I'm just saying she's shady. Be careful around her, Sky. She is not who she appears to be."

"Are you a psychic now?" Nuri asked.

Trixie shook her head. "I can't explain it."

"Alright, ladies," I interrupted. Trixie's taut jaw spoke of her distress. It reminded me of the time I'd told Kaitlynn of my abilities. That was one of the hardest things I'd ever done. Fortunately, Kaitlynn trusted me, but the fear of being considered insane was overwhelming, and Trixie's expression served as a reminder of her own struggles. "Trixie's instincts have never led us astray, so if she advises us to be cautious with Brooklyn, I'm on board."

Trixie smiled gratefully.

"So Willow's target is Drake Chamberlain, Trixie's is Brooklyn," I said. "Nuri, your target is Myra Humphreys. She's like a shark scenting blood, and I can't have her chasing me all night."

"Honey, Myra won't be a problem. I know how to handle the likes of her."

"Great." I clasped my hands together on my lap.

Willow frowned. "What will you do?"

"Doctor Joshua Moore."

Laughter erupted from my three companions.

After a brief moment of confusion, I felt a hot flush rise in my neck and cheeks. "Minds out of the gutter, people. The good doctor holds the key to Hazel's death. According to Morgana, he's the one who performed her autopsy."

With our goals in sight, we relaxed in our seats and sipped champagne from crystal flutes until the twinkling lights on the drive and trees caught our eye again.

"Wow." Trixie, closest to the door, stuck her nose to the window. "It's like a meteor shower."

Willow snorted. "That or we're being invaded. I imagine the electric bill is off the charts."

"Money isn't a problem for the Collins. It flows like water." I tugged at the bone corset stabbing my ribs and making it difficult to breathe and looked up at three dumbfounded faces. "What?"

"How rich *are* these people?" Willow asked.

"I don't have a direct line to their bank accounts. Plus, it's not polite conversation in these parts." I tugged at my poofy sleeves. Money talk always made me twitch.

"Last time I checked, it's not a topic for polite conversations anywhere," Nuri remarked, tracing his finger along the edge of his champagne glass.

Willow moved around like a toddler in their Sunday best, attempting to see beyond Trixie's head, which was fixed on the captivating light display outside our car.

"Polite conversation or not, this costs a fortune." Willow glanced my way. "How engaged are Brooklyn and Drake? Have they finalized the wedding plans?"

Leave it to Willow. When there's a legitimate bachelor with a massive fortune to inherit, all is fair in love and war. Was it shallow? Mean? Yes, and yes, however, Willow wasn't all that bad. To her, it was a challenge. She was financially independent and didn't need a man to support her. She was electrified by the chase, especially if it meant pursuing an engaged man.

The driver came to a halt at the front steps of the Collins' grand entrance. Victorian era like Honeysuckle House, the estate dwarfed that of my ancestral home although the layout was roughly the same.

We filed out of the limo onto a velvety red carpet that led up to the front door. I followed the brick path, taking in the potted poinsettias that lined it. The snow-covered flowerbeds on both sides of the path created a striking contrast with the colorful, festive plants. In spring and summer, these beds flourished with blue hydrangeas, yellow tulips, and fragrant rose bushes competing for attention. Once we reached the front door, the butler extended his white-gloved hand, half bowed, clicking his shiny black shoes in a singular motion and accepted our invitation cards, announcing us as we entered.

A stunning, winding staircase graced the foyer, but the Collins' had twice the space and twice the stairwells. On the right would be the sitting room, used for the ladies in the olden days, and on the right was the parlor, fit for the dashing men ready for a fox hunt or some sort of noble undertaking. Similar to Honeysuckle House, the back of the home would feature a kitchen that served as the heart of the house. The Collins' home was essentially identical to my ancestral home, except for one crucial element. Love.

I savored the moment. My friends were mesmerized by the stunning crystal chandelier, waiters swiftly gliding through the packed foyer offering glasses of bubbly champagne and exquisite hors d'oeuvres. This was truly extraordinary. The exhibition of wealth was evident through the white marbled floors, silver platters, and an assortment of precious gemstones. It was gorgeous, no doubt about it. I saw it now. But seven years ago? Not so much.

Raven's Hollow evoked feelings of sadness and dread in me. Morgana, along with other residents, made sure of that. For the past years, it had held no significance other than my mother's final resting place, and, of course, Hazel.

I blinked rapidly, dabbing the corners of my eyes with my finger.

"What do you think?" I whispered to my friends, who hadn't opened their mouths to speak.

Nuri placed a hand on my shoulder and leaned closer. "This is Ely's home?" When I nodded, he continued. "Girl, he must have done the undoable."

I frowned up at him. "Meaning?"

"For you to give up this." He splayed his hand in front of him with a sweeping arc. "What happened?"

"Money is the root of all evil," I mumbled.

Standing next to Trixie on my right, Willow huffed. "Money has the power to resolve many issues if you allow it."

"I agree with Skylar," Trixie said. "Money isn't everything."

Willow pursed her lips. "Imagine the possibilities, ladies, of the good you could accomplish with this money."

The intense gazes of the pairs of eyes focused on our huddled group by the door made me anxious.

"Uh, guys, let's mingle. We've all got our assignments."

They nodded in agreement and we moved towards the parlor. They stuck close to me, never diverting their attention from the extravagant decor. Who could blame them? The Collins' favored gold-gilded everything. If it wasn't gold, then it was silver. Even their furniture and wallpaper were imported from France, which must have been quite costly.

The grand foyer was filled with 1600-era regalia dressed town patrons who had money to burn and judgements to make. We'd barely taken four steps when Ely Collins materialized out of nowhere, appearing from behind a tall woman with a face resembling that of a horse. The woman had so much gold around her neck she should have been bent over.

"Hello, Sky."

"Wh-what are you doing here?" I zeroed in on his white bandage underneath his hairline. "Did you sneak out of the hospital?"

Ely chuckled. "They gave me a clean bill of health with a little pressure from my father. I can't miss the gala, right?"

I observed him with astonishment. Dr. Moore and everyone around stopped and stared when Ely skillfully maneuvered between Nuri and me, linking his arm with mine. If it hadn't been for the harp and cello players, the true awkwardness would have surpassed the night of senior prom. That was a debacle. It made me squirm just thinking about it. I'd finished the night upside down in a dumpster with Chinese food dumped on me. Chicken chow main and egg foo young, while ordinarily yummy, took some scrubbing to get out. All due to Myra Humphreys, high school cheerleader and resident mean girl. That night she blindsided me, but I learned my lesson.

I noted Dr. Moore's drawn expression and pale color. With one glance at me and Ely, he sprinted into the crowd. I strained against Ely's grip to no avail. The good doctor had vanished.

"Look what the cat dragged in."

The sugary sweet voice made me recoil. The petite, buxom brunette gracefully descended the stairwell, her eyes fixed on mine.

My heart raced when she came to a halt a few feet in front of us, tossing her wavy hair over her shoulder and squaring her exposed shoulders. Apparently, she hadn't gotten the memo about dressing vintage. However, if old habits died hard, Myra didn't give two hoots about the rules. She'd be the belle of the night, rocking a perfectly fitted Versace that outshined everyone else in terms of beauty. That was Myra. People never change. Not really.

"Myra Humphreys." I inhaled and nearly choked. Did she empty a whole bottle of perfume on her head? My eyes stinging, I waved my hand in front of my face to ward off the assault. "I see you haven't changed the napalm you call perfume."

She tapped her two-inch long catlike nails, sharpened to a point, on her jutted hip and pursed her red lips.

"Ladies," Ely warned through gritted teeth. With a smile pasted on his face, he surveyed the gathering of fascinated onlookers. "Please behave. We have guests."

The musicians had stopped playing, and now everyone in the room was focused on us.

"We?" Myra's face flashed fire as she looked down at our entwined arms. She raised on her tippy toes and fingered Ely's chin. "Does that make us official?" She grasped his other arm and pulled him toward her. It was with a pained expression that Ely let me go, sadness apparent in his eyes.

The whispers increased, and the inquisitive expressions shifted from curiosity to surprise.

Ely cleared his throat. "Ladies and gentlemen, may I introduce Ms. Skylar Night and guests? Please give them a warm welcome home."

He extricated his arm from Myra's grasp and clapped with enthusiasm. In true gentleman fashion, he lowered his head and kissed my hand. His warm lips against my skin sent my heart racing. Looking up, he gave a wink before standing up and walking confidently into the crowd, taking the energy with him and leaving a most distressed Myra.

The music started again and the intrigued participants soon returned to their own conversations, leaving me and my companions to confront an angry, glowering Myra.

"This isn't over," she hissed. "You shouldn't have come back, Sky. We don't want you here."

"We?" Willow stepped forward, her pale green pumps tapping the marble floors.

Myra redirected her wicked glare from me to my friend. "Ely is mine." A cunning smile appeared on her face. "The town is not too pleased with it either."

"Why's that?" Willow remained unperturbed despite her immediate change in attitude.

Myra scanned me from head to toe, her lips curling in distaste. "She's tainted. Always has been. The town threw a party the day you left."

My belly burned with anger, though I remained quiet. What was the old adage? If you can't say anything nice? For some reason, my tongue wouldn't cooperate. It was a thick slab of rubber cemented in place. Growing up, this was a common occurrence, which was a major factor in why I left. The other—

"Myra Humphreys."

It was both a greeting and a threat. Myra stiffened, plastered on a smile, and turned to face my grandmother. In Raven's Hollow, Morgana was the matriarch. Slight the queen bee and pay the price. By the looks of it, Myra had poked the hive. Although, with Myra and Ophelia practically glued at the hip growing up, she rarely received my grandmother's wrath. This time, though, Ophelia wasn't here to defend her or calm Grandmother, and from Myra's fidgeting, she knew it.

"I assume you're welcoming my granddaughter, Miss Humphreys. We don't want her running off again."

My grandmother stood in period garb, black in mourning, looking from Myra to me. With her black hair cascading down her head, dotted with a few white strands, it was the prominent diamond intricately woven into her updo that drew all eyes. It glistened like twenty diamonds twirling beneath the glow of the crystal chandelier.

"Hello again," Grandmother Wren said to my friends with a hint of irritation, gliding to a stop before us. "Help yourselves to the hors d'oeuvres and champagne, but save room for the main meal. Sky, you'll be seated by Dr. Moore, and your friends can find their name tags around the table. Come. Mingle. There are plenty of eligible bachelors and bachelorettes."

Her mischievous eyes sparkled as if it was a game, and I worried my friends would be charmed by her charisma and wit, forgetting *she* was the enemy and the reason for my escape all those years ago. At first sight,

Grandmother Wren seemed fantastic, anyone's dream grandmother. She was good natured, fun, and most of all, popular. Scratch the surface, and it all changed. Most of my childhood friends never saw the cruelty when we were growing up. They were fortunate to escape the beatings and hurtful words inflicted upon a grieving teenager longing for her mother. Those tendencies were reserved for those dark nights that came all too often. Whenever the bed wasn't made properly or the chicken was overcooked, it was like a witch would manifest and inflict the most severe punishments.

The mantra *I will beat that rebellious spirit out of you!* still woke me up in a cold sweat many nights.

Her black linens swishing around her feet, she disappeared into the sitting room among a few hundred other town patrons. Thankfully, Myra had left the second Morgana redirected her focus on me.

"Sky?" Nuri tugged on my elbow, concern swimming in his amber eyes. "Are you okay? You look like you've seen a ghost."

I stood up straight and smiled. "Yep. Now remember, guys, we're on a mission. Get your information and then hightail it over here. Don't press your luck, alright? If Hazel was murdered, they can do it again."

The next minute, they scattered in all directions. Nuri ambled into the parlor, his hoop skirt swishing side to side, passing by Myra. She stood among a gaggle of our old high school classmates, all mean girls. She paid no attention to the adoration of her old tribe, solely focused on the orange embers that occasionally popped and hissed from the antebellum fireplace.

After snatching a flute of champagne and downing it in one go, Nuri crossed his fingers while re-approaching Myra. Liquid courage was necessary in this case. She was a monster if provoked, and it didn't take much. Nuri was my friend. That was all it would take for her claws to come out and strike.

Nuri touched her slinky strap, and I clutched my abdomen waiting for the assault of words or a dump of champagne over his head. When Myra beamed, I was left speechless. Oh, he was good. Never would I doubt Nuri again.

I searched the crowd until I found Trixie. The blondish-brown waif stood next to her target. Brooklyn Irwin's cautious demeanor eventually faded, and the two ladies quickly began giggling while enjoying some wine.

Two down, one to go.

I approached the ballroom-sized sitting room and entered. I quickly surveyed the room and noticed the absence of furniture, which had been cleared to make space for dancing and mingling. The only thing left was the pale blue rug with gold-threaded fleur de lis on each corner. A second giant fireplace, located midway down the left wall, crackled with warmth as people in 17th-century attire conversed around it, spreading their salacious gossip about the town's scandals. The mayor's choice to sleep with a teddy bear was apparently considered newsworthy.

I fanned myself with my hand. The fire's warmth, though comforting in winter, felt like it was scorching my face in the overcrowded room.

Where did that woman get off to? I stood on my tippy toes and searched. *AHA!*

Willow's shiny brown hair dulled in comparison to her smile. Her hand lightly grazed Drake's forearm as she stood by his side, laughing at every gesture he made. Drake radiated under her fawning, and I could only chuckle at it all.

Alright. My turn. Where did Dr. Moore get off to? While I'd be seated next to him during the meal, asking autopsy questions at dinner was cringy at best. Then there were the eavesdroppers.

"Watch it!"

A woman dressed in red stood in the far left corner of the room and shoved a stumbling man, who tilted back his champagne flute.

Dr. Moore?

He flipped the glass over. When the waiter passed by, he stopped him and exchanged his empty glass with a full one.

"Hey!" Dr. Moore pointed at a man striding for the door which I knew led to the chef's kitchen. "Hey, I'm done. You hear me?" He hit his chest in frustration, but it was pointless since he was shouting at a swinging kitchen door.

I approached him and laid a steadying hand on his swaying body. His head snapped towards me, his eyes glassy and unfocused.

"Hello, Dr. Moore." I snatched away the champagne flute as it touched his lips, catching the glances and murmurs from the surrounding partiers. "Let's get you some coffee."

I tucked my arm through his and steered him toward the kitchen door. No matter who upset him, the kitchen was the only place nearly free from prying eyes and ears.

"I didn't mean to do it," Dr. Moore slurred, the reeking alcohol fumes wrinkling my nose. "She was innocent." He turned his glassy stare on me, stopping right as we entered the kitchen. Grabbing my arms and shaking me until my teeth chattered, he lowered his head and boldly stared through me. "I meant no harm."

Chapter 17

The kitchen staff filled trays with gourmet meats, cheeses, and crackers as the executive chef expertly wielded knives, preparing tonight's meal. Luckily, their attention was consumed by shouting commands and replies, so they didn't notice us.

I pried Dr. Moore's hands away from my sore shoulders and grasped them. "Who didn't you harm? Who is innocent? Hazel?"

The instant I mentioned my great aunt, it was as if a bucket of water came crashing down on him. He shook himself loose from me and tugged at his tunic, attempting to straighten his tricorn hat but only made it look off-kilter.

"Hazel—" He abruptly stopped, gaping at something over my shoulder. His face went pale with a look of absolute terror.

I turned to see what had made him sober up so quickly. Morgana, Mr. Chamberlain, and Brooklyn stood arguing over a boiling metal soup pot. The clatter of dishes and pots made it hard to catch what they were saying. Morgana zeroed in on us with the precision of a ballistic missile, and her withering glare made me queasy.

"Uh, let's get you that coffee," I said, grabbing for his hand, but he jerked away.

"I'm fine," he asserted amid a loud bong-like sound resonating throughout the room. The dinner bell. "I thank you for your help, but as you can see, I am quite fine."

His hands trembled and his steps faltered, but he pushed through the door we had entered, walking away determinedly.

"What are you doing in here?" Morgana snapped. She had somehow arrived at my side without warning.

I slammed my hand to my chest. "Stop *doing* that. It's unnatural."

"That man is no use to us drunk. Sober him up."

Morgana lifted her skirts and dashed through the door.

104

A memory from my youth, when she would scold me for things beyond my control, flashed to my mind. Then, like now, she rattled my calm.

"The Wrens are always sticking their noses in where it doesn't belong."

I whirled around and locked eyes with Brooklyn's snarky face.

"I could say the same for you. What were you, Morgana, and Mr. Chamberlain talking so heatedly about?"

"Nothing that concerns you. But if you must know, my nuptials are in four weeks, and we haven't booked a venue."

I frowned. "What's my grandmother have to do with your nuptials?"

Brooklyn grinned slyly. "Wouldn't you like to know?"

Leaving me even more clueless than before, she too walked off into the sitting room. The good doctor played a major role in the odd dynamic among those three, but what was it?

I followed the line of revelers up the stairwell, who paused in wonder at the historic family portraits. From a different era, elegant ladies in precious gems stared at us, their gazes empty. No sense of warmth radiated from them, and I found myself trailing the edge of one when a jolt of energy jerked me backward.

I hit something hard and bounced. "*Umph!*"

My ankle twisted and I careened sideways, my arms flailing.

Strong arms circled my waist and pulled me close. "We've got to stop meeting like this," came the gruff response.

I tensed. "I'm fine. You can let me go."

The pressure on my waist eased, and I gingerly placed weight on my injured ankle. I extended it left then right, blowing out a sigh of relief. No pain. It was then that I caught sight of the oddest looking pair of shoes.

"Men wore heels?" I slapped a hand over my mouth the second it came out. Why did I always speak before I thought? Morgana had chastised me for it since childhood, but it was a fault I'd never quite managed to champion.

His husky laugh boosted my mood, and I couldn't help but laugh too.

"That's what I'm told, Ms. Night. Brooklyn said they were all the rage, but I'm happy they fell out of favor. For the men that is. I appreciate them on the fairer sex."

I cocked my head. "Are you implying that women are weak, Mr. Irwin?"

He ran a hand through his hair, and he opened and closed his mouth so many times, I lost count. If it had come from any other man, I'd have flown off the handle, putting him in his place about the male patriarchy, but not him. There was something different about Robert Irwin.

Robert made a gesture towards the portrait I had been studying. "Did she bite?"

I raised a brow. "No, Mr. Irwin. Portraits don't bite."

"I might." He reached out, took a lock of my curly hair, and twirled it, half grinning.

My knees grew weak and I ran my tongue over my dry lips. "Right. Um, so, yeah." I inhaled deeply, searching for one of my friends to rescue me. "Uh, shall we?"

I hiked up my skirts and took off, ascending the last steps in no time, Robert matching me stride for stride. We followed the stream of people down a long hallway filled with furniture and objects from different centuries. French chairs, Spanish tables, and the most remarkable find of all—a full-sized knight's suit of armor from medieval England—were situated around the corner, leading to the expansive dinner room. Countless afternoons were enjoyed inside that armor-filled tomb. The memory of ancient sweat, leather, and cold metal against my young skin came rushing back. When we were kids, Ely and I would take turns hiding in it, rattling it when the maids got close. Man, how they screamed. The echoes seared my ears, but the fear on their faces made it all worthwhile. Thankfully, the staff handled it well, and in hindsight, the screams and reactions were all fake. We created a lot of noise as we wriggled around, eagerly waiting to jump and pound against the armor.

Tonight, while tracing my finger along the sword hilt before entering the grand dining room made for more than a hundred diners, my mind was elsewhere. The zap from the portrait confused me. While sensing emotions or intentions was one thing, a physical jolt was something else entirely.

"Are you okay?" Robert asked when we passed the first table filled with drinks.

I nodded, perusing the reds and white wines. The bartender was there to fulfill our drink desires.

"Midori Sour, please."

The bartender grabbed the bright green liquor bottle and mixed it with sweet and sour, then handed me the glass. I swirled the green liquid and sipped, relishing the warm burn down my throat and filling my belly.

"Ah." I smiled at Robert.

"Better?" he asked.

"Much."

Robert opted for a whiskey sour, and then we meandered around the table, admiring the setup of fine China, sterling silver cutlery, and poinsettias adorning the center of the grand rectangular table. We stopped halfway down, closest to the fireplace.

"This is me," I said.

Like a true gentleman, Robert pulled out my chair and pushed it in when I sat down. He bent behind me and whispered into my ear, "Ms. Night, women's strength far surpasses that of men. I would choose you in a fight anytime."

His breath brushed against my skin, causing the hairs on my neck to tingle. He lumbered five seats down from me and sat. The blonde in her twenties sitting to his left seized the chance and immediately engaged in conversation. Flipping her hair, giggle at the ready, she was a mean girl from Myra's crew. What was her name?

"Cherry Tierney."

"Ely," I yawned, "I'm tired and not in the mood to fend off Myra tonight. Please leave me alone."

Ely removed the cloth napkin from the ring on his plate and placed it on his athletic thighs, which were too muscular for even 17th century clothing. The years of swimming and running were evident.

"I agree. She's in rare form tonight. Must be present company. She always did have a profound dislike of the Wrens."

"Wrens, my fanny," I mumbled.

"She doesn't like the lot of you, but I've always had a soft spot for you and Ophelia."

"Why are you still here?"

Ely grabbed a bread roll, slathered it with butter, and stuffed it into his mouth. "Check out the place setting," he mumbled over the bread. He gestured towards the calligraphed nameplate.

I slumped in my chair and looked heavenward. "Of course we're seated together."

I could only hope Myra was seated somewhere far off, or at the very least across the table.

People socialized around the table, which occupied three-quarters of the room. Around one hundred guests were expected, with individual nameplates for each. I was fortunate that Dr. Moore was sitting beside me, but I hoped that Ely or anyone else didn't listen to our conversation. However, I wondered if Joshua would open up after our kitchen incident. He seemed on edge.

Now wasn't the time to fret, and it wasn't a trait I'd inherited anyway. I'd take the time to sus out any suspicious people, since Raven's Hollow had plenty of those, and also enjoy the scenery while sipping my sweet drink.

Holly dangled from the wooden beams, while a ten foot Christmas tree occupied the back right corner, adorned with blinking red, green, and white lights synchronized to holiday songs playing quietly in the background. The tree proudly showcased a shiny angel on top, along with red velvet bows draping down. Colorful presents were tucked underneath beautifully arranged red and silver ornaments. While many guests were captivated by it, enthralled by its beauty and the delightful scent of pine, I couldn't help but feel unimpressed after encountering it numerous times during my high school years. The Collins' loved a good show, and this was the best time of year to do it. Everyone eagerly awaited their invite to the annual Christmas party, and for all four years of high school, Ely made sure I was there.

I searched the room for my friends, and as fortune would have it, they sidled up behind me.

"Are we all seated together?" Trixie asked, her cheeks rosy from the warm fire crackling in the fireplace behind us.

Willow grunted. "Not by the looks of it."

She raised her skirts and leisurely walked the room's length. As expected, all of us were split evenly. I'd stake my life on the fact that Grandmother Wren was the one who arranged that.

Willow was the furthest away and closet to the tree. Halfway up from her sat Nuri, and on my side, Trixie sat two-thirds of the way down, while I was positioned between Dr. Moore on the left, Ely to the right.

I watched Grandma Wren across from me, noting the smug smile playing on her face as she flicked the napkin onto her lap. With her spectacled rims perched on her nose, she glanced at Dr. Moore before engaging in a conversation with Mr. Thane Collins, Ely's father.

"It's lobster bisque. I hope you like seafood."

Dr. Moore gazed at me with anticipation, his complexion now warm. The previous nervousness was gone, replaced by calm confidence.

I took a sip of ice water and wished I was anywhere but here, wishing Hazel was here instead of me.

"Skylar's a seafood aficionado, Dr. Moore," Ely said after a sip of wine. "There's sweet potato casserole too. I had Martha make it especially for you."

I spit my water out, coughing. Dr. Moore smacked me between the shoulder blades.

"Are you all right?" Ely's brow furrowed.

"Um, how did you know I'd be coming?" I wiped the beaded water drops on the red tablecloth with a cloth napkin.

Ely handed me his napkin and received a fresh one from a waiter in a tuxedo with a flick of his finger. Without skipping a beat, he smoothly tucked the napkin onto his lap and handed the waiter my used one. "Morgana told me."

"When?"

His set jaw twitched, but other than that he revealed no other hint of emotion. "A week ago."

I stiffened and shot my grandmother a cold stare, but she remained engrossed in her conversation with Ely's father. She threw her head back and laughed, revealing her milky white neck. Grandma Wren, like all the women in the family, didn't age. The town was impressed by her smooth, wrinkle free complexion. People in town used to talk about how my grandmother used a spell to halt the aging process. The town believed it, because how else would you explain it? It was complete garbage.

For at least a week, she had been conspiring against me. Good to know. I'd sock that one in my mental bank and save it for later. Right now, I'd best chat up Dr. Moore or there'd be hell to pay.

Just as Ely was about to speak, Myra came over and nonchalantly sat beside him.

"Did you miss me?" She leaned toward him, draping her hand possessively on his forearm, her cleavage in full view of anyone caring to notice.

Nuri winked at me, motioning towards Myra's curvaceous twins, and I stifled my laughter by biting my cheek. Ely's expression turned dark, and I saw a chance to question the doctor before Grandma Wren kicked me again under the table.

"Dr. Moore—"

He grinned. "Please, call me Joshua."

Rocking a mop of wavy brown hair on top, clean-shaven on the sides, he didn't look half bad. He sported a six o'clock shadow, and his kind, curious brown eyes gleamed. He seemed an amiable man, and one lots of women would fall for. Nevertheless, there lingered a trace of sadness, or perhaps guilt, within him.

I instinctively reached out and smiled at how effortless it was.

"You have a beautiful smile." He sipped his red wine, his eyes sparkling.

"Thank you."

Ely roughly cleared his throat. I could feel the tension rolling off him, no need to look. Jealousy was Ely's forte. Besides, Myra's incessant chatter and flirting spoke volumes. She always hated how I could steal Ely's attention. Apparently, time hadn't changed that, which was something we had in common, Myra and me. I hadn't the foggiest notion why he'd ever want to speak to me again after the way I'd treated him, and from the initial icy greeting, I'd thought he'd finally moved on. Sitting next to him, however, I realized he hadn't, and that wasn't good for several reasons. One being that Myra wouldn't waste any time putting me in my place, embarrassing me at any opportunity to prove to Ely what a waste of space I was. It wasn't worth the effort because I'd moved on, but Myra didn't know that, and no matter what I said, she wouldn't believe me.

"Tell me, Joshua..."

"Yes?" He sat up, intent.

"How long have you lived here? Last time I left, it was old Dr. Murphy."

"Dr. Murphy died right after you left," Ely cut in, turning away from Myra's pawing.

"How sad." I leaned into the seat back, deflated. "He was a nice man. Always giving me lollipops even at eighteen."

"The town had a memorial in his honor where everyone got on stage at the high school and recounted their memories of him," said Ely.

"That was kind."

"He was an esteemed physician," said Joshua.

"Did you know him?" I asked.

Joshua shook his head and his brown hair fell onto his forehead. "A relative told me about him. That's how I found out about the opening."

My eyebrows shot up. "You *wanted* to come here? To Raven's Hollow?"

"Don't sound too surprised." Joshua chuckled. "It was an established independent practice. Starting from scratch is difficult."

"What about hospital work? In a bigger city? You're young. Don't you want to meet people and live it up while you can?"

"Who says I'm not living it up? Boston's not too far away, and I take weekends every once in a while to New York City. Plus, I'm meeting people. I've just met you."

He took another sip of his wine while I looked on in surprise. Joshua Moore wasn't my usual type. He wasn't a jock, nor did he have a bulky build. Oh, and he wasn't a jerk. Wait. Was I growing?

Nuri gave me a thumbs up and a hot flush crept up my neck and face.

"What about you, Skylar Night?" Joshua grinned broadly. "Why did you leave? Was it for the big city?"

I snorted. "If you mean Boulder, Colorado, then yes. After graduation, I needed a change. Hazel understood that."

"Were you close?"

"Great Aunt Hazel was like a mother to me." I folded my hands in my lap, letting the ache in my heart settle. "She left me her home."

"The one on the hill?"

I nodded. "It's been in my family for generations."

Joshua propped his elbow on the table. "Does that mean you've come back to stay?"

I was captivated by his low and intense tone, unable to break my gaze. Tiny prickles turned my hair on end up and down my arms, and my tummy grew warm the longer he stared.

"Originally, no. I meant to sell Honeysuckle House."

"Honeysuckle House?" He crinkled the bridge of his nose in confusion.

I giggled. "My home. When the property was constructed, it was covered in honeysuckle, hence the name. That's what my mom told me."

"Hmmm..." He fingered the lace collar close to my neck.

I gulped nervously and focused on my wine glass, twirling the stem with my fingers.

"Sweet, like its caregivers," he said, his tone deeper.

It had been a long time since someone had paid me any attention, and I didn't quite know what to do with it. Based on Ely's huffs and grunts, there'd be an altercation unless I did something, and fast.

"So you knew Hazel then?" I anxiously rubbed my neck, draining my wine glass.

"Hazel?" Joshua frowned.

"Her great aunt," Ely snapped.

"Oh, yes. She came in from time to time. Honestly, she was in good health."

"Really?" I studied him. "Do you know what she died from?"

Pausing, Joshua glanced at Grandmother Wren.

"She hasn't told me," I offered.

Joshua remained fixated on my grandmother.

"It's only that Hazel was in great spirits the last time we spoke, and she made no mention of any illness other than her arthritis," I continued. "I'd really like to know what happened to her. It came as a shock to us all."

Although that wasn't exactly true, he didn't need to know that. Hazel and I hadn't spoken in a few weeks because I'd been consumed with my failing business. She had encouraged me to keep going and mentioned that her latest health tests were perfect, as they always were, except for slightly elevated cholesterol. I couldn't recall when my great aunt was last sick. She was as strong as an ox and acted like it. Last year on our hiking trip I'd huffed and puffed so much so that she'd slowed down for me.

"I shouldn't discuss her health, what with HIPPA and all." Joshua scooted his chair in, diving into his lobster bisque.

"She's my great aunt. I inherited her home. I would like to know what happened to her."

Joshua dabbed his napkin across his mouth. "I'm sorry. It wouldn't be proper. I want to avoid any issues with the medical board."

I gaped. "For telling me why she died? I hardly think they'll care."

"Yeah, Doctor, why not tell Skylar how her aunt died? Why all the secrecy?" Ely's intense stare held Joshua captive.

Joshua signaled the waiter to remove his half-eaten soup but was presently ignored. "She died from natural causes."

"Meaning what? Heart attack? Stroke?"

"Her heart stopped. Causes unknown."

I took a deep breath. "What about an autopsy? Was one done?"

Joshua gave me a pointed look, a fiery intensity burning in his brown eyes. "Why the third degree?"

"Why not answer the question, doc?" Ely interjected. "It's a simple yes or no. Was there an autopsy done?"

By this point, several pairs of eyes had locked onto us, one of which was my grandmother's, and her hard expression set my nerves on fire.

"Yes, but I'm sorry I—"

"Skylar Night?"

All eyes turned to the dining room entry, where a solitary woman stood in a pure white gown with gold piping and gold lace cuffs. She swayed and stumbled forward, pitching to the right. The gasp of the crowd filled my ears. My heart raced at the sight of the woman. I noticed the smeared lipstick, which the sloppy grin only enhanced. Her glassy stare and ratty hair stuck out at all angles from her bun, leaving no doubt the woman was three sheets to the wind.

Ely abruptly stood, sending his chair crashing to the floor, and hurried towards her, clutching her arm and trying to lead her back into the hallway. She swiped his hand away and advanced, treating each step as if it were a treacherous minefield. She moved slowly, her tongue sticking out in concentration, her hand against her chest. She held on tightly to the back of an occupied chair, her knuckles turning white. Ely scurried behind her, placing his hands on her tiny waist.

She locked eyes with me and shook her head. "You've come back." Crocodile tears dropped from her fake lashes onto her tissue-paper thin skin. "You've come back. You've come home."

"Mom," Ely cooed like a father to a child. "Mom, let's get you to bed."

She broke free from his grasp and stumbled forward, causing two guests to recoil in horror, covering their noses from the strong smell of alcohol and vomit.

My grandmother was unusually quiet and had diverted her eyes to her soup bowl.

"Father?" Ely gave Thane Collins a pleading stare, but he remained seated, ramrod straight, his lips in a thin line.

"Skylar," Lorelei Collins curled her finger at me and burped. "You've come home to save us. Please save us."

Chapter 18

Ely scooped up his mother and exited the room, her gown dragging behind, wrinkled and stained. She puffed her cheeks, flailed her arms, and wailed, her head lolling backward towards me. Clawing at the air, she screeched.

"Ladies and gentlemen," Thane Collins clinked his crystal wine glass with a fat soup spoon. "Please excuse my wife. She's unwell. Enjoy the festivities. Maestro?"

The harpist caught Thane's pointed stare and the music erupted. The rest of us gathered ourselves.

A bone-chilling cold seeped into me and I looked around the long table. A man openly stared at me from the furthest seat near the musicians. Amidst the gossip and small talk, he maintained a stoic demeanor, unwavering in his scrutiny of me.

I leaned over toward Joshua Moore and asked, "Who is that?"

He followed my gaze. "That's Lucas Hartman. He's the other real estate agent. One of the best around these parts. I got my home for a steal. Are you planning on selling Honeysuckle House?"

I tore my gaze away from Lucas. "How do you know about Honeysuckle House?"

Joshua's spoon clattered into his bowl. He hastily pulled it out of the soup and cleaned it with his napkin. "Clumsy hands." He chuckled nervously. "Poor woman. Lorelei's not been right ever since..."

"Lorelei?" I glanced at Thane Collins, who was avidly discussing something about horses with my grandmother. "What about her? How did she get into that state?"

"How well do you know Mrs. Collins?" Joshua pushed his soup bowl aside and a waiter hurriedly replaced it with a plate of Caesar salad. He picked up the salad fork and stabbed a cherry tomato.

"Fairly well."

He chomped on the tomato, swallowed, and turned his attention to a carrot, pushing it around his plate. "About two years ago, her eldest son died in a car accident. She hasn't been the same since."

"Eldest son?" I frowned. "Ely doesn't have a brother."

Joshua attacked his lettuce. "Since it's common knowledge, I'm not breaking any laws by saying it. Colter was the product of an affair. Apparently Lorelei's family's money and property inheritance were the main reasons why Thane married her, however, she loved Thane and believed he reciprocated her feelings. After their marriage, he transferred the property deeds to his name. Anyway, she can't get rid of him without losing everything, and he wasn't exactly faithful to her either. Practically anyone who has been here for a while claims he has slept in many beds. Lorelei, as a rebellious young woman, welcomed a man into her bed. The result was Colter."

He poked at another cherry tomato while I processed the information.

"If Thane had accepted him as his own, I would have known about him. Who looked after Colter?"

"Ah," he jabbed the fork at me, grinning, "that's an interesting story. Thane discovered their relationship and forbid Lorelei from ever seeing her lover again. He sent her off to Maine, where she had her son, and then he demanded she return once she had regained her youthful shape. The boy was adopted by some family there. Lorelei hired a private investigator to monitor Colter, and when he finished high school, she met him in secret. His arrival in town after college graduation caused quite a stir. Vasser, I think. Anyway, the town took him on as one of their own and he set up shop as the town lawyer."

"How was he? I mean, was he nice? Angry? I can't imagine finding a long-lost mother."

"It took him some getting used to. We became good friends. He was a good man with a world of possibilities at his fingertips. A promising law practice, a fiancé—"

"Who was he engaged to?"

"Myra Humphrey."

I slumped back into my chair and glanced at Myra. She was scooting a crouton around her plate, staring at it longingly.

"Isn't she with Ely now?" I said quietly, staring at Joshua in astonishment.

He nodded ruefully. "Not officially, mind you, but they are a couple in a certain sense of the word. They've been around town a few nights a week, but he's not the committed type, and Myra wants the whole lot."

That made sense. Since grade school, she had been chasing after Ely, where boys went from being disgusting creatures to individuals we desired and competed for. Nothing turned a friend into an enemy faster than date night.

Ely strolled in and tugged at his cuffs. He righted his chair and sat, the lingering hint of alcohol hovering about him.

"Sorry about that. My mother's not well. Sleep will help."

"Darling," Myra drawled and pawed his shoulder. "You've been gone too long. How long do we have to stay?"

Ely stiffened. "It's the annual gala, Myra. We stay until the last guest leaves."

Myra's full lower lip puffed out. "Not even a little early?" She dropped her hand from his shoulder. "I have a surprise for you."

A few seconds later Ely jerked, knocked his knee against the table, and sent the wine glasses sloshing. Red splotches faded into the tablecloth. "Myra," he hissed, "keep your hands to yourself. Please."

Ely drained his soup. The server cleared his plate and set down a salad plate, but he dismissed it. In minutes, the dinner plate arrived full of turkey, cranberry sauce, mashed potatoes and gravy, and sweet potato casserole. It smelled heavenly, and he wasted no time digging in.

Myra sat there, grumpy. She pushed the bowl away, her lower lip trembling.

"Trouble in paradise?" I hadn't meant to say it out loud, but that's my speaking before thinking issue again.

Myra leaned over Ely with a pert grin, causing his jaw to twitch. "Let's get something straight, Sky. Ely's mine. Got that? You can waltz into town, sway those hips, and do whatever it is you do to the men of this town, but I'm not fooled. Once a loser always a loser. You left, and I was here to pick up the pieces. Ely was crushed, but did you care?" She snorted. "I read the note. Who breaks up with someone with a note?"

"Myra," Ely mumbled, wiping his face with a napkin.

Myra wasn't having any of it. She'd been bursting at the seams to let me have it regardless if there were over seventy witnesses. In her case, the more the merrier. That was her style after all. Myra Humphreys, the high school bully, had now become the town bully.

"No, she needs to hear this. It took me an entire year to make him stop drinking. He stayed in bed for days and only ate when forced. I was there to get him up, showered, and out, morning, noon, and night. Me, not you." Myra jabbed her painted nail into her chest, leaving a red mark on her otherwise blemish free skin. "While I was cleaning up your mess, you were far away enjoying life. I won't stand for you taking him down again. Not when I've worked this hard to make him—"

"Myra!" Ely snapped. "Enough."

Either my grandmother forgot to kick me in the shins or she was as surprised as I was by Myra's outburst, since she gawked at Myra like everyone else, including Thane Collins, who wore an apoplectic grimace.

"Face it," Myra barreled on, ignoring Ely's warning. "You lost. I won."

She sat back in her chair, arms crossed, a triumphant grin on her face.

Her eyes filled with a wild intensity as she confidently claimed, "He's all mine."

"Aren't you forgetting something?"

We were taken aback by a woman's voice from the other end of the table. It was like a moth drawn to flame or a train rushing down an unfinished track. We couldn't take our eyes off it even if we wanted to.

"Or rather some*one*?" Brooklyn Irwin had opted for an updo, showcasing her dirty blonde hair. Her sun-kissed skin revealed extensive time outdoors, and her ordinary pink dress exuded royalty. She looked absolutely stunning with the glimmering diamond choker necklace.

I leaned over to Joshua. "Why is Brooklyn seated next to Lucas? Isn't she engaged to Drake Chamberlain?"

"You have a keen eye, Ms. Night."

"Ely?" Brooklyn pushed on. "Care to share?" She let her words sink in, fueling the crowd's excitement even more. Everyone was focused on Ely, anticipating a response. "No? Alright, I'll tell them. Ely and Charlotte Stevens are secretly engaged. Isn't that right, Ely?"

The room erupted in gasps, but Ely didn't utter a sound. Desperation clouded Myra's features and she fidgeted.

"Honey," a man seated directly across the table from Brooklyn chimed in. Around thirty, he had a groomed goatee, a square jaw, and intense eyes. By his mannerisms and speech, it was clear he was from the elite class. "Stay out of this. Please." While his speech was moderated, the warning glare was unwavering.

Joshua leaned over and whispered, "That's Chase Chamberlain. He's come back from London. An excellent lawyer if you ever need one."

"So, the prodigal son returns," I mumbled.

Chase's unruly behavior as a child and teenager resulted in him being sent to multiple boarding schools. However, once he reached college age, his father sent him to London, where he pursued a law degree. Marrying a prominent woman was his final assignment. That was what the Chamberlains did. However, Chase was different. He had always appeared distant, but perhaps he was simply unhappy living a life of constant surveillance. I could empathize to a degree.

"Ely?" Myra's voice wavered. Her eyes brimmed with tears. "Ely, honey, is that true?" Leaning forward on the edge of her chair, she licked her lips and held her fork as if her life hung in the balance.

Ely scooted closer to her. "Myra, it's been fun, but—"

"Oh no you don't." Her chest heaved, and a snarl marred her otherwise beautiful face.

"Myra, why don't you put the fork down?" I said, emphasizing each word.

"You don't get to dump *me*." Myra rose and glared down at Ely. "I'm done. Fed up with your skirting ways. I'm tired of your empty promises and mediocre gifts. I won't be here to pick you up anymore when Charlotte or Miss Goody Two Shoes here leaves town again because she will. Oh, she will, I can promise you that. Skylar Night is nothing but a loser, and Charlotte..." She looked around the table, focusing on a young red-haired woman sitting beside Nuri, whose eyes were popping out of her head. "You can have him."

The fork clattered on the plate and Myra twirled and advanced towards the foyer, executing one final spin before reaching it. Face beet red, eyes sparking with anger, she landed on Charlotte. "I'd invest in a therapist,

Charlotte. You'll need one when he gets done with you. Oh, and make an appointment with Dr. Moore. A prescription for antibiotics are in your future."

With that, she stormed off, slamming the elegant front doors behind her.

Chapter 19

After Myra's hasty exit, dinner was over. We all crowded into the upstairs ballroom, ready for drinks, dancing, and a chance to contemplate what had transpired. I glanced around the room. Elegant burgundy drapes hung from twelve-foot-tall windows in front of a spacious balcony. Decorative pots held exotic planted trees, spaced every ten feet around the room, with white-cloth covered tables scattered throughout, overflowing with alcoholic beverages as far as the eye could see. While everyone was indulging in rum, wine, beer, hard cider, and brandy, I made a beeline for the dessert table in the room on the left.

Inhaling deeply, I sighed in bliss at the inviting sweetness of cinnamon. The Collins were famous for their sweet breads, a town tradition. Each year they brought in a pastry chef just for this night. This was why partygoers spent long nights pining for an invitation to the annual gala. Plate after decorative plate held slices of sweet bread filled with raisins, figs, and spices. You couldn't eat just one.

I piled a plate high and I strolled through the room admiring its architecture. Wide beamed floors, scuffed and marked with use, shined under the three crystal chandeliers. High wooden beams covered in holly and twinkling lights cast a seductive glow upon the room's swirling couples, dancing to modern music. I migrated to a corner of the giant room where my companions were and watched the inebriated couples gyrate to the music.

"Can you believe it?" said Nuri. "The rich are apparently as messed up as the rest of us. Who knew?" He patted his purple beehive wig while tapping his pumped foot to the beat. He was dying to dance, but Nuri understood our reluctance. On a normal night out, we'd always kick up our heels and burn the midnight oil, but in these heavy gowns and whalebone corsets, there was no way I'd last a minute with the fast-paced music.

Willow squinted into the crowd. "It doesn't appear Charlotte or Ely are any worse for the wear. They're slow dancing to a fast song."

Ely had taken off his silk coat, leaving his sculpted body in full view of more than a few admiring ladies. The silky white shirt was practically see through.

"To think you dated him." Willow looked like she'd bit into a lemon.

I shrugged. "He wasn't a gigolo in high school."

Nuri chuckled, fanning his face. These old homes, while retrofitted for modern conveniences, lacked the air flow of modern day homes. Nuri's makeup dripped like hot frosting down his cheekbones. "Leave it to you, Sky. He's ruined. Too bad he's a cis male. I could make him forget you in two seconds."

I tried to hide the grin. "Two seconds? That's all I'm good for? I think I'm good for thirty minutes."

Nuri's eyes widened, and he feigned offense, jerking his head back. "Thirty? For Pete's sake, what did you *do* to the poor man?"

"He loves her."

Trixie's simple statement killed the light-heartedness.

"Ely loves himself. Full stop. The second I left town, he started rumors about how frigid I was. Great Aunt Hazel warned me he was no good. I should have listened. Instead, I wasted four years longing for him, while he pursued any brunette or redhead he saw."

"Why did you stay with him?" Trixie asked.

"Yeah, why not boot him to the harpies?" Nuri seconded.

"Because I loved him. Well, I thought I loved him. No matter." I wanted rid of the old icky feelings dredged from the past. "He can have his redhead. I'm done with Ely Collins."

"Good. Now how about a dance?"

I studied the man who had inched between Trixie and Nuri, hand held out. I stared at it as though it were an alien object.

"Dance?" Willow gaffed. "Skylar doesn't dance."

Nuri and Trixie glared at Willow.

"What?" Willow thrust out her chin. "It's true. She's got two left feet."

Willow fell silent as everyone stared at her in disbelief, while I tried to figure out what to do.

"I would love to dance."

The man whirled me onto the dance floor as the beat slowed.

"Looks like you're saved by the tempo."

He had a nice smile, and one I hadn't seen since our unfortunate incident on my Great Aunt Hazel's front lawn. The face plant to his butt wasn't my finest hour.

"It's Ryan, right?"

"Ryan Irwin. Sorry about earlier. I wasn't welcoming at all. It's been a rough day."

He pulled me close, arms snug around my waist, and swayed us around the room. I wrapped my arms around his neck and laid my head against his shoulder, closing my eyes and enjoying the peace.

"I'm a real estate agent." His voice sounded muffled against my hair. "Honeysuckle House has good bones. I hope you intend to fix it up."

I chuckled. "Why? So you can sell it for me? I bet Lucas can't wait either." I pulled my head back and stared up at him. My breath caught in my throat as his brown eyes tenderly held mine.

"You would sell Honeysuckle House?" The bridge of his nose crinkled. "Why? It's been in your family for generations."

"Aren't you supposed to want people to sell? Isn't that your job?"

Ryan swirled us onto the open balcony where we were alone. A gentle breeze stirred the beaded perspiration lining my neck and forehead. We ambled over to a secluded spot behind a Ficus tree, free from prying eyes. He leaned his elbow against the stone railing free from snow and peered out into the twinkling night.

"It's beautiful here," he said. "I can't imagine being anywhere else. As for Lucas, he's a wolf in sheep's clothing. I'd steer clear of him."

I studied his fine features. His black hair shimmered under the hazy moonlight. Ryan was undeniably attractive with a lean nose, strong jaw, and perfect cheekbones. He wasn't a model by any means, but he had a certain ruggedness about him that stirred something within me. It was odd because I usually went for the buff type.

"Your sister." I couldn't help myself. Brooklyn Irwin had made quite the scene. Curiosity maybe killed the cat, but I had to understand this man. "Why did she call out Ely like that?"

"You thought Brooklyn and Ely were an item." He smiled weakly. "Not her type. Brooklyn likes to stir up trouble."

"For Ely or everyone?"

Ryan laughed. "Everyone." Tucking a tendril of my hair behind my ear, he noted my shivering. "Are you cold?" Pulling me closer, he rubbed his hands up and down my arms.

"Thank you." I averted my gaze to the stars under his intense scrutiny.

"Skylar, I—"

"Ryan? There you are!" The tall, lithe brunette stood at the opening of the balcony, her lips turned down. "How dare you leave me alone? You know how much I hate these things. If it weren't for the food, I'd skip them altogether." She strolled over and pulled out a cigarette from her bra. She lit it, closed her eyes, and inhaled, releasing the smoke into the cloudless night.

"Brooklyn, you remember Skylar Night," Ryan said.

She opened her eyes and thrust out her hand. "Soon to be Chamberlain. Don't be fooled. I'm not marrying him for the money. Drake puts up with my shenanigans, and I adore him for it. He doesn't try to change me." She drew again off the cigarette. "Dangerous territory, if you ask me. Changing a woman?" She blew out the rest of the smoke. "Doesn't work. You wind up with a bitter person that can make your life a living hell."

Ryan smirked. "Brooklyn's a softie at heart. She appears like a lion, but she's a teddy bear."

"Am I?" She arched a brow and studied me. "Skylar Night. The great niece of Hazel Wren." Brooklyn smashed the cigarette butt against the stone railing and narrowed her gaze at me.

"That's right." I clasped my hands together and plastered a smile to the point my cheeks hurt. Ryan was such a nice person, but his sister was something else altogether. It's hard to believe she's engaged to Drake, given the intense chemistry she shares with Chase Chamberlain, which makes it seem like they should be the ones getting married.

A thought popped to mind. Worst case scenario, Brooklyn Irwin would loathe me, but it's not like we were besties anyway, plus I was curious. "Chase will make a handsome groom."

"Drake Chamberlain. I'm marrying Drake," she stated flatly, her expression one of stone. "Big brother? May I have a word?"

Ryan excused himself and accompanied his sister to the opposite side of the balcony, making sure they were well out of hearing range. However, judging by her stern grimaces and hand movements, Brooklyn Irwin wasn't exactly my biggest fan, as she had made clear at the funeral. From this reaction, though, it was probable that she and Chase had something going on.

"So this is where you've been hiding."

I couldn't help but roll my eyes. "Where's Charlotte? Cast her aside so soon?"

If I'd been the smoking type, I'd have found a way to relight Brooklyn's cigarette butt. Anything to distract the anger welling up inside.

"Charlotte and I are casually dating." Ely lifted the lacy collar of my gown. "You and Ryan are cozy."

I threw up my hands. "Enough. First, you muddy my name to anyone who'd listen after I left, and then you slept with any woman with legs in a hundred-mile radius. As if the cheating in high school wasn't enough humiliation." I scoffed and pushed past him, but he grabbed my elbow, forcing me close. His breath smelled of cigars and whiskey.

"Listen, you left me. I loved you, and you left me a note. A freaking note, Sky. What was I supposed to do? Tell everyone how great you were? Spare me the indignation. We're both at fault. At least I take responsibility for my actions. I don't run away when things get real."

I snorted. "No, you screw the next female that walks along to punish me. I'm over it, Ely. I don't want a part of this insanity anymore. Have fun with Charlotte and any other woman that comes along. My give-a-cares are long gone when it comes to you."

I pried his hand off my elbow and stormed off toward the dance floor when Ryan jogged up.

"Is everything okay? It looked heated over there."

I bit down on my lip and blinked back tears. "I'm tired. It's time to call it a night. It's nice meeting you and your sister again."

I took a step to leave.

"Hold on." Ryan retrieved his business card from somewhere in his costume. "Call me. About the house or the weather." He broke into a boyish grin. "Whatever you want, but fair warning, I make a great cup of tea."

I brushed away a tear from the corner of my eye. "You make tea?"

"The best in the area. Call me, alright?"

I glanced behind him at Brooklyn's stiff frame. She stood, hand on hip, and stared straight at me. "Your sister doesn't like me."

Ryan glanced over his shoulder at her. "She's protective, that's all. Don't worry about Brooklyn. She'll come around."

I stared at Ryan's hopeful grin a moment longer. "Good night, Ryan."

Stepping into the ballroom, I waved at my companions indicating that I was leaving, then made my way down the grand stairwell. The limo driver noticed me as soon as I stepped outside, and as I bent to sit, someone called my name.

"Skylar Night. I've been wanting to introduce myself all night, but you're a difficult person to meet. I'm Lucas Hartman." He whipped out a card and held it out. "I hear you're in need of a realtor. Don't lose money with Ryan Irwin. He can't sell his mama cookies. I'm the guy you need."

I studied the card. "I don't need a man, Mr. Hartman. Have a good night."

I scooted into the limo.

"Good night, Ms. Night. Sweet dreams."

Lucas flashed a wry grin while the driver closed the door. Once home, I crawled into my great aunt's bed and dragged the warm hand-quilted blankets up to my chin, mulling over the night's events. Parties never interested me, and tonight's was one reason why. I always attract the wrong sort of attention. As I drifted off to sleep, however, Ryan's big brown eyes smiled at me, and soon I was lost in dreams of tea parties, horses, and letters. One of which hovered in view, reading:

"*My love it cannot be. How am I to live without you? The absence of your skin's touch vexes me. The smell of it. We will be together someday soon. Until then, I'm forever yours. EW.*"

Chapter 20

Sunshine broke through the windows as dawn arrived. I got up, stretched my aching body, and dressed. The hot pot of tea shrilled on the stovetop, and I poured a mug and scribbled a To Do List of things the home needed. From new wallpaper to shoddy wiring, the bill would be astronomical, and I wondered how on earth I'd ever afford such repairs.

BAM! THUD!

I strained my neck, looking up at the ceiling. Puffs of dust fell onto the kitchen table and floors.

"What the...?"

I stood and crept up the stairwell. Following the bangs and loud sounds, I climbed up another set of rickety stairs into an old attic. Swatting at cobwebs, I used my cell's flashlight to reveal the expansive attic before me. It was large enough for a football game, but moving boxes, chests, and old furniture cluttered the space. I found a chain and tugged. Dim yellowish light cast eerie shadows around the room. My shock grew as I looked at the overflowing boxes and drawers. How had I never been up here before? Weirder yet? The banging sounds that drew me here stopped the moment I entered.

"Hello?" I called out.

Nothing.

I explored the room, turning on lights and marveling at the hidden history. One oak chest was left open with heaps of yellowed papers flowing out. I sank to my knees and searched the chest, noting long paid bills and some correspondence from years past. Hazel's pretty script leapt out at me from a couple, and my heart wrenched.

"Oh, Hazel. What happened to you?"

A broom fell to my right and I yelped. As it fell, envelopes dropped to the floor. I scanned the attic, but there wasn't a single person in sight, yet I could feel someone watching. That was crazy, right? Thinking it must have been a mouse, I made a mental note to call the exterminators and crawled over to the letters.

Goosebumps prickled up and down my arms. They were addressed to my great aunt.

I eyed the attic exit and scanned the area, but I was alone. Palms clammy, I opened the first letter postmarked a month prior.

"Hazel, Brooklyn means well. She's upset. Please don't report her. I promise that I'll talk with her. She'll see reason. Here is the listing you requested, and if you need anything else, please don't hesitate to ask. Sincerely, Ryan Irwin."

Report Brooklyn Irwin? For what?

I opened the remaining letters, all of which were from Ryan, once again urging Hazel to be patient. They provided a detailed account of the town's founding and property rights, specifically mentioning Honeysuckle House, the Chamberlains', and the Collins' houses.

Was Hazel trying to find out if Grandmother Wren owned the land rights to Honeysuckle House? Why? Did she want to prevent my grandmother from gaining control of the home? Better yet, why were the Chamberlains' and the Collins' land deeds included?

My brain was filled with countless questions, and soon enough, I had read a pile of other letters, several of them dated a century ago.

I stood, arching my aching back. A black-and-white photo fell to the floor. Squatting to pick it up, I noticed a handsome young couple standing in front of Honeysuckle House, smiling and holding each other, gazing dreamily into each other's eyes. If it weren't for my ancestral home being front and center, I would have felt like an intruder. Flipping it over, I noticed names written on the back.

"Hazel Wren and Oscar White, 1910."

Hazel? My Hazel? Surely not. She wasn't born until 1957. It had to be an ancestor, but who was Oscar White? And why weren't they Mr. and Mrs. White? It was clear they were smitten with each other.

I opened each letter until I found the photo's imprint on one. It read: *My darling Hazel, if it were up to me, we'd be married and off traveling the world. Alas, our good fortune has come to a bitter end. I will always cherish you in my heart for all eternity, my love. I take solace in the lock of hair you have given me and will wear it on a chain until my dying day. Worry not for my fate. It has been sealed as has yours. I cannot give you what you deserve, and your father is correct in marrying you to someone else. Honeysuckle House must stay under Wren control. Take care, my darling Hazel, and remember me on occasion. Farewell, my dearest. Forever yours, Oscar.*

I slid the picture into the creased letter and gingerly put it back in the worn envelope. It was clear the letter had been read repeatedly over the years, judging by its crinkled edges and creased folds. Circular stains, which I could only assume were from tears, dotted the envelope and paper inside. Such a tragedy for them to be separated when they were so in love.

I tugged out my buzzing cell from my back jean pocket.

"Hey, Willow. What's up?"

"*We're outside freezing our arses off. Let us in before we kick the front door down.*"

"Why didn't you ring the doorbell?" I picked up a stack of unread papers and hurried down the attic stairs.

"*Gee. Why didn't I think of that?*" She grunted. "*We've only been at it for ten minutes. I almost called the cops. We thought something had happened to you.*"

"Nope, I'm alive and kicking."

"*Great. Could you hurry? If Nuri sticks his frozen popsicle hands up my sweater one more time, he'll need the hospital.*"

I made it to the door and went to unlock it.

"Huh." I stepped back and wiggled the lock. The crew must have heard, as they flung the door open and stumbled inside, shaking off the wet snow like dogs.

"Praise be," Nuri crossed himself. "One moment more and I'd be an ice statue."

I stared from one to the other. "Why didn't you try the door?"

Willow stared at me like I'd lost my mind. "Who says we didn't? This place is locked up tighter than Fort Knox. Trixie tried the back door while Nuri tried the side porch."

"But it was unlocked. I didn't open it. You did."

Willow stared at me blankly. "Nonsense. It was locked. We heard you wiggle the lock."

"I wiggled it, but it wasn't locked. You opened the door, not me."

Willow noticed the stack of papers I held. "What's that? Please tell me your Great Aunt Hazel hasn't left you in debt."

"These are old letters and paid bills. I found them in the attic."

Trixie bunched her nose and stared up the oak stairwell. "There's an attic? I bet you could find all sorts of fun stuff up there."

I loved her enthusiasm for everything old, which stood in stark contrast to her celebrity clients. As a yoga instructor to the stars, she'd been purview to Botox, tummy tucks, and butt lifts. New meant better in her world, but all that insecurity and money never phased Trixie. She remained grounded and focused on health and well-being, and that meant spending ten hours a week on the elderly or anyone else who needed help strengthening and centering their lives. She donated her time and expertise in making sure the underprivileged got the same type of treatment that celebrities do. She was tops in my book.

"I haven't touched the tip of the iceberg either. It's the size of a football field."

Willow studied my face. "Something wrong? You look preoccupied."

Intuitive as ever, Willow nailed it. Ever since the letters to Ryan and finding the picture of some relative, I'd been preoccupied alright. I handed over the letters and picture to Willow. She opened them, reading them one by one while I informed the others of my morning adventures.

"Wow." Willow held out the picture while the others huddled around her to look. "That *is* interesting. What do you know about this Hazel Wren? She's too old to be your Great Aunt Hazel."

I gestured for them to follow me into the kitchen. "Unfortunately, I don't know anything about my ancestry."

"Nothing?" Trixie filled the kettle with water and set it on the stove.

"Nope. Anything past Grandmother Wren hasn't been discussed except that Honeysuckle House was one of the founding homes of Raven's Hollow."

"Didn't you ask?" Nuri sat at the kitchen table and shivered.

I grabbed more mugs out of the cabinet and set them on the table. "I spent my youth avoiding my grandmother."

The kettle soon whistled, and Trixie pulled it off the stovetop and walked it over to the table, pouring it over the tea bags in each cup.

"Isn't it time to ask?" she said, setting the hot kettle on the stove again. "I can come with you."

"Thanks, Trixie, but I wouldn't subject you to that."

"Subject her to what?"

I gasped, hand on my chest. It was like the woman could teleport. "Stop *doing* that," I hissed.

"Calm down. What's got your panties in a wad?" Grandmother Wren snatched Nuri's warm mug and sipped.

I filled up another mug and handed it to a thankful Nuri before stomping over to my grandmother. Folding my arms against my chest, I stared at her. "Who was Hazel Wren from 1910? And why was Great Aunt Hazel corresponding about land rights to Honeysuckle House?"

Grandmother Wren flinched, but only momentarily. "Trixie, my dear, order takeout," barked my grandmother. "Whatever you want. It's my treat. Skylar, follow me. This won't be pretty, but you need to hear it nonetheless."

Grandmother Wren stalked out of the room leaving me staring after her.

"Trixie?" I called over my shoulder. "Get some rum and Coke while you're at it. I have a feeling I'll need it when this is all over."

I stormed out of the room and found my grandmother in the front parlor staring up at a portrait above the fireplace in practically the same stance as the mysterious man.

"She was a fool to trust him."

I padded to a stop behind Hazel's favorite sofa chair. "Who?"

Grandmother Wren turned. A bitter frown marred her otherwise smooth complexion. "Let's start from the beginning. Please," she motioned to the chair, "sit."

I obliged, sitting on the edge of the sofa chair with my hands folded in my lap and waited patiently for her to continue. Uncharacteristically, she paced in front of the fireplace several times before speaking.

"Honeysuckle House was a founding home back in the 1600s, which you already know. One thing you might not understand is that it was built by a woman. Cleantha Wren, Clea to her family, came over to the Americas for a fresh start. She was a formidable force in her day, and it wasn't common for women to strike out on their own as you can imagine." Grandmother Wren smoothed her long A-line black skirt as she was still in mourning over

Hazel's passing. "Her roots go back to Ireland, Wales, maybe Scotland. I don't know for sure, but she is our matriarch. She never married, which caused quite the scandal, but according to the letters, she liked it that way. Marriage was bondage, and she was a free spirit. Tell me, what have you heard of the Druids?" Grandmother Wren abruptly stopped pacing and stared right at me.

"Um, not much." I held up a finger in confusion at the sudden turn of conversation. "Excuse me, but what has this to do with our ancestry and Hazel's death?"

Grandmother Wren pinched the bridge of her nose. "Patience," she scolded. "I'm getting to that. First, tell me what you know about the Druids?"

"They worship nature. That's what the television shows depict. Other than that, nothing. Oh, and there are festivals. Lots of festivals."

Grandmother Wren scoffed, and tiny wrinkles crinkled about her eyes and forehead. "How did you manage to learn nothing in the time you grew up here?" She paused. "Never mind. You'll learn now."

I slumped in the chair. She pushed on, ignoring my irritation. "Druidism dates back to Wales," she flicked her wrist, "but that's not important. What matters is you know where you come from."

The chair legs snagged on the worn maroon rug as she yanked it over to sit in front of me. She rested her elbows onto her thighs and brought her hands to her chin. "We're druids," she whispered, her lips curling into a mischievous grin.

I blinked at her, dumbfounded. "Wh-what?"

Grandma Wren rolled her eyes, a trait I'd inherited from her. "Druids, Skylar. We're druids. Honestly, why couldn't it have been Ophelia?" She glanced toward the ceiling as if talking to someone and raised her hands.

Morgana slapped her thighs, lips pressed together. "For pity's sake, child." She stood and peered down her fine nose at me through her sparkling spectacles. "I thought you'd be—"

"What, Grandmother? You'd thought I'd be happy? Gleeful? Chagrined? What? Should I throw my hands in the air, squealing with delight? Or should I gasp in horror and dare never to tell my friends for fear of persecution?"

All of this was bordering on the fantastical, and I'd lost patience years back when my grandmother would beat my back porch red with a switch off one of the many trees at Honeysuckle House. She'd resorted to physical pain when the grounding or cellar confinement failed to drive her points home. Oh, and her sayings nearly drove me bonkers. If I woke a minute late, she'd say, "Wrens are prompt or forgo their breakfasts," and then there was the often dreaded "Sprites never forgive lazy humans!" Whatever that one meant. From one quip to the next, they grew more bizarre, but I chalked it up to her eccentricity and never gave it much thought past the first year of captivity. The first year after Mom's death.

Grandma Wren's nostrils flared. "Persecution nearly wiped out our family line, young lady."

"Our family was persecuted? When? How come I've never heard this before?"

The chime of her phone stopped her retort. "Ah!" Morgana's face lit with joy as she answered, her voice sugary sweet like honey. "Ophelia, my darling. Just the person I wanted." She paused, tapping her finger on her bony hip. "When? Oh, honey, we've got lots to do. Tonight? Fantastic. See you soon."

Morgana slid her cell into her skirt pocket and faced me. Hands on her hips, chin held high, she beamed. "Reinforcements are coming. By the end of the day, you'll be well versed in family history, and then," she rubbed her palms together gleefully, "let the magic begin."

Chapter 21

"That was weird." I plopped into the last open chair and faced my companions' inquisitive stares. The tea mug had grown cold.

"Skylar," Willow started, her fingers tugging at her pendant necklace, "what do you know about Ryan Irwin?"

I raised a brow. "He's a real estate agent. I'm sure he's interested in Honeysuckle House." I snorted and stood, refilling my cup with hot water from the kettle and dipped another tea bag in to steep. I leaned against the counter. "Brooklyn Irwin is his sister. She's nice enough, but when she found out I was a Wren, something changed. I get the impression she doesn't like Grandmother."

I sat again and absentmindedly dipped the tea bag over and over, rethinking the party from the previous night. It was like I'd stepped into *Alice in Wonderland*, except I was now Alice, and every corner had a sinister shadow. If only Hazel hadn't died, then I could be miles away worrying about all the past due bills mounting in my absence and maybe save my shop.

I refocused on Willow, who had carried on while I reminisced about days gone by.

"These letters," she stabbed one with her French manicured nail, "mention tension between the Irwins and Hazel. What about the property rights? Why were they mentioned? Apparently Hazel had a vested interest in finding out who owned them."

The scolding from Morgana the day before rushed back to mind.

"My grandmother owns the land rights." I dunked the tea bag, unable to watch any of their expressions. "Apparently she's resistant to selling Honeysuckle House."

"Resistant?" Willow studied me like a specimen under a microscope.

I wrapped my hands around the hot mug and sipped. "Grandmother Wren won't let me sell. I believe Hazel realized this and was sorting out land rights so that when I inherited Honeysuckle House I'd be able to sell it."

Nuri tsked. "That gives your grandmother motive."

"Wait." I held up my hand. "Morgana is a lot of things, but a murderer?"

It wasn't possible. The sisters always argued, but they'd stuck by each other through thick and thin, and it was inconceivable to believe Morgana would kill her own sister.

"If the shoe fits." Nuri harrumphed, crossing his legs.

"There's got to be another explanation," Trixie piped in, offering me a small smile.

"What is there?" Willow held up the letter and shook it for emphasis. "It's written here. Hazel was looking for land rights, and your grandmother doesn't want anyone to sell Honeysuckle House. I get wanting to keep it in the family, especially considering it's one of the original homes in this area, but why else would Hazel be searching for land rights? Plus, what about the Irwins? What was Brooklyn so angry about? I don't like them. Something's up there."

Trixie laid her hand on mine and gently squeezed. "Why not fight your grandmother in court? I'm not a lawyer, but land rights usually refer to oil or something of that nature, right? You could still sell Honeysuckle House and your grandmother can keep the land rights."

Willow nodded. "She's right." She set the letter on the table. "What aren't you telling us, Sky?"

Nuri, Willow, and Trixie all stared at me while I gulped the dread down like week-old bread.

"I didn't want to tell you this but I'm in debt. Huge debt."

They launched into rapid-fire questions, getting louder and louder until I clapped my hands together and stood. "First off, it's none of your business."

Willow eyed Nuri to her right. "Except Nuri."

Nuri hopped up and sashayed to the kettle, pouring another mugful and keeping his back to us all.

"Nuri," I stared at his back, wishing I didn't have to spill the beans, "sold his half of the business."

"When?" Willow asked looking from me and back to Nuri, who continued staring out the kitchen window into the backyard.

"Recently." I swiped a solitary tear off my cheek and tried grinning. "Grandmother Wren told me about it yesterday. She's bought him out, and she's paid off all the debt."

Trixie squealed. "That's wonderful! You don't have to sell the store."

I hung my head. "No," I said, barely above a whisper. "Now that she's majority owner, she sold it and is currently closing its doors. The shop is no more."

Trixie gasped, but Willow steadied her gaze on Nuri, who had tears flowing down his cheeks.

"I didn't know. I didn't know it was your grandmother. She promised me that the shop was in good hands, and that she'd work with you, Skylar. I had no idea. Please forgive me." He hiccupped, his hands gripping the countertop behind him.

"It's okay, Nuri. I understand. The debt was quite enormous. I'm the one who owes you an apology. I should have talked with you sooner."

"No." He stared at me, a muscle twitching in his jaw. "I didn't sell because of the debt."

"If not the debt, then why?" Willow asked.

His features tightened in pain as he sobbed, his shoulders trembling.

I got up and went over to him, wrapping my arms around him. He laid his cheek on my shoulder and shook with the force of his sobs.

"I... I was... they offered me a job. It was my dream job." He clung on to me for dear life.

"They?" I asked after his sobs turned into whimpers and his grip lessened. "What dream job?"

Trixie walked over and handed him a tissue. He dabbed at his eyes and nose.

"New York. I'm moving to New York."

"When?" Willow asked. She was rubbing his arm.

"After Sky sold Honeysuckle House, I was to get the next plane out of here. I'm to be the lead drag queen."

I clapped my hands and beamed. "That's fantastic! The one you've been raving about for the last five years? That one?"

Nuri smiled weakly. "One of their owners was in Colorado on vacation and happened to see me perform. Within a week, they offered me the job, and..." He shrugged.

"I'm so happy for you." I hugged him and let the tears flow. "This deserves some champagne."

Willow and Trixie nodded, each taking their turn to hug and congratulate Nuri.

"We'll sure miss you," said Trixie.

"Some more than others apparently," Willow scoffed, but we all grinned at her.

Nuri and she had a turbulent start, but their strong wills and stubbornness bonded them, and I suspected Willow would miss Nuri fiercely.

"Yes." Nuri pumped his hands high in the air and wiggled his hips at our enthusiasm. "Time to celebrate, but first we have to find out who murdered your aunt. I'm not leaving until we do."

"Absolutely." Willow nodded. "We're staying put until the killer is brought to justice. Oh! I have an idea."

Nuri, Trixie, and I groaned. Willow's plans usually ran afoul in the most spectacular ways.

"Hear me out." She raised her hand against the moans. "This Ryan Irwin, we saw you two together last night."

"So?"

"So, there was chemistry," said Willow.

"Uh, no. No there wasn't."

"Come on." Trixie giggled. "There was definite chemistry between you."

My friends' amused looks persisted despite my crossed arms and shaking head.

"Ryan Irwin is an aloof blowhard who wants nothing more than to sell Honeysuckle House. He'd probably wine and dine anyone selling this place. There are the letters, clearly he's invested. Plus, there's Lucas Hartman. He's the other realtor who wants the commission from selling Honeysuckle House."

"Which one was Lucas Hartman?" Nuri asked.

"He sat by Brooklyn last night."

"Ah, yes," Trixie said, wrinkling her nose. "He's the one who stared at you like a piece of meat, Sky."

Willow raised a brow. "Do tell."

"There's nothing to tell. I barely met the man. He's just some realtor."

Nuri tsked. "They're circling like vultures."

"That gives motive," said Willow. "First things first. You need to sugar up Ryan. He's clearly got the hots for you. It'd be easier to extract information from him. We'll work on Lucas later. Call Ryan up. If he's interested in Honeysuckle House, then he'll agree to a date."

"A date?" My eyeballs nearly popped out of their sockets. "No way. Not happening."

"It's not a real date." Trixie grinned. "Don't you want to find out who killed your great aunt?"

I'd been cornered. There was no backing out of Willow's plan now. They'd pulled the great aunt card, and I did owe it to Hazel to find out who murdered her and why.

"Fine. But it won't be a date. Only coffee."

"If it helps you sleep at night, sugar." Nuri patted my arm and chuckled.

"Ladies."

We all turned and faced the kitchen entrance where Grandmother Wren stood. She peered over her spectacled rims. "Tonight is a special occasion for family only."

"Grandmother—"

"She's right." Ophelia stepped out from behind Morgana.

"Whoa." Nuri tapped me on the shoulder and whispered, "Are you sure you're not identical twins?"

"She is my fraternal sister," I hissed back. "We look nothing alike."

"You keep telling yourself that," he replied without taking his widened eyes off my sister. "She's your twin down to the dimple on your right cheek, except for the black hair."

"Moon sisters," Trixie mumbled, trancelike.

"Ophelia Wren," announced my grandmother, "meet Nuri, Trixie, and Willow. They are staying at the local bed-and-breakfast. You missed them at the funeral. Ophelia here was doing as she was told and not running off with Ely Collins."

"Well, well, big sister," Ophelia tsked. "Looks like you finally found your tribe. Good. You'll need them."

"What's that supposed to mean?" I asked.

"Nothing." Morgana clapped her hands, sending everyone scattering for their coats. Strange how that never worked for me. "Off with the lot of you until tomorrow morning. Skylar, Ophelia, and I have lots to catch up on."

"Love you," whispered Willow as she held her hand up to her ear, which meant to call her later. "Sorry to run, but that woman scares the crap out of me."

"See ya, honey." Nuri air kissed both of my cheeks while pulling on his white faux fur coat.

"Good luck, Sky. She may be younger, but you're stronger." Trixie hugged me and then all three scurried past Ophelia and Morgana.

"You've finally returned, big sister." Ophelia's grin failed to reach her cold brown eyes.

"Right in time," offered Grandmother Wren. "Sit. We've a lot to discuss. First up, psychics. Who wants tea?"

Chapter 22

" No, this is ridiculous. I'm not some psychic." I waved off yet another round of tea. We'd been at it all night, and I was bleary-eyed, worn, and ready for a hot shower and some food. Anything but to keep rehashing psychics, clairvoyants, witches, and druids. It was enough to make me bonkers.

I groaned and rested my head on my folded arms on the table. "Next, you'll be telling me that dragons, trolls, and fairies exist."

Morgana and Ophelia exchanged glances.

"For pity's sake, give it up. You've had your fun. I get it. I'm the black sheep. You want me back in the fold, and I'm here. Enough already."

I stood and stomped toward the kitchen door, but Morgana whipped about me, barring my exit.

"Remember the boy?" Morgana pointedly stared at me.

Had she lost her mind? None of this was getting us any closer to catching who killed Hazel, if anyone *did* kill her.

"The boy, Skylar. You were eight and in the backyard by the honeysuckle."

That didn't help. The whole backyard was filled with honeysuckle in the summer.

"He was about ten, and he wore knickers."

"Please tell me you haven't been drinking, Grandmother?"

"Blond hair, wasn't it Ophelia?" She glanced behind me to my twin, who was standing so close her breath tickled my neck.

"Yep. Blond hair and hazel-green eyes," my sister responded.

Both of them seized my shoulders in that instant and shouted, "Remember!"

A flash exploded in front of me, followed by the deafening sound of gunfire and the smell of smoke. I gagged, thrusting a hand up to my mouth, bile scorching my throat. Gone was Hazel's kitchen, replaced by fields covered in knee-high grass and men yelling commands. Their mouths twisted in concentration as they bolted beside me, close enough to ruffle my hair. I turned and beheld the ghastly horror of war, and not just any war.

BOOM!

I took off running, hopping over dead, disfigured men clad in torn and sullied stockings, ripped breeches, and what could only be described as hunting shirts. Others wore the characteristic red coats of the British army. Over tricorn hats and felled rifles, the smoke smothered my airway, making me cough and my eyes burn.

A blast erupted behind me, splintering a tree two feet away. I dashed behind another tree on the right, its trunk just big enough to shield me, and knelt down, too fearful to peek.

"What are you doing here?" someone yelled. "Tis not a place for a woman."

From behind trees in the woods, men opened fire on the redcoats. I screamed and clamped a hand over my mouth when one fell on my foot, eyes wide open and glassy. Blood seeped from a chest wound and stained his white frock crimson. I scrambled backward, slamming against a tree, bark scraping my neck and tangling with my hair.

"Miss?!" a man shouted above the roar of cannons. "Are you hurt?"

Men everywhere dropped to an eternal sleep while I frantically searched through the smoke and woods for the source of the voice.

"Miss?"

A young man all of twenty knelt in front of me. He leveled his rifle at some redcoats and fired. The muzzle expelled a plume of dirty white smoke.

I clamped my hands over my ringing ears while the man spoke, unable to understand any words. Focused on his lips, I discerned "hurt." He pointed at me, his face awash in worry.

My mouth bobbed open and shut. In one swift motion, he threw me over his shoulder like a sack of potatoes and jogged deeper into the woods.

Flying splintered bark scratched my face and hands, sticking in my hair as a red-eyed man shot at our pursuer. He barely acknowledged us as we jogged by.

The trees parted, exposing a clearing. The landscape was scattered with makeshift tents and fire pits. Fortunately, we were by ourselves, and the ringing in my ears had subsided somewhat.

"Miss, are you hurt?" His nimble fingers worked their way around my ankles, up my calves, and to my knees. It wasn't until he reached my thighs that I blanched and smacked at his sooty hands.

"If you are injured, I must help." He gestured towards my abdomen, and I dismissed him with a wave.

His appearance matched the others, except for his brown hair was pulled back into a ponytail. He'd be attractive if he wasn't so thin.

"I'm fine." I wrapped my arms about my waist and took in the scenery. "Where are we?"

The young man pointed at my legs. "It's not proper attire for a lady."

"What?" I glanced at my jeans and sweater and confusion soon turned to clarity. "They're jeans."

The young man's forehead scrunched in confusion. "Whatever they are, a proper woman wouldn't be wearing them. Women should be treated more fairly, but pulling this stunt won't win you any support. Although, you are quite the seamstress. How did you get those stitches so even and neat?"

I brushed my hands against my jeans, dirty from skidding to a halt and taking cover.

"What's your name, miss?"

The blasts increased in volume. I twisted my body to scour the woods.

"They won't come for another couple of minutes," the man continued. "Long enough for me to find out what a young lady is doing out in these parts wearing pornographic clothing."

"Pornographic?" I stood to my full height. "I am not a lady of the night, prostitute, or any woman of ill repute, Mr....?" I tilted my head at his bewildered, yet amused expression.

He sat back on his heels. Rifle still in hand, he rummaged in his rucksack, bit off a wad of white paper, dropped a pinch of powder on the flash pan of his rifle, and then he poured the remaining powder down the muzzle, followed by a ball, paper, and finally he shoved a steel rod in to tamp everything down. After he finished, he looked at me curiously.

"Lieutenant Raine White," he half bowed, "at your service, Miss?"

A hot flush swept across my face as the man eyed me from head to toe, lingering on my thighs. His appreciation for my feminine curves in these jeans made me hesitate to question further. This was no coincidence that I'd met yet another White family member. But how in the heck did I get here, and why Raine White? What in the blazes was going on?

"Skylar Wren." From the narrowing of his eyes, I cursed myself silently.

"Wren?" He cocked his head even though the shots blared behind us. "Miss, I've lived in these parts my entire life, and the Wrens are close family friends. Not once have I heard of a Skylar Wren."

"I'm a cousin," I blurted. "From out of town." I was itching to run, and wondering how in tarnation I'd get back to my time.

Wait. Did I time travel? The man touched me, which meant it wasn't an illusion. He was as solid as any human. Could time travel exist? How? Was it Morgana and Ophelia's doing? I felt the blood drain my face. Were they... were they witches?

I put a hand to my forehead. All the smoke, gunfire, and revolutionary war soldiers I'd hopped over sent my stomach into a nosedive. "What year is it?"

The amusement vanished as he scrutinized me further. He reached his hand to touch my forehead. "Did you hit your head? Are you ill?"

The warmth of his hand felt so real on my skin. This couldn't be a dream, but if it wasn't a dream, then everything my grandmother and sister had told me had to be true, and that wasn't something I could digest right now.

My knees gave way, but just before impact, I was lifted into the air. I let my head rest against his chest. He set me on a cot inside a tent. He lifted my head and put some old trousers underneath it and stared down, worry reflected in his soft green eyes.

"Rest easy, miss. You're safe. I'll call the Wrens. They're close by. I'll get you home."

My heavy eyelids closed, and all I recall is his rough hands caressing my face.

Chapter 23

"Explain." I sat, drooped over the kitchen table, and massaged my aching temples.

In one moment, I was in a Revolutionary War tent with a man who had the same last name as someone in a picture with my ancestor. In the next moment, I woke up on the kitchen floor with my sister and grandmother standing over me. They picked me up and sat me at the table. Currently, Ophelia was making tea while Morgana studied me from across the tiny table.

"Who did you see?" Morgana pressed, refusing to answer.

A throbbing pain threatened to split my skull in two, and I'd lost all patience. Not that I had much left when it came to my family, though my first coping strategy had been to run as far away as possible. Colorado had been great, up until now. In hindsight, Japan would have been a safer option.

I leaned my head onto my folded arms, finding solace on the cool surface of the table. "A man," I mumbled. "He had brown hair, green eyes, and was a lieutenant in the Revolutionary War."

"Which side?" Morgana asked.

I closed my eyes, recalling the man's attire. From the ragtag linens, breeches, and snagged tights, there was only one option.

"He was a part of the Colonial army."

The screech of a chair leg against the wooden floorboards was followed by a sharp poke in the ribs.

I sat upright and rubbed my aching side, glaring up at my sister. She handed me the hot mug and nodded towards our grandmother, who stared at me with a stern expression.

"What's his name?"

I took a sip and winced when the hot tea burned my tongue and throat. "Could you make it any hotter?" I set the mug down onto the table.

Ophelia smirked and sat down beside me.

They both stared at me so intensely that I started fidgeting in my chair.

"His name," Morgana barked.

"Raine White."

I caught a knowing look shared between them.

"The Whites go way back in this town," Morgana said with a nod at Ophelia. "They were friendly with the Wrens."

"Could it be the descendant of—" Ophelia clamped her mouth shut at Morgana's stern glare.

I grunted, irritated at their secrecy.

"I don't know who Raine descends from, but I gather Oliver White is his child or grandchild," I said.

Both of their heads whipped in my direction.

"Oliver White?" Morgana's expression immediately changed from pensive to startled, while Ophelia's expression was strained. "It's as we thought. Skylar, did Raine White say anything to you? Mention anything about the Wrens?"

I scowled at both of them. "Only that he knew the Wrens. He was familiar with them."

"How?" Morgana asked. "What did you say exactly?"

What had gotten into them? Their angst was highly bizarre considering it was only a dream. Time travel didn't exist.

"He asked my name, and I told him."

Ophelia rubbed her face, mumbling, "Smooth move, sis."

I shook my head. "What's wrong? It was a dream."

Ophelia chuckled. "Has it not sunken in? That wasn't a dream, Sky."

Shivers ran down my spine. "What?"

"Sky," Ophelia leaned her elbows on the table and sipped from her steaming cup. "Raine White existed. You didn't invent him in some dream. Whatever you say in trances can and will change the future, but it's mostly for gathering facts."

I gaped at her. "Trances?" I pried my tongue off the roof of my mouth. A cool breeze set me shivering in the otherwise warm kitchen. I wrapped my hands around my torso and rubbed them up and down my arms. "I'm not a psychic. I'm no clairvoyant or medium. You've got this all wrong. I'm Skylar, remember? The screwup, the failure, the flighty girl from Raven's Hollow."

Morgana clucked. "Ophelia speaks the truth, granddaughter. You *are* psychic. No? Okay, then tell me about the man you saw."

"I already told you."

"Humor me."

I sighed. "Fine, but you're both crazy. There are no such things as witches, ghosts, or psychics. Raine White, if such a man existed, was around twenty years old, thin, but that's probably because of rations. I remember in one of my college history courses that they barely had food, and many died from dysentery and other diseases probably because food was scarce. Anyway, his greasy hair was pulled back in a ponytail, his clothes were dirty, and from the stench, they hadn't been washed in ages. He had green eyes, and he found me amusing."

"How?" Ophelia cocked her head in interest.

"He found my clothing unconventional."

Ophelia burst out laughing, sending her tea sloshing over the cup's rim and onto the table. "He said you were a prostitute?"

"No." The fire of heat spread up my neck and shoulders to my flaming hot cheeks. "He scolded me, saying a woman shouldn't have been there, and he said a proper woman wouldn't wear this type of clothing," I motioned to my jeans, "and that they were pornographic."

Ophelia slapped the table multiple times in humor and wiped tears away from the corners of her eyes. "And you still don't believe you met the man? Come on, Skylar. Did he touch you?" When I failed to respond, she continued. "I'll take that as a yes. Was he solid? Warm?"

"I didn't time travel."

"It's a trance, sis. And yes, it's like time travel." Her sparkling eyes beckoned me to protest, but it fell flat on the tip of my tongue.

"I refuse to believe people can time travel."

"No?" Morgana waggled a finger at my head. "What's that in your hair?"

I grasped my hair, hands roving all over my head, when a sharp prick scratched my palm. I tugged at an odd-shaped object and tugged it free. My mouth dropped open. "B-b-bark?" It slipped from my grasp when I jumped up from the seat, knocking it over. It banged against the floor while I gasped, pointing a shaky finger at it.

"Th-th-that's not possible," I stuttered. My knees shook violently while yet another cool breeze tickled the hair on the back of my neck.

I rounded on Ophelia. "You put that in my hair."

"No, Sky, I—"

"Stop lying!"

I stepped away from the table, stumbling over the chair.

"Skylar, pick up the chair before you break your neck," my grandmother snipped.

I frantically searched the room, eyeing the back door. "I have to get out of here. This is crazy. This is nuts!"

I stalked toward the back door, but when a shove on my shoulder toppled me into the door, I whirled. "Leave me alone!"

My skin tingled with apprehension, and a cold sweat broke out upon my neck. Both my grandmother and sister were feet away, looking at me like I'd lost my mind.

"Skylar?" Ophelia's forehead wrinkled in concern. The first real sign of compassion I'd seen on her in ages. "Where are you going?"

I backed against the door, felt for the knob, and twisted it. "Somewhere to think. Don't follow me."

"Skylar—" my sister protested.

"Leave her alone, Ophelia." To me, my grandmother said, "Skylar, when you're ready to talk, we'll be here."

My cell buzzed in my jean pocket. It was Willow. "I can't talk now," I answered on speaker phone out of habit.

"It'll only take a minute." She rushed on. *"I bumped into Brooklyn Irwin. Her wedding planner bailed, and guess who's stepping in? Me!"* She squealed with delight. *"I'll have easy access to her for the next two weeks. I'll check her phone for any info and get back to you. It's fate I tell you."*

"Willow, no. It's too dangerous. We don't know if she has anything to do with it, and even if she did, then she's already killed once."

"Exactly, and I'll be the one to find out if she did. I'm a big girl, Sky. I'll be careful. Don't worry. We'll talk later. She's coming back to the table now. Got to run. Bye!"

"Willow? Willow?!" The line went dead.

"It's Youngblood, right?" My grandmother had snuck up behind me. "Is she originally from the northeast?"

"Leave my friends out of this," I snapped.

"It's out of your hands, Sky. She's fully in, but I wouldn't worry. Brooklyn Irwin is an arrogant donkey's butt, but Willow's barking up the wrong tree. If she's anything like the Youngbloods of Connecticut, she'll be well armed."

"Well armed?" I felt the raging headache come to full bloom. "I'll deal with my friends. I'll be back later, and when I do, you'd better be gone."

I stalked out onto the back porch and slammed the kitchen door shut behind me. Whoever, or whatever, pushed me was disconcerting enough, but Willow's eagerness cut the proverbial cake. She was always rash, only this time it could get her killed. Regardless, the twisted sisters, as I called them, that stood in my kitchen spewing utter nonsense would take my hesitance on the porch as an opportunity, so I stormed out into the cottony blanket of snow and stalked off toward the woods, trying in vain to understand how that piece of bark ended up in my hair when I'd never left the confines of my kitchen.

I'd soon marched through the wet snow about a quarter mile, huffing, puffing, and with a cool sweat trickling between my shoulder blades when a sound whipped my head to the right. A snap of bark followed by the shuffling of boots.

"Who's there?"

The headache that threatened to bring me to my knees vanished. My eyes darted left, right, left again, and I spun in a circle, searching the woods for an intruder.

"Show yourself or I'll call the cops."

I held out my phone like a light saber, slashing with each sound. A bird fluttered out of a bush to my right. I yelped and jumped sideways.

"Careful."

Two arms wrapped around me and saved me from falling flat on my butt. I scrambled to my feet and jerked away, turning on a dime to face the intruder.

"*You.*"

Chapter 24

H is wavy brown hair blew gently in the frigid breeze while he folded his hands behind his back, and those intense eyes studied me for what felt like an eternity.

"We have not been formally acquainted." He bowed, crossing his right arm against his chest, then stood upright. "Ebenezer White. And you are?"

I remained mute, staring wide-eyed.

"This isn't the third degree. I merely request a name." His smile brought a spark to his eyes.

"Um, I'm Skylar." After the ordeal in the kitchen, I wasn't about to utter my last name for fear it would bring a fate worse than death upon my friends and me. However, the mere thought of that left me giggling. I was officially losing my mind.

The gentleman looked at me oddly. "Is something humorous?"

"No," I held up my hand, "it's just that my family told me time travel exists. Isn't that bonkers?"

I chuckled again when a playful grin broke his stern features. It softened his face, much different from the brusque nature he'd greeted me with in the parlor yesterday. From Oscar White, to Raine White, to Ebenezer White, all these men had a likeness to each other.

"Indeed," he agreed. "Time travel, as we would see it, poses many ethical dilemmas, but does that weigh heavily on your mind, Miss Skylar? Wouldn't you rather walk among the honeysuckle or attend the latest ball?"

I stared at him unblinking. *Attend a ball? Walk among the honeysuckle?*

It was only then that I became intrigued by his clothing. Yesterday, I'd chalked his style up to Ely's family's party, but why was he still in colonial era clothing today?

"Are you still in the party mood?"

"Pardon?" The bridge of his nose crinkled.

I pointed at his clothing. "The party from last night?"

"Miss, these are not party clothes as you say. What party? Where?"

I tugged at the top of my turtleneck sweater. The cold had seeped in, and I started to regret my hasty exit from the warmth of my Great Aunt Hazel's home.

"The Collins family had their annual party last night." I stuffed my hands in my jean pockets as they were turning from red to a light purple, and my fingertips were numb.

"Oh, the Collinses. Yes, their parties are quite good, but I dare say the Wrens beat them in hospitality. Ely, you say? I don't recall an Ely."

"Wait. We don't hold parties. Not since I've been born." Unless, of course, Hazel had picked up the habit in my absence the last seven years, but she would have told me that. Wouldn't she?

Nothing was making sense, and with each passing second, my limbs grew colder. My skin stung even under my clothes, and that meant I'd better get a move on back into the shelter of Honeysuckle House. I hoped Morgana and Ophelia had left like I'd asked.

"Listen, I've got to get back. It's freezing out here." I turned to stomp back the way I'd come, but Ebenezer had started before me.

His sturdy frame weaved back and forth, retracing my footsteps until we were safely on the back porch.

He opened the back door to an empty kitchen. "At least come in to warm up. I'll see if Sarah can make some tea."

I blinked, trying to speak, but could only squeak. He ushered me inside and shut the door, then stepped through the kitchen and out the door, calling for this mysterious Sarah.

I followed. Down the hallway leading to the foyer, I jogged to keep up with his longer strides. By the time I approached the base of the stairwell, he'd topped the landing and disappeared. I scrambled up the staircase and stopped on the landing, listening for any sound that would indicate where he'd gone.

"Ebenezer? Hello. Are you there?"

I swept through the rooms to no avail. It was like he'd disappeared without so much as a puff of smoke. How odd.

When I failed to find Ebenezer, I wandered back to Hazel's room and sat on the foot of the bed bewildered. This Ebenezer must have been the handyman Ryan mentioned, and I didn't have time to worry about it. He was a nice enough man, and he hadn't killed me yet.

Beep!

Willow. She'd texted that Ryan Irwin was expecting me at the local coffee shop in thirty minutes. She was smart not to have called. I'd have refused, but seeing as how I didn't have much time to back out, and the simple task of doing so would bring on yet another anxiety headache, I dragged myself to the closet and quickly undressed. The bottoms of my jeans were soggy from the snow.

I stepped out of the large walk-in closet and over to the nightstand where I'd left my cell when I spotted the picture of Hazel and Oliver dead center of the bed. Beside it was a monogrammed handkerchief with the initials E.B. in pale blue thread.

My heart tripled in speed as I scanned the room, rooted in my spot. The only sound was the rapid beat of my heart.

I picked up the objects. How did these get here? I couldn't remember where I'd left them, but it certainly wasn't the center of the bed. They'd been intentionally left in just that way to grab my attention.

I sat on the edge of the bed, searching on my phone for an Ebenezer White in Raven's Hollow.

As I scrolled, my fingers trembled.

Could my grandmother and sister be telling the truth? Did the magic of the Druids really exist? Was Raine White a real person who I encountered via time travel? From the bark in my hair, the odd man named Ebenezer in my family's parlor as well as in our backyard, the correspondence between Ryan and Great Aunt Hazel, which spoke of tensions and land rights, to a photo of another Hazel and Oliver White taken in 1910 in front of Honeysuckle House. It all was curious independently, but put them together and add it to Hazel's suspicious death, and it made my blood run cold.

I swallowed hard as I clicked on the link and read.

Ebenezer White, Raven's Hollow original founder and patriarch to the White fortune, died unexpectedly on the eve of his marriage to Cleantha Wren. He was aged 35. There were no dependents, and as such his fortune was inherited by his cousin, Chauncey Chamberlain, 33, whose descendants became avid philanthropists, mayors, and shop owners, making Raven's Hollow what it is today: a thriving town tucked in Connecticut free from corruption and where families can raise their children without fear of crime or taint.

I skipped to the next article written in the 1950s by a Foster Irwin.

Contrary to popular belief, Chauncey Chamberlain was not the rightful inheritor of the White fortune back in the 1600s. Upon extensive research, I have the smoking gun to end all the rumors of infidelity and can champion the naysayers that the rightful owner of Raven's Hollow and the original fortune of Ebenezer White does not belong to the Chamberlain descendants but instead to an illegitimate offspring. This would rewrite history and transfer the fortune, house, and land, including land rights, to the rightful heirs. I shall not be silenced.

Further scrolling produced little more information, but color me intrigued. An illegitimate child? That's not surprising considering the era in which they lived, except back then it was more scandalous. Who was this child? Better yet, my own ancestor, Clea Wren, was engaged to this man?

Could I be an heir to this man's fortune?

The sound of footsteps in the hallway outside my door were followed by a creak of the floorboards. I stayed glued to the bed while the sounds grew closer to the bedroom door.

"Skylar?"

Black boots thudded to a halt at my door. Ophelia's straight black hair fell evenly over her shoulders. "Don't fret. Everything will be fine. Scoot over."

She ambled over and sat beside me. Patting my thigh, she inclined her head to see what I was holding. "Ah, Hazel and Oliver."

She took the photo and studied it. Her nose bunched up as she stared at the two people smiling back. "They were truly in love. Too bad it didn't work out. Ugh." She handed the photo back and leaned back onto her hands. "I hate curses."

"Curses?"

"Supposedly a Wren woman falls for a White descendant in every generation, but the Whites ceased to exist a long time ago."

I frowned. "Then how did Oliver White exist? If Ebenezer White died in the 1600s, how was there an Oliver White in 1910?"

Ophelia sat up and folded her hands in her lap. "Ebenezer? How do you know about him?"

I stared. Should I tell my twin, the sister who'd been a thorn in my side, stealing boyfriends, jobs, and familial attention since birth, about Ebenezer?

"Spit it out, Sky. You're a horrible liar."

She tossed her straight black hair over her shoulders and waited.

"Ebenezer was in the parlor yesterday, and today he was in our backyard. I lost him somewhere upstairs. Do you think he understands that he's a ghost?"

I stared down at the handkerchief and traced the pale blue initials. Someone had crafted it with such care and precision.

Ophelia's eyes about bulged out of their sockets. "Ebenezer's here? Right now?" She jerked her thumb toward the hallway. "Get out of here! Why didn't you say so earlier? Geez, Sky, you had us all fooled. I knew you believed in ghosts. Why did you give us such a hard time?" She chuckled. "Morgana will be relieved."

"I don't believe in ghosts. At least I didn't, until now. As for psychics and all the rest, I can't wrap my head around it. It's too—"

"Crazy?" Ophelia grinned. "Yeah, I felt so too when Morgana told me years ago."

"When? Why wasn't I told?"

Ophelia drew in a deep breath. "Morgana wanted to give you time."

"Time?" I snorted. "Time for what? When is it a good time to tell your granddaughter that ghosts exist, psychics exist, heck—trolls freaking exist? And why do you keep calling her Morgana? It's creepy. She's our grandmother."

I rose and stalked toward the closet, grabbing the first coat I saw. It was my Great Aunt Hazel's favorite. Emerald green and puffy, it still smelled of her. I drew it close and inhaled, relishing the scents of lavender and honey.

Ophelia touched my shoulder as I swiped a tear away. "This is overwhelming for all of us. Problem is, you've only learned the tip of the iceberg. Morgana, uh, Grandmother Wren wanted you to have a childhood. She sensed something different about you, Sky. It was her gift to keep you out of this for as long as possible, and when you ran away, she was relieved. She thought maybe you'd outrun your destiny."

I tugged on the coat and zipped it up, stuffing my hands in the pockets, careful not to wrinkle the picture or the handkerchief. Ryan had a little explaining to do, and as it was, I'd be running late.

"Destiny?" I groaned. "This will have to wait. I'm late for a coffee appointment. Can we talk later?"

"Sure, but don't take too long. Things are tricky."

"What's that supposed to mean?"

"Not important right now. First, you've got a date. Don't make Ryan wait too long."

I sighed. "I'm not even asking how you know it's Ryan. Plus, it's not a date, and Ryan can wait as long as it takes."

"Tell Ryan hello. He's a nice guy. His sister on the other hand..." She whistled. "She's a piece of work. Stay clear of her, Sky. I mean it. Big sister or not, you were never one to defend yourself well. Remember dance class?"

I stuck my tongue out at her. "How could I forget? You've reminded me ever since."

"Someone's got to look out for you. Myra Humphreys is a right twit, and she deserved the knuckle sandwich. On the bright side, she finally got the nose job she'd wanted."

Ophelia grinned wickedly.

"You're rotten to the core, you know that, right?"

Ophelia pulled me in for a hug. "You're welcome." Before stepping back she whispered in my ear, "You look ravishing. Now off with you. Don't keep the man waiting."

I traipsed down the stairwell a few pounds lighter, grabbed the keys from the hall stand basket Hazel always used, and swung the door wide.

"Hello, beautiful."

"Ely?" I looked behind him, expecting Myra in tow. "What are you doing here?"

"Aw, you missed me. What's for lunch?"

Chapter 25

He pushed past me into the foyer and down the hall toward the kitchen. "Great," I mumbled, checking my watch. "Uh, Ely," I scampered after him and hooked his arm right as he entered the kitchen. He looked down at me, a wistful smile on his face. "You can't stay. I've got to go."

"But I just got here."

When I tugged on his arm, his smile faded. "Listen, we need to talk. Last night—"

"Was a disaster, but we're not together, Ely, and you don't owe me any explanations. Now scoot." I shooed him toward the front door. "I've got places to be."

His expression grew cloudy and he ran a hand through his thick hair. "Let me drive you. It's been awhile since you've been back, and there's two feet of fresh snow on the roads. You'll be sliding all over the place. I've got my LandRover. I promise to drop you off wherever you want and leave. Pinky swear." He wiggled his pinky in the air, and I couldn't help but grin.

"Fine, but I'm used to snow. Colorado has plenty of it."

"Colorado has dry snow, we have wet. Whole different ballgame."

We were creeping down the road toward town when he finally spoke. "I owe you an apology."

I held up my palm, but he plowed ahead. "When you left, I was miserable. Worse than miserable, but that's not the point. I shouldn't have sullied your name. That's my fault."

I cast a sideways glance at him. Had he grown up since I'd last left? Miracles did happen.

"Apology accepted."

"Myra's not really my girlfriend," he continued as if I hadn't said a word. "We were never a thing, and I thought I made that perfectly clear to her from the start."

"So she was what? A stand in? Or was it a brother thing? Colter tried her on and you couldn't resist?"

Ely gripped the steering wheel so hard it creaked and his knuckles turned white. "How do you know about Colter?"

I hunched in the seat, feeling two feet tall. I'd crossed a line. "Someone at the party talked about them."

"I'm not talking about Colter."

"Fine. What about Charlotte?"

"What about her?" Ely drifted to a stop at the lone traffic light.

"Are you engaged?"

It was a simple question, but he remained quiet. A different tactic was in order.

"How did you meet Charlotte? She seems nice."

Though I'd never met her, the poor girl looked like a drowned rat left out in the cold and I couldn't help but feel for her. I remembered Ely's "skirting ways" as Myra had called it, and the receiving end of it wasn't fun especially in front of your expected in-laws. Based on Thane Collins' tight expression, his son's engagement was not only a surprise but also unwelcome.

"Charlotte is my father's receptionist."

He offered no further details, and I wasn't jumping down that rabbit hole no matter how juicy the tidbit dangled in front of my face.

Ely circled the town square then pulled into a spot on the opposite side of the cafe. He took my hand in his and squeezed.

"I love you, Sky. Always have and always will. If you tell me to end my engagement with Charlotte, I'll do it."

I slid my hand from his, and his shoulders deflated.

"I've lost you. Haven't I?"

Ely returned his hands to the steering wheel and jammed his foot on the accelerator, sliding us backward out of the parking space. I threw my hand up and grabbed the handle above the door for dear life. He took the street corners at a precarious speed, sloshing and sliding, and finally slid into a parking spot outside the coffee shop.

I scrambled to unbuckle my seatbelt, my hands shaking.

Ely reached over and unlocked me in one click. "Go. Enjoy your date."

I opened my mouth several times to speak but thought better of it and got out, shutting the door. He immediately reversed and sped down the street and off the town square.

I sighed and said aloud, "I can really screw things up."

I hiked through the sidewalk snow and entered the coffee shop a bit dazed, confused, and shaken, yet also determined to find out answers to some of my questions.

I scanned the cafe, which was crowded even in this abysmal weather. Ryan was sitting at a table for two in the far right of the shop. I unzipped my coat and zigzagged through the crowd to him.

"Hello." I smiled awkwardly and thrust out my hand. "Sorry I'm late."

He motioned to the chair on the opposite side. "I ordered you some coffee. I hope you don't mind."

"Not at all." I hung the coat on the back of the chair and sat.

We stared at each other for a few minutes. When the coffee arrived, I gratefully sipped and searched the crowd. It was awfully full. "Is there some event?"

Ryan nodded. "Last night's party is the talk of the town. Gigi's has become gossip central. Rain, snow, sleet, or shine, the town converges here to discuss."

I smirked. "Some things never change. Although," I circled my finger in the air, "apparently the location does. When did Gigi's open?"

The coffee warmed me up in minutes. "Yum. This is wonderful."

Ryan cracked a grin. "Gigi is short for Giorgio. He's a coffee enthusiast who once traveled through here on vacation."

I raised a brow. "Who vacations to Raven's Hollow?"

"Ah, no. He was passing through to New York City from Boston. Anyway, he developed a fondness for the town and made a vow to return and establish a bakery/coffee shop because Americans don't know good coffee."

I raised my mug in salute. "He's right. We don't. This is marvelous."

Ryan leaned back into his chair, mug in hand. "Willow said you wanted to meet. Is there something I can help you with? Are you looking to sell Honeysuckle House?"

The longing in his eyes startled me for a second. "That was the original plan. To sell, I mean, but apparently it's the family home so..."

Ryan set his mug on the table and leaned forward. "Do you own the house? Didn't Hazel give it to you in her will?"

I tilted my head at the mention of the will. "About that. How well did you know Hazel?"

"Well enough. It's a small town. Everyone knows everyone."

"Right, but how well did *you* know her? Was she a friend?"

"Not particularly. We were friendly enough."

"Why did you write my great aunt about land rights? Why was Brooklyn so angry with her?"

Ryan's face resembled a white sheet as he rubbed his stubbled chin. His foot tapped so rapidly our table shook, rattling the mugs. He clamped his hand on the clattering mug to stop it from spilling. Planting his elbows onto the table, he leaned forward. "I told her to be careful. I warned her." He rubbed his hand over his mouth.

"Careful?" I searched his face, but he remained mute. His leg bobbing got so bad, my coffee sloshed out of the mug. I picked it up and examined him when his leg stopped bobbing.

"She was looking into land rights," he finally said.

"That much I know."

Ryan's gaze darted nervously around the room. "She had me look back into the records as far as I could. I thought it was weird at the time but now..." He shrugged.

"How far back do the records go?"

Ryan chuckled nervously. "All the way back."

I leaned even closer to him, our heads nearly touching. From an outsider's point of view, it appeared as if we were lovers, whispering sweet nothings, but the tension that rolled off him made me nauseous. A wave of doom and gloom came over me like nothing I had ever felt before.

"Ebenezer White," I whispered.

He immediately shushed me. "Not so loud. That name appeared more than once." He glanced at the patrons all busy gossiping about last night and sipping their drinks. "He was an original founder. Nah, scratch that. He was *the* founder of this town. That man was loaded. Although he came from English wealth, surprisingly, he was a decent man. From what I can tell, though, his house was the first built."

"Is his house still standing?"

Ryan snorted. "Yep, it's standing."

The tingling at the base of my neck grew. "Which one is it?"

I held my breath, hoping against hope that it wasn't Honeysuckle House because if true, then that could have been a reason for Hazel's demise. It wouldn't be surprising if a long-lost relative, upon finding out about the possibility of an illegitimate child through a web search, resorted to killing Hazel to gain possession.

The sound of broken glass by the front counter startled us.

"Watch it. This is Armani," snapped Brooklyn Irwin.

"It's nothing." Chase Chamberlain scrubbed at a spot on his navy pinstripe suit with a napkin.

Brooklyn's nostrils flared and she stomped her foot. "No. You deserve an apology. This town wouldn't even be on the map if it weren't for your family."

Chase's jaw twitched in agitation. "Enough, Brook. Let it go."

The waitress was scurrying about on the floor picking up the shards and cutlery, dabbing ineffectively at the spilled drinks. He squatted and lent a hand.

Brooklyn gasped. "What are you *doing*? Everyone's watching."

"Here, let me help."

Willow? I slapped a palm against my forehead. She did say that Brooklyn needed a wedding planner, and she'd weaseled her way in, but I wasn't expecting to see her here.

Willow knelt beside the waitress and Chase, picking up as much as she could.

Brooklyn tapped her leather boot against the floor, looking around the room. "Ryan?" she gushed. "Ryan, is that you?" Disgruntlement forgotten, she wiggled her fingers high in the air, a brilliant smile lighting up her face. She promptly strode to our table.

I settled into my chair, feeling the weight of the attention focused on us. Willow merely shrugged an *"I'm sorry"* look my way.

With her pink manicured finger, Brook poked Ryan's shoulder. "Big brother, why didn't you say you wanted coffee? We could have picked something up for you."

She focused an unfriendly gaze on me. "What's *she* doing here? Haven't we had our fill of the Wrens?"

"Brook, please," Ryan pleaded to no use.

"No." She jut out her slender hip and jabbed a finger at me. "Your aunt should have minded her own business. What's all this crap about land rights? She wasn't getting her grubby hands on our land." With a wag of her finger, she cautioned, "If you so much as consider chasing us off our property, I'll—"

"Enough!" Ryan snapped so loudly the next town probably heard.

At this point, Chase had collected the last shard of glass and tossed it in the trash, accidentally brushing against Willow's hand as she discarded coffee-stained napkins. Their hands stayed connected for a brief instant amidst the chaos of Brooklyn before Willow abruptly pulled hers away and stepped back, adjusting her cashmere sweater and blushing.

"Brooklyn," Ryan continued, each syllable stilted and clipped, "this is not the place. The Wrens are grieving. Have some compassion."

Chase Chamberlain walked up and pulled at his cuffs, his face tensing when he spotted Brooklyn. He placed his hand on the small of her back. "Honey, let's go." He nodded and smiled at me. "Skylar Night, it's good to have you home. Your grandmother must be grateful. Brooklyn, Drake awaits."

Despite her reluctance, he steered Brooklyn towards the exit without any verbal objections. Chase had a way of eroding her resolve. This intrigued me all the more. It was evident that Brooklyn knew how to get her way, which at the moment was Chase Chamberlain and property.

"Sorry about that." Ryan scratched his scruffy jaw. "She's not a bad person."

"What's she talking about? Property rights? Does Ebenezer White play a role in this?"

Ryan shushed me again, but the crowd had grown bored the moment Brooklyn sashayed her tiny derriere out the door.

"No. Yes. Ugh!" He ran his hands down his face. "I don't know. Hazel asked me to look into the land rights, and I did. When I found out that Ebenezer White had founded the town, she insisted on learning more about his land rights and any potential heirs. When I stumbled upon Cleantha

Wren's engagement announcement, I realized that she might have been exploring Ebenezer White's property for personal reasons."

"Hazel had her hands full with the existing property, with no want for more land. What about Brooklyn? What is she ranting about?"

"Our property, the Irwins' property, was granted to us by the town's founder."

"Ebenezer White? Why?"

He sipped on his drink. "It was included in his last will and testament. That was a shocker. I'd never heard my father speak of it, but it was there in black and white. Our land had been deeded to us."

"Are you any relation to the Whites? I don't recall any in town growing up."

"No, my family originated from Boston during Ebenezer White's era. Perhaps they were friends."

"Some friends. Leaving a parcel of land? That's not usual."

"I agree, but there you have it. Hazel wasn't satisfied though. She said there was a scandal."

I puffed out my cheeks. "An illegitimate child?"

His eyes widened. "Yes, she kept talking like it was fact, but that's led my family down a dark past. One we don't care to rehash."

The realization finally struck me. "That's why Brooklyn was so upset."

"She remembers the horror stories about Grandpa Irwin. He was convinced there was an illegitimate child."

"I read that online."

"Grandpa Irwin was the laughingstock of the town, but to his credit he died convinced the land belonged to another family."

What did Foster Irwin and Hazel have to gain if there was?

"Ryan, who lives in Ebenezer White's home presently?"

Ryan paused, circling his spoon in his cup. "The Chamberlains."

I leaned back in my seat. The Chamberlains practically owned the town. Every shop, restaurant, heck, even the hospital was either owned or invested in by the Chamberlains. It had been that way forever, but I'd never thought about why. Chase was nice enough, not arrogant like his parents or grandparents, but that didn't mean anything. If they weren't the rightful owners of the property, then that meant at least some of it could be taken away, and lots of the money too.

"I see. And your property? If the rightful landowner were to stroll into town and lay claim, would you lose it?"

Ryan stared down at his coffee. "Probably."

No wonder Brooklyn was irate, and I couldn't blame her, even though the way she went about things wasn't ideal. It also meant Brooklyn, and as much as I hated to believe it, Ryan, could have killed Hazel. I definitely needed to see Hazel's autopsy results.

The front door chimed and Myra Humphreys walked in, along with the resident doctor, Joshua Moore. She clung to him like glue, pawing at him and giving him adoring glances. It was nauseating.

"She moved on fast." Ryan motioned toward the pair.

"Myra never wastes time. However, this looks like a desperate attempt to win back Ely's affections."

Ryan grinned. "Does that ever work?"

"Not with Ely Collins."

Willow walked over and blocked my view, not that I cared. "That was interesting." She dabbed at her sweater where spots of coffee had stained it. "This is ruined." She tossed the wadded napkin onto the table, pulled up a chair from the table beside us, and sat, eyeing the two of us. "So how's the date? Will there be another?" She grinned like the Cheshire Cat when I kicked at her under the table.

"Ow!" Ryan yelped.

I sank further into my chair. "Ryan, I'm so sorry. That was meant for Willow."

"See how she treats her friends? I bet she's great in—"

"That's enough, Willow," I interrupted. "Don't you have some place to be?"

"Not in the slightest." She crossed her legs and sat back.

I pressed my lips together, knowing resistance was futile. Willow did as Willow wanted, and nobody could change her. She was great to have in a pinch, and she'd stayed by my side through the store's ups and downs. Willow was the best friend I could ask for.

Ryan rose and offered his hand. "It's been a pleasure. Perhaps we could do this again sometime?"

Unfazed by Willow's snicker, I shook his hand. "That would be lovely."

"How about I pick you up tomorrow night? About seven?"

"Seven sounds fine."

He fumbled for his keys on the table and nearly knocked over his coffee mug before striding for the door.

Willow's snorts rolled into a belly laugh once he was out of earshot.

"Stop it." I swatted her arm. "He's nice."

"I bet." She rested her chin on her hands, batting her eyes at me. "What if he's a killer?"

Lost in thought, I stared at the door. "He's not."

"Pish posh. You're smitten and not to be trusted around him. Are you not the least bit interested in what I gathered from Brooklyn?"

"Let me guess." I sipped on the now cold coffee. "The land rights Hazel was investigating were owned by Ebenezer White, the town's founder. On top of that, he granted the Irwin ancestors some property without any apparent explanation, leaving Brooklyn furious at the possibility of losing their property if an illegitimate descendant of Ebenezer surfaced. How's that?"

Willow cursed under her breath. "I spent the entire afternoon listening to her complain about the distinction between blush and pink, and berating the catering staff and florist all day."

I grinned. "I told you I'd handle it. Sticking your nose into this stuff could get you hurt."

Her cheeks grew pink with pleasure. "You didn't mention the autopsy."

I sat forward. "Tell me you found something."

Willow tossed her hair back and deliberately crossed her legs. "Hazel was indeed killed."

I grabbed her arm. "How?"

Willow leaned close and whispered, "She was poisoned."

Chapter 26

" Poisoned?" I glanced at Joshua and Myra, who were seated at a nearby table. He was laughing, and every time he did, she'd playfully pat him, leaning in close to expose her ample bosom.

"A few days ago, Brooklyn confronted the good doctor over there."

"That's against the law," I said. "She's not family."

"It's true, but Brooklyn has leverage over everyone in this town." Willow looked at the two pawing each other.

"What's Brooklyn got on the doctor?" I asked.

"That's the juicy part. He has a hidden past, and he's prepared to pay a high price to keep it hidden."

A sudden coldness gripped my core. "What?"

"She wouldn't say, but I'd keep that lady on a short leash. Guard your secrets, because she's a viper."

"Duly noted."

We watched the pair a few moments longer before turning our attention back to each other.

"What will you do next?" Willow asked.

I tapped a nail against the table. "I think it's time for a physical."

"Oh my. That sounds kinky."

"Get your mind out of the gutter, Willow. If the good doctor has secrets, then Brooklyn doesn't need to keep them all to herself. What better way to find out than to get an appointment with him? I'm overdue for a physical, and he's got some answers. He hasn't allowed my family access to those autopsy reports, and I want to know why."

"I like your style, lady. Be careful though. If he has anything to do with this, you're going in alone. Want some backup?"

"I'm a safety girl." I held up my keychain and jangled the bear spray in front of her face. "I'll be fine." I tapped her hand. "They're leaving. Now's the time."

I hopped up and grabbed my empty mug, scooting past Willow.

She smacked my butt. "Strike while the iron is hot, girlie. See you later?"

I placed the mug on the counter. "Text me when you want dinner. Gotta go."

The second I was out the coffee shop door, I swung left like Myra and Doctor Moore did. They were only a half block away. Fortunately, they were heading towards his office, strategically positioned between the pharmacy and Chase Chamberlain's law office on the other side of the town hall.

I thanked my lucky stars I'd worn my winter boots because the sidewalks, while salted, were still slick with ice. They were too engrossed in each other to notice me slipping and sliding behind them. About halfway there, I shimmied up to a storefront as Myra darted for her sporty car. Doctor Moore waved farewell to her and she sped down the road, oblivious to the weather. He then trudged the rest of the way to his office. Two minutes later, chilled from the frosty air, I entered his office. In the quaint rectangular reception area, a table showcasing magazines was complemented by a stunning poinsettia. Five cream-colored sofa chairs were positioned around the table. The walls were a muted gray with wide white baseboards and crown molding. Someone had strung fresh garland across the top of the room with large red velvet bows every five feet or so. Standing in the corner was a professionally decorated six-foot tall flocked Christmas tree. Ribbons of gold and silver flowed down from the top, featuring a white dove as the focal point on top. The silver balls sparkled next to the hundreds of blinking white lights.

I approached the reception desk, but the lights weren't on.

Strange.

I knocked on the plexiglass separating the reception from the work areas and waited a minute. No response. The door was a foot to my right. I twisted the handle, and it opened. Sticking my head inside, I called out. "Doctor Moore? Hello?"

There was a corridor in front of me about twenty-five feet long, with doors lining both sides. The check-out counter was on the left, the restroom the first door on the right. The room was faintly illuminated by security lights.

I stepped inside and called out again. "Hello?"

A drawer slammed somewhere further down the hallway. I crept forward, a cool tingle down my back. I pulled out my keys and held the bear spray in front of me.

I shouldn't be here.

I turned to leave when a voice rang out.

"That's not good enough." It was Dr. Moore, and he sounded angry. "We're almost there. Give me two more days. If I don't have it by then, I know what to do."

"Don't lose your nerve," said another voice, gruff and low. "I've got so much dirt on you, don't think I won't use it. Are we clear?"

I scurried into an open examination room and huddled by the door, straining to hear. This wasn't a good idea after all. I held my breath, heart slamming against my ribs, gripping the bear spray and holding it out in front of me.

"No," he hissed. "I haven't lost my nerve. This is a delicate situation, and I—"

I leaned forward to hear and the old floorboard creaked, halting the two in their tracks.

"I thought we were alone," snapped the other man. "Imbecile!"

I heard a thud followed by a grunt, and then what sounded like a metal door slamming.

I threw caution to the wind and jogged forward, sticking my head around the corner. Positioned on the right side was an area equal in size to the reception room with a waist-high ledge along the right and back walls. This space served as a desk area for computers and lab equipment. Slumped against the far desk counter, Joshua Moore was cupping his bleeding forehead, breathing heavily.

"Are you okay?" I asked, keeping at least six feet between us, noting the metal door, which I assumed led out to the back alley, on my left.

"What are you doing here?" He stumbled into an examination room on my right and rummaged through multiple drawers until he found gauze, antiseptic, and gloves.

"I need a physical and wanted to set up an appointment."

He bit open the gauze bandage and dabbed at his forehead. He pulled out a handheld mirror, set it against the examination glove boxes, and kept dabbing at the gash until it staunched the blood flow.

"I'm a little busy." He rubbed some antiseptic ointment on the wound and winced. "Call and leave a message. I'm sure I can fit you in sometime tomorrow or the next day."

He ripped open another gauze pad, applied it to his forehead, and taped it.

"Won't that need stitches?" I asked.

He set the mirror down, replaced the bandages and ointment in their respective drawers, and faced me. "Last I checked, I was the doctor Miss Night." His voice was cold and hard.

"I am only trying to help. Let me call the police."

I grabbed my phone with my free hand while still holding the bear spray.

"No," he barked. "That won't be necessary." He plastered on a smile. "That was... a friend who is in trouble."

"Some friend."

"No matter. It's being handled."

I gestured to his bandaged head. "That's assault. If your friend has drug issues—"

"Nothing of the sort." He lowered himself onto a swivel chair, hand to his forehead. "We had a disagreement, but it won't happen again. I promise. Now," he clapped his hands together, all doctorly again. "You need a physical? I've got a spot open right now if you're ready."

I bit my inner cheek. Something was amiss, but if I left now, I may not get another chance. Fortune favors the risk takers, or something like that.

"Fine."

He gestured to the examination table. I hopped up, trying to hide my immense trepidation. Almost as an afterthought, I quickly texted 111 to Willow before pocketing my phone.

Joshua drew out a tongue depressor from a drawer and walked over, his footsteps thudding loudly in the still air. "Open and say 'Ah.'"

I stuck out my tongue and nearly gagged on the wooden depressor as he shined a light down my throat. Next, he felt along my jaw and along my neck before grabbing his stethoscope from around his neck. "Take a deep breath and let it out, please."

He checked several spots on my chest and then stood back.

"Sounds good." He pocketed his stethoscope in a deep laboratory pocket and pulled out a small hammer. "Time to check your reflexes."

He tapped on my knees, which obediently swung out so fast he jumped sideways to avoid getting whacked. "No problems there."

"Sorry about that."

He waved dismissively. "I've gotten good at avoiding things."

"It must be a hazardous job."

"You have no idea," he mumbled. He scooted his doctor's stool over and sat, folding his hands onto his lap. "You seem fit, but I'll need labs for any definitive answers. I can draw blood now, or you can come back sometime tomorrow when my nurse can do it. It's your choice."

While the idea of darting out the door was tempting, coming back tomorrow wasn't high on my list. "Now will be fine. I'm already here." I rubbed my sweaty palms on my pants.

Joshua planted his hands on his thighs. "No time like the present." He popped up and stepped outside the room to gather the necessary supplies while I twiddled my fidgeting thumbs. Needles weren't my thing. Spiders? Fine. Rats? They were okay too. Needles? *Ugh*. The sight of them made me squirm. However, I'd cornered myself on this one, and there was only one way out.

I cleared my throat. "So you and Myra, huh?"

The metal drawer clanged shut, and I flinched. What was he getting? A bone saw?

Joshua entered, dragging a medical cart behind him. After prepping my arm with alcohol and the rubber tourniquet, he donned gloves, letting the last one smack onto his palm. "Myra is a friend."

Friends don't hang on each other, but if he wanted to delude himself, then far be it from me to correct him. He must have seen the skepticism written all over my face, because he paused, holding the needle in the air.

"Myra's attractive and has everything a man would like."

I grinned. "Fake boobs, a butt lift, and Daddy's money?"

"Skylar, you've got to date better men. Hang on, this will sting."

I looked away from the needle, out into the lab area. Mistletoe hung over the back door. I imagined it was the exit used by the other man. On either side of the door there were poinsettias, some wilting. Crumpled leaves littered the floor, though there were a couple that stood out from the rest. These weren't red and green like the poinsettias. It was a red flower with toothy, segmented leaves.

"There. That ought to do it." Joshua capped the last vial of blood and set it in his hand-held carry cart. He bandaged my arm, discarded his latex gloves, and turned toward me, arms crossed. "Now that that's out of the way, why not tell me the real reason you're here."

I gripped the edges of the exam table and opened my mouth to speak, then my phone buzzed. "Sorry. I've got to take this."

Joshua simply stared.

"Hello, Ophelia. I'm coming home right away. I'm at the doctor's office, so it'll be about ten minutes."

"Wait. Why are you at the doctor's office? On second thought, never mind. Get here as quickly as possible. The front door's unlocked."

I hopped off the exam table, offered my apologies to Joshua, and raced down the dark hallway and out the door. The winter air hit me before I realized Ely drove me.

"Crap."

"Need a ride?"

A black convertible revved its engine beside me and I jumped, startled.

"I promise not to bite."

I hesitated briefly before jogging around to the other side and hopping into the passenger seat. "Take me to Honeysuckle House, and step on it."

Chapter 27

"The prodigal daughter, or should I say granddaughter, returns."

Chase Chamberlain concentrated on the bumpy terrain, the car slipping along the ice-patched road. He'd gained muscle since the last time I'd seen him, and the business suits suited him. They weren't the glitzy, high-dollar kind like his father's though. Chase preferred simple and refined, an attractive quality. Yet he and Drake, while only eighteen months apart in age, were polar opposites. Chase wasn't a skirt chasing, beer chugging, arrogant prick in high school, and while people could change a little, he hadn't.

"One could say the same for you," I said.

"Touche."

"What prompted you to offer me a ride? It's not like we're friends."

Chase glanced at me then back to the road. "We're friends."

I chuckled. "Since when?"

"Okay, so maybe we aren't the closest of friends, but we knew each other."

I studied his symmetrical features. He was a dead ringer for Ryan Gosling from *The Notebook*, but less extroverted. Chase preferred fencing practice to socializing, keeping to himself. While he excelled at fencing, he lacked the life-of-the-party charisma the ladies liked in high school. For that, I liked him, though we were never close.

"You barely nodded at me in the hallways, Chase. I hardly think that makes us friends."

"Fair enough."

We pulled out of the town square and merged with traffic. Time didn't stop for mourners. Garland hung from all the storefronts, signposts, and even the street signs. Huge, red, velvety bows adorned the streetlights, and Christmas music blasted through the town hall's outdoor speaker system. It was supposed to be used during natural disasters and the like, but the town council made an exception for the holidays years back, and it's been a town favorite ever since.

"I'm sorry to hear about Hazel. How are you faring?"

I wrapped my arms tightly about my torso. "She will be missed."

"When my mom died, it about killed me."

I stiffened. The night Theodora Chamberlain passed was etched into my memory. She'd been running errands and never came home. When the police were notified, they found her car crunched in a ditch two miles outside town. Bags of Christmas presents filled her back seat. No one ever figured out what had happened. Although it was reported as an accident, something about it never sat well. At home and around town, it remained a mystery, though nobody spoke of it. Initially, I believed it to be out of respect for Chase and Drake, but when their dad married less than three months later, I wondered if it was due to his indiscretions. It was all so hush-hush.

"Does it ever get easier?" I asked.

"Everyone says it gets easier, but it comes in waves, and when I least expect it. Grief is strange."

We pulled in the driveway and bumped along in silence for a moment.

"Sky, be careful with Brooklyn."

I took note of his creased forehead and taut jaw.

"Are you two a thing?"

His eyebrows shot upward. "A thing?"

"A couple. Are you two dating?"

Chase snorted. "Not likely. She's engaged to my brother."

He pulled to a stop behind Ophelia's black SUV and hopped out of the car, running around to my side. He opened my door, averting his gaze from me, and looked instead at Honeysuckle House.

"Ophelia home?"

I glanced at the house, unsure of what to say. Alerting him to a possible intruder wasn't exactly something I wanted to involve him with.

Ophelia's head popped out the front door. "Skylar! There you are."

"What are you doing inside? Get out of there!" I scolded. "Have you called the police?"

"The police?" Chase looked alarmed.

Ophelia excitedly waved at me. "Keep it down and get your butts in here," she hissed.

We both hightailed it to the door and slid in.

"Why aren't we staying outside?" I whispered to Ophelia, who was now tiptoeing past the stairwell toward the swinging kitchen door.

BANG! Slam!

We all froze mid-step.

Then we heard the back door slam.

"Ophelia, stop," I whispered.

No use. She was off, the kitchen door swinging in her wake. Chase brushed past me in hot pursuit.

I hit the swinging door running, and one step in I slammed into Chase, unable to avoid the door smacking my butt. I yelped.

"Shush!" Ophelia held her index finger to her lips.

Hunched over, Ophelia in the lead, and me as the caboose with Chase sandwiched between, we crept to the back door, our hands on each other's backs. When we reached it, Ophelia peeked out. Her body tensed. Out of nowhere, a hand landed on my shoulder.

I spun and punched, pulse pounding in my ears.

"Whoa!"

"Ely?!" I placed a hand against my chest. "Why are you sneaking around my house?" I balled my hand into a fist and punched him in the chest. "You about gave me a heart attack."

"Sorry. Someone called for the police. What's going on?"

"That's my fault." Ophelia raised her hand. "Looking fit as always, Ely." Her lips twitched into an admiring grin. "How about you check the house? The front door was unlocked when I got here, and knowing miss safety girl over there," she hooked her thumb in my direction, "that was not intended."

"Fine. Everyone stay put until I give the all clear."

Ely trotted up the kitchen stairwell out of sight.

"Someone was here," Ophelia said, staring at the back door. "Look."

Chase and I stepped forward and peered through the glass at the snow.

"Footprints," I murmured. Was this a ghost thing? Or was this a real intruder? If so, what did they—

I bolted up the kitchen stairwell, my sister calling after me to stop. I skipped two steps at a time until I was upstairs. Chest heaving, I pushed on past a myriad of rooms until I reached Hazel's bedroom.

"Oh my gosh."

Clothes hung out of half-closed drawers. The sheets and pillows on the ransacked bed were torn and shredded, white bird feathers strewn about the bed and floor. I ran to the nightstand and opened the book I'd placed the newspaper clippings in from the cellar. The book's binding fell apart in my hands, and pages fell to the floor. I sank to my knees. Shuffling the papers around over and over again, I searched in vain. They were gone.

"Skylar?"

When I turned to look at Ophelia, my blood ran cold. I shot up and rushed into the connecting bathroom.

"Skylar, what's wrong?" Ophelia asked.

I dropped to the floor, banging my knees on the hard tile. "No," I whimpered. "No, please, no." I dragged Willow's limp body into my lap and checked her neck for a pulse.

Ophelia clamped a hand over her mouth and gagged, stumbling backward into the bedroom.

Chase popped his head in, took one look at Willow's bruised and battered body, and shouted, "Ely! Get in here fast."

The thud of Ely's boots stopped behind me. "Officer Collins to dispatch. Send an ambulance to Honeysuckle House."

I looked up at Ely, a well of tears blurring my vision. "Why?"

Ely looked at me, then Willow. "I don't know, Sky. But we'll find out. That I promise."

Chapter 28

The paramedics came and went. The hustle and bustle of the police force scampered through my house yet again. Chase had fixed the mattresses and led me to them after the ambulance arrived while Ely took charge of the crime scene. For once, Ophelia sat by me, holding my hand. She'd even called Nuri and Trixie, telling them to meet Willow at the hospital and to call with any updates.

I sat numb on the edge of the mattresses, staring blankly at the bathroom floor across from me. Why was Willow in my bathroom? There had to be a reason.

"Sky, honey. Morgana's coming. Let's meet her downstairs."

I kept staring at the bathroom like it would telepathically tell me what had transpired.

"You go." I numbly patted her hand. "I'll follow."

Ophelia hesitated. "Sure. Don't take too long." With a final glance at me, she exited the bedroom flanked by police officers.

"Skylar," Ely startled me out of my stupor. "You need to leave. Grab a bag. You can't stay here. It's officially a crime scene."

"What?" I stared up at him. "Oh, yes. Right."

In a daze, I stood and walked into the closet to the left of the bathroom, collecting a bag and some clothes while Ely looked on, uncertain whether to stay or leave. When I emptied my underwear drawer into the bag and stuffed some leggings and sweaters, Ely finally left. The zipper strained against all the contents as I zipped it closed. Wiping a fresh round of tears away, I stepped toward the threshold.

"What were you doing?" I mumbled, scanning the entire room for a trace of what happened.

Hazel's toothbrush still stood in its glass container by the sink. Her talcum powder, soap dispenser, and shampoo bottle had fallen in the struggle, crashing onto the floor, scattering shards everywhere among crushed red and yellow petals. The trail of talcum powder showed two sets of shoe prints. I cocked my head and stared at the fine white powder, noting a disturbance toward the base of the clawfoot tub nearest the wall panel. Careful not to disturb evidence, I cast a quick glance over my shoulder. I was alone, but not for long. I picked up a petal of each flower, tucking them into my coat pocket for later perusal. I reached for the wall panel and nudged. There was a soft click, then the panel depressed and moved away of its own accord. I strained to reach it, wiggling my fingers.

A flush of adrenaline tingled my entire body.

Reaching as far as I could without stepping foot into the bathroom, my fingers finally latched onto a plastic bag. Carefully pulling it out, I clutched it tightly to my chest.

"What are you doing?"

I whirled around, keeping the baggie pressed to my side. "Nothing." I bent and grabbed my bag, scurrying toward the bedroom door.

"Not so fast." Ely grabbed my arm. "What are you holding?"

I tucked the baggie into my coat pocket and turned to face him. "The bag."

Ely's brows knitted together. "What were you holding against your chest?"

I held up the heavy bag. "I'm only carrying this, Ely. That's all."

The corners of his eyes crinkled, but he released me. "I've booked you a room at the B&B. Someone will let you know when you can come back."

I hurried out the door without looking back, waving a hand in farewell. Soon, I was down the stairs where Ophelia and Morgana waited by the door.

"Say nothing," Morgana said, opening the door.

We filed out and got into Ophelia's SUV.

"Take me to the B&B, please," I said, clutching my bag to my side.

Morgana fixed a hard gaze at me from the front passenger seat. "You'll stay at my place where it's safe."

"With all due respect, Grandmother, no. My friends are staying at the B&B, and so am I. Ely booked a room for me."

"Right." Morgana leaned into her seat facing forward. "We've a killer to catch. No sense in wallowing over your friend."

Ophelia slammed on the brakes, and the car skidded sideways. "That's low even for you, Morgana." Ophelia's even voice held a hint of steel. "The killer and the attacker are probably one and the same. We'll deal with this in due time. For now, let Sky attend to her friend. You *do* remember friendship, right?"

Grandmother Wren heavily sighed. "Fine."

OPHELIA DROPPED ME off at the B&B and promised to return later. I wasted no time inspecting the items inside the Ziplock baggie. The first item was a yellowed letter. Carefully, I unfolded it, noting the date: May 1650. My hand splayed across my chest as I stared down at it. The fancy handwriting indicated a man.

My darling, I fear someone is after me. At first, I dismissed it as an overworked mind until Hercules. Someone tampered with his hoofs. Our farrier mentioned it when Hercules turned up lame the day after he threw me. If my trusted servant has delivered this to you, then my worst fears have come true, and I am deceased. It is up to you, my love, to know the who, but I fear I am unable to answer. If this pains you, then I most humbly apologize. All the evidence points to someone who wishes us not to wed. Please marry well. Live your life to the utmost and remember I will always be with you.

Your beloved,

EB

Flipping it over, I searched for a name, anything to tell who this was addressed to, but there was nothing. I placed the worn letter on the bed and picked up the flower. The toothy red petals reached out from a disk in the center. Simple, but beautiful. I could stare at it for hours and not come up with its significance. This required a flower specialist. Luckily, Raven's Hollow hosted a yearly flower festival on Christmas Eve. The winner was named Ms. Holly-days and featured on the front page of the *Raven's Gazette*. As a fundraiser for our local animal shelter, prominent men and women of Raven's Hollow clamored to win. The cutthroat planning for next year's winner commenced on December 26th. In their quest for the title, people sabotaged gardens nonstop all year. Although I always found it silly and still do, perhaps last year's winner could help identify this specific flower.

I slid the flower into the plastic baggie and took out Willow's scrap paper. She'd written names with arrows connecting people to dates and places. She'd linked Hazel's threatening messages to Brooklyn, and Brooklyn to Ryan, noting he was acting rather aloof, which to Willow meant suspicious. There wasn't much we hadn't discussed, and I spent the next hour scouring the piece of paper for any insight that would have made her enter my house without telling me.

I turned the paper upside down. "Land rights" was emphasized with an exclamation point next to a crude drawing of Honeysuckle House. Alongside it, the name Noble Foster and an address were written.

I mapped it on my phone and frowned. It was the library's address.

I placed Willow's notes along with Ebenezer's letter into the Ziplock bag and tucked it into my coat pocket. Grabbing the hotel room keys, I dashed out the door into the frigid wind. One thing was for certain, Noble Foster held the key to all this, and I wasn't about to waste any more time finding out why. I only hoped Willow lived to tell the tale.

Chapter 29

" Hi, Trixie. How's Willow?" I trudged through the snow, head lowered, resisting the strong gusts. The library was only two blocks away from the B&B, and it was next to the police station, so I figured it would be safe.

"She's still unconscious. The doctor said it's blunt force trauma. They've detected brain swelling. Sky..." her voice trembled, *"...she put up one helluva fight."*

I blinked back tears.

"The doctor said she's suffered multiple rib fractures, hand and arm fractures, plus someone tried... they tried..."

Swallowing past a lump in my throat, I pushed the library door open and entered with a determined stride, stomping my boots on the welcome mat. The rage rolled in waves from my shoulders to my knees and I ground my teeth, squeezing my lids shut.

"Trixie," I squawked. "They tried? But they didn't." I clenched and unclenched my fists repeatedly, wanting to hit something.

Trixie sniffled. *"No, but there was bruising and cuts. This person's an animal, Sky."*

"Right." I headed to the librarian's desk. "Keep me updated."

I hung up and shoved the cell into my coat pocket.

The bright-eyed librarian greeted me with a smile. "How can I help you?"

"The town's founders. Give me all the information you've got on them. Newspaper articles, land rights, birth and death records, whatever was recorded, I want."

The young librarian stuffed a slip of paper into a book and closed it, pushing it aside. "Is there an event I haven't heard of? There's a lot of interest in our town's founders these last couple of weeks."

She rounded her circular desk counter and gestured for me to follow. We passed two stacks of books and then traveled down one toward the back of the building.

"Out of curiosity, how many people have asked about the town's founders lately?"

We stopped in front of a door on the back wall surrounded by library stacks. The librarian typed in a code on a keypad and a beep sounded. She opened the door, and we entered a room filled with tables of old books, some with broken spines. We navigated around the tables and ended up in yet another room next to it. The room was filled with desks topped with green lamps, and it had the scent of dust and bygone days.

The librarian paced straight back and stopped at the end of one stack of books. She ran a finger along the spines, tongue stuck out of the corner of her mouth in concentration, and pulled out a large book. "Aha!"

She hefted it over to the nearest table and set it down with a thunk.

"Ryan came in a few weeks ago," she said and donned white gloves, motioning for me to do the same. "He spent hours nosing through tomes of old town records, but he was mostly focused on land rights. Brooklyn, though, she sifted through book after book on not only land rights but the town founders."

I shot a glance at the librarian, but she was busy transporting loads of books. "Brooklyn Irwin had an interest in the town's founders?"

The librarian set the latest tome on the stack of other olive green-colored books and wiped her forehead with her forearm. "More specifically, Cleantha Wren." She cocked her head at me. "That's your family, is it not?"

Her brown eyes searched mine.

I stuck out a hand. "Sorry, I'm Skylar Night."

The librarian shook it. "I'm Lizzy Swift, head librarian since last year."

"What happened to Martha Cushman?"

"Retired. She's happily relocated to Florida where she's enjoying the beach and sun, not to mention the warm winters." Lizzy lugged the remaining green-colored volume over and set it beside the others, flipping it over and carefully sifting through the pages. "Here. This is what Ryan first looked at." She grinned. "As for Brooklyn, take a look at these." Lizzy picked up the top tome off the pile and set it beside the already opened one and found a particular page. "Cleantha Wren. I'll leave you to it, but if you need anything, come find me." She walked off and left me staring down at a document as old as the hills.

I quickly became engrossed in town hall meetings, birth announcements, and similar events. Only when my tummy growled in protest did I check the time. 4:42PM. Crap! It was near closing. Thankfully, Lizzy had provided me with a pen and paper, and I wrote until my hands hurt, but I struck gold. Cleantha Wren, the matriarch of my family, originated from Ynys y Cedairn, Wales, now known as Anglesey. She arrived sometime in the early mid-1600s, exact date unknown. She bought 100 acres of land as a pioneer, though not without a scandal. According to a town court document, Cleantha Wren was charged with illegally owning land due to her gender. Curiously, Ebenezer White's name appeared as her benefactor, stating that Cleantha was residing on his lands. Another document entered into town history was a bill of sale from Ebenezer to Cleantha. In the 1920s, a newspaper article revealed that Cleantha had actually purchased the land using her father's name. Upon her arrival, the townspeople violently attacked her, and Ebenezer White came to her rescue. She spent a night in jail, underwent a court hearing, then ultimately went home to set up shop and build Honeysuckle House. If not for Ebenezer, Clea would have been an outcast and left to die. Deed after deed, newspaper clippings, and reported town hall events linked them both. Was it possible they were engaged?

Lizzy tapped the desk with the butt of her pen. "Closing time, I'm afraid."

I closed the book and picked up the notepad. "Lizzy, have you read anything on Raven's Hollow founders?"

Lizzy snickered. "Martha beat it into my brain before she left. Why?"

I shrugged into my coat, buttoned it, and followed her back through the repair room. "What can you tell me about Charlotte Noble? She's mentioned as being engaged to Ebenezer White."

The library's lights were dimmed when we walked into the main area. She held a finger to her mouth. "Charlotte Noble? Yes," she nodded, "Ebenezer White was engaged to a Miss Charlotte Noble when he passed. She hailed from a prominent family in Boston. I believe they were wealthy merchants, and her father desired a landowner for his daughter. Back in those days, land meant power."

"His daughter was a bargaining chip," I stated flatly.

Lizzy stepped behind the counter and tapped on the computer keyboard, absentmindedly bouncing her navy-booted toe against the ground. "Yes and no. From what I remember..." She hit the enter key and the screen lit up. "Here it is." She spun the monitor so I could see.

"A marriage of love?" My eyes widened. "It was a love marriage?"

Lizzy's face brightened. "The article describes how his parents wanted another young woman. Uh, let me see. Yeah, here. His father had arranged a betrothal from a Winthrop, one of the Boston Brahmin families, and our Ebenezer refused." Lizzy gazed dreamily at the computer screen. ""He's my kind of guy," she murmured.

"Would you mind researching Charlotte Noble for me?" My cell buzzed. It was a text from Trixie, insisting that I rush to the hospital. "Uh, I've gotta run. If you find anything, would you mind texting me?" I scribbled my number on a piece of paper and hurried towards the door.

"How fast do you need it?" Lizzy called.

"As soon as possible."

I exited the library, zipped up my coat, and tucked my hands into my pockets, making my way to the B&B. Willow needed clothing, and since I was only two blocks away, I figured I'd do it and leave Trixie and Nuri to attend to Willow just in case she awoke from her coma. I bounded up the front steps, and halfway into the house, my phone buzzed. It was from Lizzy.

"Don't want to get your hopes up, but I think it's related. I set the search for any name with Noble in it, and I got a hit. According to town court documents dated from the late 1690s, a Noble Ebenezer Foster had petitioned the courts over land rights. Do you think it could be related to Charlotte? If you want, I can continue searching."

Heart in my throat, I wrote back: *Great work! Please continue and let me know if you find anything else.*

I rushed up the stairwell and entered my room, grabbing the first items of Willow's clothing I could find. I packed toiletries, hair gel, mousse, nail polish, and fresh underwear in the duffel bag before rushing out of the room again, with one more stop before the hospital.

The Uber drove up the second I stepped outside, and I hopped in.

"Where to?" asked the driver.

I glanced down at my watch: 5:20PM.

"Irwin Reality, and step on it."

Chapter 30

The driver dropped me off in front of Gigi's. The front chalkboard advertised a Bailey's and Cream Coffee Mixer tonight, along with a Secret Santa event that drew the entire town. I snuck into the alley next to Gigi's, tiptoed past dumpsters, avoiding a rat eating a sandwich, and made a right turn. Ryan's realty office was two businesses down from the cafes.

As I stole up to the back door, two figures exited the building. I jumped behind a ratty sofa chair with holes the size of softballs and squatted. Peeking around the chair, I spotted a man and a woman engaged in an avid discussion. Before long, their raised voices were easily discernible.

"Take your hands off me." Brooklyn yanked her arm free.

"Brook, this is for your own good." Drake stood in shadow, his distinct voice holding a thread of steel to it. "Keep digging, and you're bound to get hurt."

Brooklyn scoffed. "I'm a big girl. I can handle it."

Drake stepped out of the shadow, extending a hand to rub her arm up and down. "You're in over your head. Please, for once, listen. I'd hate to see that pretty head of yours hurt."

Brooklyn went rigid as she stepped backward at an angle. "Is that a threat?"

Drake stuffed his hands in his pockets. "Take it as you will. All I'm saying is you're messing with fire. I'd hate to see that pretty skin get burned."

"What are you hiding? Why are you defending the Wrens?"

Drake's face contorted. "The Wrens should all be exterminated. Their kind has seen the last of Raven's Hollow."

Brooklyn crossed her arms. "What do you mean?" Her face drained of color. "What have you done?"

Drake wrapped an arm along her lower back. "Nothing. Let's get to Gigi's before we're missed."

Brooklyn hesitated, but at the last moment stepped alongside him down toward me.

I huddled against the soiled brick wall, the stench of urine and rotten meat overwhelming me. I hoped they'd pass by without spotting me.

"Father has a special announcement for our wedding."

A rat scampered across my boot the moment they came in sight. I clamped my mouth shut to stop a squeal and held my breath.

Brooklyn stopped and pivoted, examining Drake. "Your father? Why? I've done everything you've asked. What more do you both want?"

Drake's even white teeth gleamed in the moonlight. "An heir, of course." He straightened his tie, smirking. "I'm looking forward to it. It's time you learned who's boss, Brook." He swatted her bottom. "Get a move on. We're late."

Brooklyn's eyes seethed with anger as she walked towards the back entry to Gigi's. They entered, and the door closed.

I sagged to the ground, exhaling noisily.

What was that? Brooklyn *wasn't* in love with Drake Chamberlain after all. What leverage did they use to manipulate her into a marriage?

I peeked around the chair and, seeing it was clear, I darted for the realtor's alley door and unlocked it with a hairpin. In undergrad, Kaitlynn taught me how to pick locks after we got trapped in a frat house with a murderer.

I slid into the office, only turning on my phone light when the door was safely shut. Aiming the light downward, I waited for my eyes to adjust, noting the office layout. Two desks were situated on each side of the front door, and next to them were whiteboard listings on the adjacent walls. The desks each held a computer and not much else. In the back right corner was a closed office that held a larger desk and copier. A picture of Ryan's smiling face next to a middle-aged, salt and peppered haired man in spectacles was hung right outside the office.

I stepped in and promptly began searching the desk drawers, removing several folders that contained nothing of interest. With a swift movement of the computer mouse, a password prompt appeared on the screen along with a striking horse portrait in the background.

Great. What would his password be?

Inside the center desk drawer were the typical contracts and property details of the latest home sales. I put them on the desk and extended my hand, exploring the sides and bottom of the open drawer. With a grin, I extracted a strip of paper from the left side.

"Gotcha."

The computer files were categorized into listing types – single home, townhome, or rentals – except for one file that was different.

I clicked on "Founders" and picture after picture popped on screen. Land surveys from the 1600s up to the present day loaded on screen along with loads of newspaper articles involving not only Ebenezer White but also Cleantha and other Wrens.

Honeysuckle House?

I zoomed in and my mouth dropped open. The original land deed showed a hundred acres with Cleantha Wren's and Ebenezer White's signatures on the lower left corner. I came across another hand-drawn map, dated twenty years later, that depicted the same hundred acres and included property boundaries and a family cemetery. However, the most unsettling thing I found was a file labeled "Wren." Letters, journal entries, town hall documents all splayed across the screen, leaving me numb and confused. The current detailed map of Raven's Hollow had red arrows pointing at Honeysuckle House, but the most bewildering part was Hazel's own picture staring back at me. I wiped away tears, trying to understand why Ryan had saved all this on his work computer. Who were the Irwins, really? Why did Ebenezer gift them land all those years ago. What was I missing?

I reached out a finger and traced Hazel's cheek, remembering the last time I saw her. She was fit, healthy, and alive. Her soft, creamy skin, those wise brown eyes, and that bobbed gray hair made me yearn for her and times long past.

Clicking off the file and exiting out from all the files, I shut the computer off and re-situated the desk like I'd seen it. As I slid the chair under the desk, I heard a screech coming from my right.

I grabbed my phone and raised it. A picture of the old town square was framed on the wall tilted. I breathed a sigh of relief and started walking towards the office door, then something stung me on the back of my neck and my knees buckled. I slapped a hand against my neck, staring at the drop of blood left on it. I fell to the floor as the room shifted. The last thing I could remember was the thumping of boots on the carpeted floor.

Chapter 31

I lifted my heavy arms to my throbbing head, opening each eye in turn. Everything was blurry, and my leaden eyelids drooped. Outside my door, carolers sang while the smells of alcohol and coffee filled my car.

With a groan, I turned my head towards the passenger side. On the seat, there was a white paper bag and a cardboard carton containing a hot beverage. Fumbling for the bag, I opened it and stared down at cranberry scones. Stuffed beside it was a napkin with writing. I lifted it up and allowed the cafe's glow to illuminate the words.

Keep sticking your nose into things, and you'll end up like Hazel.

I crumpled the napkin and tossed it to the side, rubbing my temples.

What happened?

I remembered the alley, Brooklyn and Drake arguing, and the office. *The files!*

Scooting up, I patted my coat pocket and found my phone. I dialed and listened to the ring.

Knock, knock!

Gaping out the window, my hand instinctively went to my chest. Rolling the window down, I peered out. "Yes?" I asked, squinting against the hard lights. Whatever hit me addled my brain.

"Get out of my car."

Brooklyn held a coffee cup, looking down her nose at me.

"What?" I looked around the car's interior. A hot flush crept through me. "I'm so sorry." I scrambled out of the car.

Brooklyn glanced at the car then me. "How did you get in my car?"

If it wasn't so painful, I would have shaken my head. Instead, I rubbed it and stared blankly.

"Honey—" Chase jogged up and stopped short at the sight of me. "Sky? Are you alright?"

Brooklyn let out an annoyed huff. "She was in my car. Call the cops."

Confusion filled Chase's face as he stared at me, brow wrinkled.

"No need." I clutched the paper bag and took a step, then stumbled.

"Whoa." Chase offered a steadying hand. "Can I call someone for you?"

"No. I mean..." I tried to straighten on unsteady legs, I said, "No thank you. I'll be fine."

Brooklyn held her cell tightly to her ear. "Hello, police? Yes, I'd like to report a crime."

Chase objected, positioning himself between her and me, hands raised. "I'm sure there's a reasonable explanation." He glanced at me with a pleading look.

Brooklyn tapped her shoe on the snow-covered lot. "Yes, theft. Someone broke into my car."

"Wait." I flinched as the throbbing in my head worsened and I strained to make sense of it all. "How *did* I get into your car? Who had access to your keys?"

Brooklyn deliberately lowered her head and studied me, staying quiet.

"Someone stabbed me with something, and the next thing I know I'm in your car. Who had access to your keys?"

"Where were you stabbed?" She asked, covering the cell's speaker.

I massaged the back of my neck.

Brooklyn glanced at Chase. "Check it out. But if you're lying..."

Chase lifted my hair and stroked my neck with his thumb. "She's not lying." He lowered my hair and stepped toward Brooklyn. "There's a puncture mark."

Brooklyn tilted her head like she was mentally weighing the evidence. "Never mind," she said into the phone and hung up. "Where were you when this happened?"

"Uh, I was," I shifted my weight, "I was walking in the alley to throw away my trash." I raised the white bag.

"In the alley?" Brooklyn sounded unconvinced.

"Yeah, I was following a little kitten. Have you seen it? It's too cold for it to be outside."

Okay, I pulled that one out of my backside, but thanks to Chase, Brooklyn visibly relaxed.

"The gray kitten?" Chase asked. "Yeah, I've seen it for the last week. Always by itself."

"Fine." Brooklyn gestured to the car. "How did you get in without breaking a window? This vehicle comes with top-notch security."

"That's true."

We all looked on as Drake confidently approached Brook, smoothly hopping off the curb onto the street, kissing her on the cheek. She blanched but allowed him to do it.

"Father's vehicles come with nothing but the best."

I pointed at the car. "This is Mr. Chamberlain's?"

Drake beamed at his fiancé. "It's a gift for our marriage. She loves it, don't you, babe?"

Backing up, I stumbled and caught my foot on the curb. "I've got someplace to be. Excuse me."

I darted into the café without looking back. Being in a crowd provided me with a sense of safety and allowed me to have some thinking time.

I sat on a bar stool by the front counter, set my bag down, and pulled out my phone to request an Uber.

"Why can't you find another town to terrorize?"

I sighed. "Always a pleasure Myra." And then on second thought. "Myra, how long have Drake and Brooklyn been engaged?"

Myra smirked. "Why? Haven't you broken up enough relationships? Leave Drake alone and stay away from Joshua."

"Ely's engaged to Charlotte, and I have no interest in Joshua."

Myra banged her hands on the counter. "Really? Then why were you at his office?"

"Easy, Myra. I just want Hazel's autopsy report."

The fire in her eyes faded. She sipped on her beverage. "Drake and Brooklyn got engaged three months ago."

"That's fast."

Myra chuckled. "It raised a few brows. The town gossip is she's pregnant, but I say hogwash. She'd be showing now. If it were a shotgun wedding, they'd have done it already."

"So you don't think it's a love match?"

Myra lifted her palm up as if to say *Who cares?*

"Why marry then?"

She stared at me intently, leaning into her barstool. "Why else? It's always about money or looks with the Chamberlains. Brooklyn is a beautiful woman. I suppose she likes the wealth."

"Myra!" I hopped off the barstool and planted a kiss on her cheek. "You're brilliant. Thank you!"

I rushed to the door, leaving a shocked Myra in my wake.

"Driver, head for Raven Wood please."

I sank into the back seat and watched the festive lights blur. There was only one person who could tie these dots together. I only hoped she was in a good mood tonight.

Chapter 32

"Take your shoes off and leave them by the door." My grandmother whisked about her sitting room, tidying up the burgundy and black diamond quilts on the red velvet couch. She picked up a feather duster and flitted through the room, touching every picture frame, vase, and table top.

She lived in a comfortable cottage a mile down the road from Honeysuckle House. The lot was original to Cleantha Wren's claim, but Hazel had gifted her a couple acres when their mother passed. High wooden beams, cathedral ceilings, and dark wooden walls always gave off a warm, earthy vibe. Lit candles dotted the ledges, windowsills, tables, and even beams. How she managed to light them was beyond me. I'd often wondered how it didn't burn down with all the candles.

I kicked off my boots, hung up my coat, and flopped onto the velvety couch against the back wall, embracing a golden pillow.

"What troubles you?"

She lit new candles and placed them on the melted remnants of the old ones, glancing at me.

"Ebenezer White."

Morgana stood tall and tilted her head, peering through her oversized glasses. "Ophelia mentioned you'd asked about him."

"My ears are burning." Ophelia walked in, glass jars clinking in her arms. "Skylar's asking about Ebenezer."

Ophelia heaved the jars filled with dried herbs onto the wooden counter situated to the left of the couch. She lined them up next to the other jars of various sizes. She flicked a strand of hair out of her eyes and admired her work. "I told you to tell her, Grandmother."

Morgana placed the feather duster on a worktable in the center of the room under a glowing green pot hanging above. It was a weird light fixture, but to each their own. She snapped her fingers. "Bring me the rosemary and thyme, Ophelia."

My sister sifted through the glass jars, picking up two of the bigger ones, and carried them across the room to our grandmother.

"Skylar, care to join us?" Morgana asked, pulling off the jar lids and picking out one of each, laying them upon a piece of wax paper.

"What are you doing?" I asked, rising from the couch.

"Watch and learn." Morgana lit the bundle end of rosemary and waved it around, cupping the smoke, and inhaled. "Bless this home, ward it from ill intent, guide us on our journeys. Keep us safe while on our mission of truth and justice."

A spark and a burst. Flames shot in all directions.

I jumped, but it all disappeared as soon as it began.

In the midst of the pungent camphor-like smoke, Ophelia and Morgana fixed their gazes on me.

I wrinkled my nose and coughed. "What was that?"

Morgana pointed at a wooden chair behind me that was in the same style as the couch. "Sit."

She and Ophelia pulled up similar chairs and sat beside the worktable.

"What have you learned about Ebenezer White?" Morgana asked, hands folded in her lap, not an emotion evident.

"He's *the* founder of Raven's Hollow. What's more, his name is on Cleantha Wren's land deed. Before crossing the Atlantic from Wales, she purchased the land under her father's name, but after she arrived, the laws prevented her from taking possession until Ebenezer stepped in. I've seen the document, the hand-drawn maps, and the articles about Clea's and Ebenezer's engagement. I've also seen this."

I pulled out the note Willow had found and handed it over. Morgana read it, her mouth turning down at the corners. She handed it back. "It's as I suspected."

I stared from Ophelia to Morgana. "Were they engaged? Are we the product of Ebenezer White?"

Ophelia's mouth slackened. "Grandmother?"

Morgana rose abruptly. "They were in love, yes." She strode for the counter, reached behind the jars, and touched something on the wall. With a creak and groan, the wall slid forward a few inches.

"Whoa!" I leapt to my feet.

"Come." Morgana beckoned with her finger and disappeared behind the false wall.

Ophelia's hands fell to her sides, but she followed our grandmother as I looked on in disbelief.

"Are you coming?" Ophelia asked.

I walked forward. There was another room, about the same size as the sitting room, hidden behind the false wall. Jar-filled shelving lined the walls from waist high to the floor. They were crammed with herbs, bugs, and what appeared to be dried fruit. In the center was yet another worktable filled with wax paper, hemp string, and linen bags. Above the shelving were portraits marked with plaques. Morgana admired the first portrait on the right.

"Skylar and Ophelia, meet Cleantha Wren. She's our matriarch."

We both approached.

"But... but that's..." Ophelia gaped.

"Oh my gosh." I openly stared at the blonde woman, her emerald green eyes reflected back at me. I extended a trembling finger in her direction. "That's me."

Morgana moved over to the portrait on the opposite facing wall. "This is who you're wanting to ask about."

I tore myself away from my mirror image and walked over to stand beside Morgana. A wavy-haired twenty-year-old woman with kind eyes and creamy white skin stared back, a glimmer of mischief to her eyes. The plaque read Charlotte Winthrop.

"Wait," I said. "This is the woman in the article. Ebenezer was engaged to her, not Clea."

"Ebenezer was a complicated man," Morgana replied.

"Meaning?"

"He loved Clea with all his heart, but she refused to marry. In proper society, he had no choice. Ebenezer took a wife."

"That was Charlotte Appleton."

Morgana lowered her head and made her way to a couch by the back wall and sat on the edge. "It was a secret marriage. When he died—"

"No one knew?" I asked, eyes bulging. "Then what happened to Charlotte?"

Morgana pulled at a black thread on her skirt. "She married Ebenezer's best friend from Boston. Noble Foster."

Chapter 33

"Nobel Foster?" I asked, staring at the portrait of Charlotte Appleton.

Morgana motioned to the couch where all three of us sat behind a coffee table. She flipped open a photo album and turned to a page. "This is a copy of Charlotte Appleton's portrait, and this one is of Noble Foster. Charlotte bore a son, who was also named Noble."

"After his father?" Ophelia asked, her head bent over the album, studying the portrait.

Morgana flipped to the next page. The birth record of Noble Ebenezer Foster was beside a written note.

Loving and kind lady,

We are of good fortune to receive from the most high a healthy baby boy named Noble Ebenezer Foster. It is with great privilege that I call him son. His mother fares well and sends her best wishes. You may come as you wish and at your pleasure for this would never have come unless by your hand. We wish you most well and humbly thank you.

Noble Henry Foster

I pointed at the letter. "Clea arranged this. Noble Ebenezer isn't his son, is he?"

"He is not." Morgana turned the page. "Noble Ebenezer was the offspring of both Charlotte and Ebenezer. As I said, they married in secret. Less than a month later, Ebenezer passed, and poor Charlotte was in dire straits. Unmarried pregnant women, regardless of nobility, never fared well in those days. Cleantha intervened and arranged the match between Noble Henry Foster and Charlotte. Noble Henry loved Charlotte, and she was grateful to him for taking on her son as his own. Charlotte's son grew to become a prominent businessman."

"Was anyone else aware of this at the time?" I asked.

"No. Clea, Charlotte, and Noble Henry all arranged for this to be kept secret. Clea took it to her grave, and neither Charlotte nor Noble spoke a word of it. Any documentation shows Noble Henry Foster as the biological father, and no one questioned it. They ran in the same circles in Boston, and they'd always been friendly. Most Bostonians understood Noble's infatuation with Charlotte."

"Brooklyn's been researching her background. Lizzy said she's searched land rights and family records, including the Irwins, the Chamberlains, the Fosters, and the Collins."

My cell buzzed. It was Ryan. I held up a finger to Morgana and Ophelia. "Hello?"

"*What were you thinking? Breaking and entry is illegal. Worse? It almost got you killed. Are you insane?*"

"You have video surveillance," I mumbled, fingers to my lips.

"*Who doesn't these days?*"

"Did you see who attacked me?"

"Someone attacked you?" Ophelia asked, in shock. "When?"

"*They wore a ski mask and all black. There's no direct picture, except their frame, which if I were to guess was female.*"

I cursed under my breath.

"*What were you doing in my office?*"

"Why do you have a file on the Wrens?" I countered.

Morgana shut the album, stood, and walked around the couch, putting the album between a couple books on the shelf.

"*You got onto my computer?*"

I held the phone out from my ringing ear and waited for the tirade to stop. "Answer my question. Why is there a file on my family on your computer, Ryan?"

Morgana strode across the room while Ophelia and I looked on.

I covered the phone speaker with my hand. "Hey, where are you going?"

"*Brooklyn believed we're related to the Wrens, and she was determined to prove it. When Hazel asked about the land rights, I kept a copy and did some digging.*"

"Morgana, stop," I whispered as Ryan kept on.

"*Sky, there's something else you need to know, but maybe you've already found out since you've broken into my office. Anyway, even if you wanted to sell Honeysuckle House, you couldn't. There's a petition against the will.*"

"A petition? By whom?" I asked.

My grandmother made it to the false wall and turned, her face a stone mask.

"*I'm sorry, Sky, but Morgana claims to be the legal owner of Honeysuckle House.*"

I hung up and stared at my grandmother.

"Why are you fighting the will?"

Ophelia leaped up from her seat.

"Morgana? Is it true?" Ophelia's arms fell to her sides.

A rigid glare appeared on our grandmother's face. "Honeysuckle House is mine. It was never meant for Hazel. I'm the one with the gift." She pounded her palm against her chest, her cheeks flushed.

I drew myself up to my full height, flexing my fingers and drawing them into fists. "Did you kill Hazel?" My voice was low but measured.

Morgana jutted out her chin, nostrils flaring. "Hazel was my sister. Honeysuckle House is my home. It's my life."

I recoiled, swallowing hard. "You disgust me."

I briskly made my way to the door, pushing past her and picking up speed until I reached the outside, taking deep breaths of the cold air. Doubled over, I rubbed my sweaty palms on my thighs.

"Skylar, I didn't know." Ophelia appeared on my left, her arms clutched to her chest. "Please, Sky, you've got to believe me. She's mad."

Brrring!

I swallowed the bile that had leapt into my throat and drew in a breath. "What's up Trixie? Now's not a good time."

"*Sky, he stopped breathing. I don't know what happened. One minute he's fine, then the next he's not. He's blue. He's blue and—*"

"Whoa. Slow down, Trix. Who's blue?" I placed a finger on my other ear, unable to make out her words amidst her sobbing.

"*Nuri!*" she wailed. "*Nuri's ill. They're doing chest compressions. Sky, I don't think he'll make it.*"

Chapter 34

I bolted down the drive, legs pumping faster and faster until I hit the main road. My lungs were on fire, but I kept sprinting down the road towards town. The hospital lay on the outskirts a little over two miles away.

Tires from a passing car sloshed dirty snow onto my boots, and the passenger window rolled down. "Get in."

I yanked the car door open and threw myself in, snapping my seatbelt as Ophelia jammed her foot on the pedal.

"Is it Willow?" Ophelia cast a worried glance at me.

I kept my eyes focused on the road.

We arrived at the emergency room doors five minutes later, and I hopped out of the car before it came to a stop.

Nurses and doctors swarmed one particular bed, and I made a beeline for it. A pink-scrubbed woman straddled Nuri on the bed, rhythmically rising up and down performing chest compressions while another filled a syringe full of a clear liquid and jammed it in his thigh. A firm hand landed square on my chest.

"Stop!"

My leg muscles tightened, ready to run. "He's my friend!"

"Miss, your friend is in good hands. You're tying up valuable space and time."

Gasping for breath, I observed my surroundings and clung onto the male nurse, his bruising grip unwavering. He guided me to the waiting room. I started shaking uncontrollably, staring but seeing nothing.

"Sky? What's going on?"

I blindly stared into my sister's milky brown eyes swimming with concern.

"Nuri," I gripped her hands so hard my knuckles turned white, "he's in cardiac arrest."

"Sit." Ophelia lowered me to a chair. "Stay here. Let me handle this."

Off she jogged, raising her credentials to the triage nurses, who buzzed her into the emergency room. Fifteen minutes later she was back, Trixie in tow. She knelt in front of me while Trixie stood quietly behind her, shoulders slumped.

Ophelia took my hands. "Sky, he's stable."

Unable to hold back, I let out a sob.

Ophelia gently stroked my hands, her brow knit together. "He's not out of the woods."

I eyed the exit as the room closed around me. "I don't understand. What happened?"

"From what I gathered, Nuri's been poisoned."

The room spun. "Poison? What poison? When?" I licked my dry lips, haunted by the images of his lifeless body and the way it contorted from the electric shock.

"We don't know yet. They're doing blood tests. We'll get the results as soon as possible. The best thing for you and Trixie to do is wait here. I promise he's in good hands, Sky. He's in the best place possible. Let me handle this."

Her athletic frame crossed the waiting room and disappeared into the emergency room.

Trixie sat beside me. "It happened so fast. We were talking about Willow and how she needed pink nails when he got dizzy. I raced to get him a chair, but he collapsed. Sky, I'm so sorry." She sniffled, dropping her head in her hands.

"No, honey." I rubbed her back. "It's not your fault."

It wasn't. The blame was all mine. If I hadn't brought them here, then Willow would be off on a wild date in Colorado, and Nuri would already be in New York. And poor Trixie. She's such a sensitive soul.

"Sky," Ophelia called out from behind the ER doors. She beckoned us both over. "Follow me."

Trixie looked at me hopefully as we filed in behind Ophelia. Gone were the crash carts and rush of healthcare professionals. The ER room curtains were drawn, obscuring prying eyes. We arrived at Nuri's, and Ophelia drew the curtain aside.

I latched onto Trixie, a smile spreading across my face.

"Nuri?"

"Hey, ladies. Don't look at me. They took my wig."

I ran forward, hugging him so tightly he squealed. "You're suffocating me!"

"You gave us a fright. Don't ever do that again." Trixie playfully patted him on the shoulder.

Nuri pushed himself up in bed, a palm to his head. "I don't know what happened."

"What were you doing ten minutes before the dizziness?" Ophelia asked. She stood by his feet, holding a tablet, scrolling through his chart.

Nuri tapped a purple fingernail against his chest. "We were talking about Willow, and I said she'd look good with pink fingernails. Then the dizziness hit. I set the drink down and then everything went black."

Ophelia's head snapped up. "Drink?"

Nuri nodded. "Some soda. Nasty, I know, but when in Rome, right? It's not like hospitals are known for their fine cuisine and beverages."

"Was it from the cafeteria or vending machine?" I asked, fluffing his pillows.

"Neither."

Ophelia frowned. "Then where did you get it? The nurses' station?"

"Ryan stopped by to check on Willow." Nuri snatched my hand from tucking the sheets up to his chest and squeezed. "He's a nice guy, Sky."

"Ryan?" I asked. "He gave you the drink?"

"Yes, uh, no. Well, they both had it," said Nuri.

"Both?" Ophelia set the tablet on the sink counter.

"Ryan and Brooklyn Irwin. She's the one who handed me the drink."

"Where's the can?" I immediately looked into the trash can.

"It's not in here. We were with Willow."

Ophelia and I both bolted, leaving Trixie and Nuri staring at us, perplexed.

"Are you thinking what I'm thinking?" I asked, eying my sister, who jogged the remainder of the ER rooms, shoving aside the curtain of the last one.

The white bandages on Willow's face were stained dark red, her long brown hair clinging to the side. Her face was pale, and she lay motionless, except for the gentle movement of her breathing. The monitor beeped in sync with her heartbeat, while IV lines extended from her arms and hands, connected to various bags on a nearby pole.

I peered over at Ophelia as she snapped a purple glove on her hand, bent over, and pulled out a soda can from the trash can.

"Bingo," she said, hoofing it to the nurses' station, me right behind her. "Have this tested for narcotics, digoxin, and insulin, ASAP. It's urgent."

The nurse took the can and disappeared down the long corridor while my sister and I walked back toward Nuri's room.

I laid a hand on Ophelia's shoulder two rooms away to stop her. "First Willow, now Nuri." I paused. "I think they should leave."

"Leave?"

I leaned closer to her, whispering, "Someone's attacking my friends. Trixie will be next, and I can't..." I choked on the last word.

"Hey, we won't let that happen." She took both my arms and stared directly at me. "We won't. Trust me. Let's get the latest labs back, and then we'll talk. Alright?"

We returned to Nuri's room and unexpectedly encountered Dr. Joshua Moore.

"Dr. Wren." He extended his hand, smiling widely. "It's a pleasure. You looking for a job? We've got a position open if you're interested." He looked at me. "She's quite the medical doctor, Skylar. I bet she kept all of you on your toes growing up."

I crossed my arms and painted on a smile. "You have no idea."

"Dr. Wren?" The nurse from moments before stepped into the room and tapped Ophelia on the shoulder. "We received preliminary reports from earlier. The latest will take another hour, but I thought you should see these."

Ophelia took the tablet and scoured the page. Her eyebrows shot up. "Nuri, do you have a heart condition?"

"What? No."

"So you don't take heart medication?"

"Ophelia, what's with the third degree?" I asked.

Ophelia handed me the tablet and pointed at the potassium level.

"What am I looking at? This is all Greek to me."

Ophelia slipped her hands into her jean pockets. "Nuri's potassium is elevated. It's a standard panel we run when someone is admitted. If my suspicions are correct, someone laced his drink with digoxin."

"How easily accessible is digoxin?"

"In a hospital? Easy. It's commonly used for heart failure and arrhythmias."

Dr. Moore stepped toward Ophelia, lowering his head toward hers. "You suspect someone in the hospital did this?"

"Most likely," Ophelia replied.

"Which is why we need to get them out of here. Isn't there a nearby hospital they can be moved to?" I asked Ophelia.

"Sacred Heart in Hartford could take them," Joshua suggested. "I can arrange it if you'd like. No one has to know except us."

Ophelia nibbled on her lower lip, a trait I'd also inherited. "Do it."

Joshua left, calling someone on his cell, and disappeared down the hall.

Nuri stared at Ophelia and me. "Where are we going? What about Willow? And Trixie?"

I rubbed his feet over the blankets while his voice rose. "Everyone's leaving. You're safer in Hartford until we get this all figured out," I said, trying to sound reassuring.

"No, I'm not leaving you. Someone's out there trying to kill us, and you're next. We're safer in numbers."

I puffed out my cheeks. "Nuri, I appreciate the sentiment, but both you and Willow are in the hospital. You're no match for a killer right now, and it would bring me great peace of mind to know you're all safe. Please, do this one thing for me. Please?"

Nuri was stubborn, but also pragmatic. "Fine, but watch your back, Sky. No heroics."

"Agreed."

When Ophelia and I turned to leave, Nuri said, "Oh, one more thing. The Irwins weren't the only ones who brought gifts."

My skin prickled and I turned around. "Who else?"

Nuri took deep breaths, his gaze flitting around the room. "Uh, don't get mad."

"Who, Nuri?" I demanded.

"Morgana. She brought us coffee and baked scones."

=

Chapter 35

"Where are the cups?" Ophelia asked while I paced to the nurses' station.

Planting my hands on the counter, I lowered my head and silently counted to ten. Ophelia had sent a nurse to retrieve yet another cup from another trashcan outside of Willow's room. She was telling my fidgeting friends the evacuation plans, but I was lost in thought. My own grandmother. Was she a murderer?

"Sky?" Ophelia called. "It's time."

I wiped my cheeks, blinking rapidly before turning. Clapping my hands together, I walked to them, hugging them each in turn.

"Take care of yourselves. I expect an update on Willow whenever you can." I squeezed Trixie's hand. "Love you."

I stormed off, stopping at Willow's room. Her serene expression reminded me of Snow White. Bending over, I brushed her forehead with a kiss. "I promise you I'll find whoever did this to you. You focus on getting better, you hear?"

Stepping away, I blew her a kiss and fled. Out the back door, I ran to the exit. With a clunk, it closed, and I slumped against the chilly brick wall, allowing the tears to pour until I was completely drained.

On the Uber ride to the B&B, Ely called.

"Honeysuckle House is officially yours."

I snorted. "Not if Morgana has a say."

"Ah, family trouble. That didn't take long. You two were always oil and vinegar."

I blew into a tissue. "I hate it when people say that. Oil and vinegar make the best salad dressing."

Ely's rich chuckle tickled my ear with the vibrations. *"Whatever you say, Sky. I can wait for you here to give you the keys, or I can place them somewhere to retrieve if you'd like."*

In high school, I'd risked life and limb telling Ely where our spare key was hidden. Morgana never found out, but if she had, I'd probably still be in the cellar, a bag of bones by now.

"Leave it under the rock. Thanks, Ely."

We hung up, and I redirected the driver to Honeysuckle House after grabbing my bags at the B&B. When I entered Hazel's room, I was covered in sweat from carrying the bags up the stairwell. The police left everything messy, so it took an extra hour to tidy up.

I glanced around the room, taking in all the details. It was like Hazel could walk in at any moment.

I ran a brush through my untidy hair, undressed, and took a long shower, wrapping up in Hazel's old bathrobe afterward. Stepping into the bedroom, I sank onto the bed, staring up at the pink and green tatted ceiling. I curled into a fetal position and something crinkled under my fingers.

I sat up, smoothed it out, and recognized Hazel's distinct handwriting.

Be they noble, be they foul

Man's fortune lies within

I read the message over and over again.

"Man's fortune?" I mumbled. "Be they noble...?"

Could this be?

The inheritance.

Knock, knock.

Disbelief turned to shock.

The man who'd rescued me from the cellar, the same man who'd greeted me in the parlor that first day, now stood in the doorway, intently staring at me.

He wore a pair of khaki pants, a navy button-down shirt, and brown loafers. A grin spread across his face as he stared down at the letter on the bed.

"Ebenezer," I said, and he glanced up at me. "You're Ebenezer White, aren't you?"

Hands in his pockets, he leaned against the doorframe. How did he not fall right through?

"Clea, you're more beautiful than ever. I can't believe I didn't recognize you in the parlor that first day. It must have been your distracting clothing."

Rising from the bed, I moved across the room. He remained completely still, watching me intently. A foot in front of him, I reached out a finger, poking him.

He was solid.

With a trembling finger, I traced his face. He closed his eyes and sharply inhaled, causing my breath to catch.

"I've missed you." His voice was low and deep.

He opened his eyes and stepped forward. I craned my neck and searched his face. There were similarities between the two other gentlemen I'd encountered. That same wistful smile, the lean, sturdy shoulders, and those gentle eyes. I could get lost in them.

"H-How?"

His lips parted and he brushed my hair away from my face. His touch made my heart leap.

"Clea, I've messed up." He cupped the base of my neck with his hand and rubbed his thumb up and down, making my pulse jump. "You should have married me. We could have stopped them."

Tears prickled my eyes. "I'm not Clea." His hand froze on my neck. I placed my hands on his chest and pushed, stepping back. "I'm Skylar Wren."

He narrowed his eyes. "Skylar?" He dropped his hands by his sides. "I don't understand."

I let the tears fall. "Clea's my ancestor. It's 2023."

He rubbed his jaw. "It can't be. Clea, it's me. Ebenezer."

My chin quivered. "I'm Skylar." My voice sounded empty, distant.

I went to the bed and retrieved my phone, showing him the first news channel I could find, and played it for him.

His eyes bulged but then he stepped forward and took the phone. "No," he whispered, "this can't be. You look exactly like her." He lifted a hand toward my face but dropped it halfway.

"Ebenezer, what is the last thing you remember?"

He handed back my cell. He blew out air and sat on the edge of the bed. Scrunching up his face, he said, "Um, I was riding. Yes, I was riding." His words came more quickly as his memory returned. "Hercules and I were riding the property line. Fences needed tending for the nuptials. Charlotte insisted." He grimaced at the memory. "I'm sorry, but you look exactly like Cleantha."

From the portrait in Morgana's secret room, I had to agree. We were identical.

"What next? You were out riding Hercules. Were you coming back? Going out?"

"I was returning. The house was just in view, but Hercules grew restless and he reared. Everything went black, and the next thing I remember was in the parlor when you arrived ..."

"Right. So, you've jumped a few hundred years."

He rubbed his hands down his face. "A few hundred years? What happened to Clea? Charlotte?"

"We'll get to that. First, why did you write this note?"

I scrambled toward my coat and dug out the paper, giving it to him.

Ebenezer lumbered to the window between the bed and bathroom. He drew the daisy yellow curtain aside and peered out, lost in thought. "I had my suspicions. There were fires, gunshots, and carriage accidents that on their own appeared accidental, but put them together..."

"Fires?" I perched on the edge of the bed, which better allowed me to study his clouded profile.

"Sarah, our maid, put out a fire in the parlor. A moment longer, and the house would have burned completely."

Ebenezer squinted at something in the distance. "Who built the barn?"

I shrugged. "It's been around longer than me. I could ask my grandmother."

He waved me off, staring out at the hazy sky. Soon, snow would fall, and everything would be coated in another layer of white.

I cleared my throat. "What about the gunshot?"

Ebenezer glanced at me. "Hercules and I were on our daily rounds, checking the posts and fencing, when a bullet grazed my trousers." He absentmindedly rubbed his hip as if remembering the event. "It wasn't enough to alert the constable. After all, it was hunting season."

"What about the carriage?"

Ebenezer stepped into the bathroom and picked up a perfume jar, sniffing it. "Someone tampered with the harness. Our horses broke free and the carriage careened into a ravine, killing my stable man." He set the perfume down and moved on to my toothbrush, inspecting it.

"Forgive me," I said, "I'm terrible at history, but didn't that happen on occasion?"

Ebenezer held up the toothbrush. "What's this for?"

I stifled a chuckle. "It's for your teeth. We call it a toothbrush. Dentists love them."

He cocked his head. "Dentists?"

"They're people who take care of teeth and prevent tooth decay. If you brush your teeth daily, it helps keep our teeth healthy."

Ebenezer fingered the bristles and set it down. "Carriages were looked after," he said, "but yes, accidents happened. However, the axle broke on an even surface. A gentleman witnessed the dreadful thing. He stated that the carriage careened unexpectedly and he saw the wheel flying off. Poor Branson stood no chance. When they investigated, they found someone cut a V-wedge into the axle. Branson took the carriage at the last minute." Ebenezer leaned his shoulder against the bathroom doorframe and stared at me. "I was to drive it that morning. Everyone in my household knew it."

He was right. Add everything up, and it reeked of foul play.

"Why not take all this to the police? I mean constable?"

"We handled things differently in my time. It was my word against his."

"His? A man killed you?"

Ebenezer's eyes widened. "Indeed. I dare not say a woman would do such a thing," he scoffed.

I struggled not to roll my eyes. He *was* from a different century.

"It's not past the realm of possibilities. Kaitlynn taught me that."

His gaze narrowed. "Who is this Kaitlynn?"

"She's my best friend." I glanced at my phone on the nightstand. She hadn't messaged me in a while, and I was starting to get worried. Although, I'd had enough on my plate since arriving home.

Ebenezer tread forward, each step calculated.

"What are you doing?" I asked, tensing.

"Trying not to scare you."

"Why?"

He reached out, tracing my face with his finger. "How can it be?" he whispered. "You're the spitting image of Cleantha." He dropped his hand by his side. His intense gaze bore remnants of hurt and yearning.

"So I've recently found out. My grandmother has a portrait of her." I drew my legs up underneath me. "May I ask you a personal question, Ebenezer?"

He sized me up. "I expect nothing less from a Wren."

"Why did you marry Charlotte if you loved Clea? I understand about societal demands and what was expected of you, but you were a man."

He cracked a grin. "Obviously."

"What I mean is that you had a choice. That has not been afforded to women for centuries, and even now we struggle. Why didn't you decide to stay unmarried?"

Ebenezer stepped over toward Hazel's chest of drawers by the bedroom door. He picked up a picture of Ophelia and me as children. It was a bright, sunny day, and Hazel had us swinging on the swing set. We'd pumped our legs so hard that day they hurt for a week.

"When Clea refused marriage, I bed another. Charlotte came from a prominent family, and she was what my parents expected in a wife. She came to see me two months later, telling me of our child to be." He tilted his head back, looking toward the ceiling, the strain of consequences evident. "It was a mistake. One I couldn't take back. I regret that decision. It not only hurt Clea but Charlotte as well."

"And your son."

"A son you say?" His eyes brimmed with tears. "What is his name?"

I bit the inside of my cheek. "Noble."

"Noble?" He grasped my hand. "Did Master Foster marry my Charlotte?"

The urgency with which he squeezed my hand melted my heart. "Yes. Charlotte married Noble within weeks of your passing. His name is listed as your son's father."

Ebenezer beamed. "She found my letter. The letter giving her the estate."

"What?" I shook my head. "No. I'm so sorry, Ebenezer. Your fortune didn't go to Charlotte or your son."

He stared at me for what felt like an eternity, and when he spoke, it was but a whisper. "Where did it go?"

"Chauncey Chamberlain. Your first cousin inherited lock, stock, and barrel."

Chapter 36

"Bachelor's son!" Ebenezer roared. He paced to the door and slammed his fist into the doorframe.

"Is that a confirmation that he's not your favorite cousin?"

Ebenezer hung his head against the frame.

I got up and crossed the distance between us. "Who do you think murdered you?"

Ebenezer's face was a flurry of anger. He wagged a finger at me. "He urged me to leave, go to Boston. I have a house there, and he said I'd be safer there while he figured out what was happening here."

"He was supposed to get to the bottom of the accidents you mean?"

"After the carriage accident, I'd had it, and when Chauncey suggested I leave for Boston, I adamantly refused. This was my home. My life. I don't run from problems. How did this happen?"

I held up my hands to calm him. "You said your will gave everything to Charlotte. Who had the will?"

"A will?" He looked confused. "There was one letter to Charlotte. Since I was unmarried, I wrote my lands and fortune were to be inherited by her. After I found out about her...condition."

"Ebenezer, I understand this is difficult, but think. Who knew about the letter to Charlotte?"

He stared down at me, hands by his sides. "Only myself, my maid Sara, Chauncey, and Noble Foster, my best friend."

"Okay, do you think any of them could—"

"No!"

"Right. Then what enemies did you have?"

"My father was an importer of silks, spices, that sort of thing. He owned lots of land around Raven's Hollow and Boston. Lots of enemies were made in his lifetime. Some of whom I inherited, I suppose."

Land was a hot commodity, and as an importer or silks and spices, Ebenezer's father was ripe for murderous deals.

"Ebenezer? May I try something? I promise it won't hurt, but you'll have to stand still."

He'd been pacing between the window and bedroom door so fast that I thought the rug would catch fire. Ebenezer halted at the foot of Hazel's bed. "What do you have in mind?"

I slowly approached. "Stand still."

Closing my eyes, I mentally reached out. Like fog on a humid morning, clouds floated, obscuring any mental view. "Give me your hand."

Ebenezer's touch was warm in mine, and the clouds cleared almost instantly. A man's face popped into view. He was of Ebenezer's age and time with dark brown hair and eyes. He bore a stern countenance, as one who considered himself above others. I focused on him and the vision twisted, so I was staring into the most inquisitive eyes.

"Clea!" I gasped.

Ebenezer yanked his hand, but I held fast.

Clea's lips moved in rapid fire fashion, saying, "Fleur de lis." She vanished, and in her place was a young woman with ivory skin and sky-blue eyes. There was a sadness about her. Unlike the others, she didn't hold my gaze. It was as if she was lost in time. A residual impression.

I broke free from Ebenezer. Beads of sweat dotted my brow and I brushed a hand across my forehead. On wobbly knees I stumbled for the bed, plopping onto the foot of it just in time.

"Fleur de lis... does that mean anything to you?"

"It's French." Ebenezer kept mumbling *fleur-de-lis, fleur-de-lis* until he stopped cold. "Wait. That's on Noble's family crest."

"As in Noble Foster, your best friend?"

Ebenezer raised he hands to his head. "Of course! The person who locked you and your companion in the cellar wore a signet ring with a fleur-de-lis on it."

I hopped up, grabbed my coat, my cell, and headed for the bedroom door.

"Where are you off to?" Ebenezer called.

"I've got to see a woman about a flower." I raced down the stairwell and out the door as fast as my legs could carry me.

I SCHEDULED ANOTHER Uber as I jogged down my drive, meeting it at the road. We drove into town, stopping at the local high school where bushels of flowers were being unloaded from hordes of trucks. People flooded into the gymnasium where a multitude of tables were laid out in rows, each with their own floral arrangements.

Raven's Hollow held the Holly-days Festival every year on Christmas Eve come rain, sleet, snow, or shine. Wealthy patrons barked at anxious employees, arranging flowers to their exact specifications. The winner not only got the bragging rights for the year but a sizeable donation to their charity of choice. The festival generally brought out the worst in people.

"No, not that way." Mrs. Chamberlain swatted the teenager's hand, snatching the silver vase away. "Honestly, Morgana, the youth these days don't know their heads from a hole in the ground."

My grandmother stood next to Mrs. Chamberlain in front of the high school stage, which was reserved for the winners and judges' panel. At the stage lip, the three judges observed the busy bees below working on their tables, creating extravagant flower arrangements.

I weaved past a few harried young men and women sent off for fresh water, clippers, and ribbon when I caught my grandmother's stern gaze.

Her cold eyes followed me as she spoke. "I'd say they've forgotten where they've come from. A shame really. There's no place like home."

Mrs. Chamberlain patted her helmet head of hair and admired her latest concoction of red and yellow.

I picked up a stiff, hairy, upright stem that branched in multiple directions. The oval leaves clung to the stem and on top bloomed the brightest red, dome-shaped, toothy petals. Spinning it between my thumb and forefinger, I inhaled.

Huh. No smell.

I picked up another red flower. It was double the height of the first. The bloom size was larger but flatter than the first, though the petals were larger.

"She takes after you, Morgana," Mrs. Chamberlain said approvingly.

I held up the two similar, yet distinct flowers side by side. "What are these?"

Morgana crushed an empty water bottle she'd used in the vases. Voss water. They spared no expense for these beauties. "If you'd paid attention growing up, you'd know the answer."

Mrs. Chamberlain stared at my grandmother as if she had suddenly grown antlers. "That's a great question, Sky." She plucked the flatter shaped flower from my hand. "This one is a zinnia, while the other you have is a dahlia. They're easily confused since they come from the Asteraceae family, like daisies, chrysanthemums, and sunflowers. Beautiful, aren't they?"

She inserted the zinnia stem she'd taken from me into the vase, fussing over its height with the other zinnias and dahlias.

"Aren't these summer flowers?" I asked.

Mrs. Chamberlain's face lit up. "Why yes, the zinnias are. However, dahlias can flower until first frost." She leaned over the table, lowering her voice. "We have our own nursery and horticulturist, but don't tell anyone. It's how we win every year, and I can't have Betty Allen win. She always wins everything, except this."

Mrs. Chamberlain winked and went about arranging more dahlias and zinnias in reds, deep purples, and yellows until they were towering in a mass of decadence. If she didn't win, I'd be shocked.

"Why the newfound interest in flowers, young lady?" Morgana asked, picking out a zinnia from the mass still on the table and holding it out.

I noted the head of the flower. A central head. "Mrs. Chamberlain?" I asked. "Would anyone else grow these up here?"

"No, dear. As far as I know, we're the only ones growing these two flowers, although Betty has her own horticulturist for roses."

"Mrs. Chamberlain, thank you. Thank you so much. You've been a tremendous help."

I stalked off, feeling the burn of my grandmother's stare boring into my back. The pieces were fitting together, but a few suspects were left. Next stop, the library.

Chapter 37

“ Hello, Skylar.” Lizzy greeted me at the library door, book in hand. “Here are the first records of the town leaders and their property lines. I've included another on the family crests and insignias you requested, but the book on poisons has disappeared. I'll take another look around the tables and see if someone has left it there.”

“Thank you, Lizzy.” I headed for the back wall. Lizzy had given me the code as long as I promised not to disclose it to anyone else.

The door clicked behind me after I walked through the book hospital and into the rear room full of the town's oldest documents. The second I stepped in a book slammed shut.

“What are *you* doing here?” Brooklyn stood by the section of town founders and stuffed pieces of paper into her jeans pocket.

I circled the room, keeping distance and tables between us. Everything about her screamed unease and suspicion, and with Willow and Nuri in the hospital and a killer on the loose, I could not be more careful. She had a huge motive to kill Hazel, and whoever *did* wouldn't think twice about offing me, library or not.

I sniffed. “I could ask the same of you.”

She was halfway to the book hospital entry. I scanned the table in front of me and grabbed a pen someone had left.

“You're smart.”

“Pardon?” I asked.

She gestured to the pen in my hand. “If I were you, I'd be aware that protecting myself is the only alternative.”

“Do I need protection?” I eyed the only exit door; I'd have to beat her to it. Would anyone hear me scream?

Brooklyn studied me for a moment. “Trust your instincts. Two of your friends are hospitalized at Sacred Heart. That wasn't because you believe you or your friends are safe.”

I angled toward the fire extinguisher against the wall by the furthest window, never taking my eyes off her. "H-h-how?" I licked my dry lips. "How do you know about my friends?"

Her hard gaze softened as she backed toward the door. "I'm not the only one who does. Ask yourself, Sky, who stands to lose the most?"

"What?"

"I'll see you soon."

Brooklyn backed out of the room. "Sorry about Hazel. She was a good woman."

I sank into a chair next to the fire extinguisher and exhaled. On the next table, a few books were stacked on top of each other. Setting down the books Lizzy had given me, I walked over and flipped one over.

Poisonous Plants sat atop *Lethal Medicine.*

I wandered back to my own books, flipping to the pages Lizzy had indicated with scrap paper. Record after record showed land markers and boundary lines along with their owners. If Ebenezer White had lived, he would have practically owned the whole town. Generous to a fault, he'd either sold cheap plots to those less fortunate or gave them outright, only taking a small portion of profitable crops or products produced from the land. He was the truest of philanthropists, which was in direct defiance of his father, who'd robbed, cheated, and stole his way to wealth. It seemed Ebenezer aimed to give back what his family stole.

"Finding what you need?"

Startled, I jerked, then relaxed when Lizzy breezed in.

"Sorry to say that the book of poisons isn't anywhere to be found," she said.

I motioned to the next table. "Is there a way to check who last had that?"

Lizzy picked up the book. "If they didn't check it out, then probably not, but let me give it a go. Maybe we'll strike gold."

Whipping out her cell, she tapped away.

"Ah, here we go." She frowned. "That's weird. Joshua Moore last checked this out a month ago, but according to our system, it has not been returned. Maybe he never took it home."

"Dr. Moore?"

"The one and only. Although, why he'd need a medical book when he's got loads of them at his office is beyond me."

"Exactly." I fumbled for my buzzing cell. "Ophelia?"

"*It's Morgana,*" my sister said. "*She's up to something, and it involves you.*"

"What?"

"*She's got it in her head that you're the answer to taking back the town. Whatever the blazes that means. Anyway, that's a heads-up. On another topic, I received Hazel's autopsy. It took some wrangling, but—*"

"Poison," I interrupted.

"*I'm not asking how you know that. Don't tell me you're privy to Nuri's diagnosis?*"

"That's all you, sis."

"*Sorry to say, but it's what I suspected. Digoxin.*"

I hunched over the table, placing the cell phone on speaker and setting it down. "I never doubted you."

"*This changes things.*"

"Tell me about it. Hey, what do you remember about insignias?"

Ophelia paused long enough for a set of beeps and alarms to go off. She'd been hauled into working at the hospital after all. "*Unless it's about the founders, then nothing.*"

"Were there any with a fleur-de-lis?"

"*That's fairly common in French ancestry, but yes. There was a family. Uh, let me think, it's not a founder family. That's from a guy named Foster, I believe.*"

"Are you certain?"

"*Positive. Morgana drilled it in me. I can't sleep without dreaming about it.*"

"Did someone say Foster?"

I'd forgotten Lizzy was in the room. She walked over from Brooklyn's pile of books.

"*Who's that?*"

"Ophelia meet Lizzy the librarian. She's been helping me research. Lizzy, please meet my twin, Ophelia."

Lizzy leaned her palms on the table and studied the maps I had been looking at. She pointed at a plot adjacent to Cleantha Wren's.

"Here. This was Noble Foster's. Ebenezer White sold this to him about a year before Ebenezer died."

I examined the plot of land, mainly counting the acreage, and sucked in a breath. "Geez, there's got to be over two hundred acres here. Ophelia, Noble Foster's land covered much of what Raven's Hollow boundaries are today, including the Chamberlains' and the Collins' properties. Lizzy, who owns this land today?"

Lizzy tapped on her phone a few more times, holding it up for me to see. "The Chamberlains?"

"The Chamberlains own the exact land that Noble Foster owned way back when? How?"

"They own everything except what the Collins gobbled up," said Lizzy. "Somewhere along the way, Noble Foster's descendants either sold it or lost it."

"Lizzy, can you find out who the Foster descendants are?" I asked.

"Sure, give me a second."

After another few taps on her phone, her eyebrows shot up. "Wow. I didn't see *that* coming."

"What?" Ophelia snapped.

Lizzy held the phone out for me, and I swallowed hard. "Huh. That takes the cake. Ophelia, Noble Foster's descendants are none other than Ryan and Brooklyn Irwin."

Chapter 38

"But the Irwins' land is tiny compared to what they once had. What happened?" I asked.

"From the articles and land sales, it appears that the descendants all fell on hard times," said Lizzy. "Over the generations, they sold what they had to in order to stay above water. The Irwins are currently struggling to hold on to what little they have."

"*Hang on, guys.*" Ophelia's muffled voice broke through in spurts, though nothing coherent until, "*Skylar, Willow's awake.*"

"Can I talk with her? Does she remember anything?"

"*Slow down. One thing at a time. Dr. Moore informed me that she awoke an hour ago. Her vitals look good and she's got a good prognosis.*"

I relaxed into the chair, feeling the tension release from my shoulders. "Thank God."

"*The only thing she remembers is a man and woman arguing. She may remember more in time, but these things are tricky. Sometimes they never remember. Hey, Jared? Would you please give Sky updates? Willow has her on the HIPPA form contacts.*"

"Who's Jared?" I asked.

Lizzy and Ophelia simultaneously said, "Dr. Moore."

Lizzy giggled. "It's his nickname. One of his friends came to town last summer. He had stories, let me tell you. Apparently Dr. Moore was quite the bad boy before his doctoral pursuits."

"*Hey, Sky. I'm being paged. Gotta run. We'll talk later about Morgana. Congrats about Willow. We'll drive up and see her whenever this stuff blows over.*"

We hung up, but I kept staring at Lizzy. "Jared Moore?" I tapped my finger against my phone. It sounded familiar, but where had I heard it? Searching the web, I came up with nothing for several minutes until I entered Jared Joshua Moore of Boston.

"Bingo."

Lizzy pulled out the chair beside mine and scooted close.

I enlarged the article titled "*Dirty Doctor,*" and read:

Dr. Jared J. Moore, of Boston, was arraigned today on charges of malpractice in regard to an underage female.

I skimmed through the remaining part of the article and settled back in the chair.

"Oh my." Lizzy snatched my phone away. "This is salacious. If the town gets wind of—"

"It's a problem."

Lizzy handed my phone back. "Should we tell someone? Surely the hospital has done a background check on him, right?"

I closed the books and stood. "Thanks, Lizzy. I appreciate the help. Would you do me one last favor?"

"Anything."

"Wait for thirty minutes and call the police. Tell them there's a break-in at Irwin Realty."

"Wait to call the cops?" Lizzy squealed. "Are you sure?"

I waved a thanks, calling out, "I'm sure. Thanks, Lizzy. Lock up after I leave just in case."

I rushed out of the library and into the parking lot where an Uber was waiting. Hopping in, I directed the driver to the realtor's office a short ride away. It gave me time to think and send a couple of texts. If my plan went well, we'd have our killer.

"Thanks," I said to the driver and got out when he pulled up. Sliding over a few icy patches, I made it to the front door and peeked in. The lights were off. I rapped a few times on the door, but no one came. Strolling around back, I waited by the alley entrance. The sound of tires caught my attention as a ten-year-old Volvo pulled up. I glanced at my watch; it was close to sundown.

The car door shut, and I squared my shoulders, inhaling a steady breath. "Hello, Ryan."

"To what do I owe the pleasure?" His husky voice left me wobbly. What I was about to say could have a permanent impact on both our lives.

"Shall we go inside where it's more private?"

Ryan opened the back door and held it open. I stepped inside while he switched on the lights.

"Let's go to my office," he said.

He led the way, and I dutifully followed, noting the portrait of a chestnut horse over his office chair.

I gestured to it. "Hercules?"

Ryan's forehead crinkled in surprise. "How...?" He shook his head. "It's time I stop underestimating you, Ms. Night. Or should I say Nightshade?"

I jerked my head back. "Nightshade?"

His eyes widened. "Maybe that's best left for Morgana. What can I do for you this fine evening?" He motioned to the seat in front of his desk. "Please have a seat. Would you like some coffee? Tea? Something stronger?"

I tugged at my earlobe. "Something stronger, please."

He opened a desk drawer and pulled out two bottles. "Pick your poison."

I grimaced, but he failed to notice.

"Tequila or bourbon? They are of the finest quality. That's something my father insisted on teaching us."

I smirked. "He taught you about hard liquor?"

He shrugged. "It's in our history."

"About that..." I accepted the offered glass of bourbon, leaving the tequila for him. "How much do you know of your genealogy?"

Ryan sat, leaned his elbows on the desk, and swirled his tequila in the glass before slugging it back. Refilling with bourbon, he leaned back and stared across the desk at me. "Enough."

He wasn't making this easy. "The land grant given to your family by Ebenezer White that you spoke of earlier, are you aware of how much was given?"

Ryan shook his head. "From what I've gathered through my mother, it was rather sizable. We lost a lot due to financial hardship. Oh, there was a story about losing a bet, but who knows if that's true?"

"Ryan, are you aware of the original owner's name of this granted land?"

He narrowed his gaze. "No, but from the looks of it, you do. The real question is, will I like what you're going to say?"

"How far back can you go?"

He set his glass on the desk and scratched his chin. "There's a Percivus Irwin, I think."

"So you're only familiar with the Irwin name?"

Ryan tilted his head. "Is there another?"

I knocked back the bourbon and licked my lips. "Mr. Irwin, why do you have a portrait of Hercules in your office?"

He frowned. "It was my mom's, and the last thing we've got of hers. Everything else was lost in a fire years back. How do you know the horse's name?"

He refilled his glass and tilted the bottle towards me in question.

I pointed to my glass and nodded. "Hercules was the horse of a town founder."

Ryan set the bourbon bottle down on the desk top with a thunk. His look conveyed a blend of fiery determination, icy detachment, and exhaustion. He swallowed. "Which one?"

"Come on, Ry."

We both jumped in surprise and my heart thumped against my ribcage.

"Hands where I can see them."

"Drake," Ryan raised his hands in the air, "what the hell?"

Drake Chamberlain stalked around the desk, stopping beside it, facing both Ryan and me. He waved the gun at me. "Hands up. Don't make me repeat it."

I obliged, hoping Ryan wouldn't make any gallant effort of defending me.

Ryan glanced at the gun nervously. "Whatever's going on, I'm sure we can come to an agreement."

"The Wrens." Drake sneered. "For centuries you've meddled. Why can't you leave well enough alone?"

Ryan glanced at me. "What's he talking about, Skylar?"

"Tell him, *Wren*. Tell him who he descends from." Spittle flew from Drake's mouth as he readjusted the gun in his hand, swinging it from me to Ryan and back.

"Ryan," I eyed the horse above his head, wishing Ebenezer could somehow reach through the portrait, "Ebenezer White had a child with Charlotte Appleton. They were secretly married right before Ebenezer died.

When she found out she was pregnant, she panicked. His best friend Noble Foster ended up marrying her to protect her honor, though it was more than that."

"Stop with the love crap and get on with it," Drake barked.

I closed my eyes for a split second and drew in a breath. "Ryan, you and Brooklyn are descended from that union. Noble Foster's name is listed as the father, but it was really Ebenezer White."

Ryan's taut face grew white. "Then... then that means...but wait." Ryan gaped up at Drake. "Why are you upset? What am I missing?"

"It wasn't because of a bet that you lost your familial lands and money, Ryan," I said. "It's because Drake's ancestor stole them by murdering Ebenezer White."

I shifted my gaze from Ryan's confused face to Drake's angry one. Sweat beaded on his brow, and his flushed cheeks stood out from the paleness of his neck and ears.

The pistol was pushed against my neck, its cold steel sending shivers down my spine. Ryan abruptly stood.

"Sit down or she dies!" Drake yelled.

Ryan sank into his seat, never breaking eye contact with me.

"It's okay." My voice shook. "It's okay, Ryan."

Drake pushed the gun deeper into my neck. "No, this is *not* okay. Why couldn't you stay out of it? You *and* your kind. Hazel didn't have to die."

"Oh God!" Ryan paled. "Drake, tell me you didn't."

Drake's face twisted with rage. "She meddled. What else was I supposed to do? She deserved it, but good luck proving it. Get up. Now."

He yanked me up from the chair with a bruising grip and pushed me into the corner near the file cabinets, signaling for Ryan to follow.

"Kneel," Drake growled.

I stood my ground.

"I said kneel, witch!" he screamed, cocking the gun and leveling it at my head.

"If you're going to shoot me, then do it," I said through gritted teeth.

He slammed the butt of the gun into my skull and I crumpled to the floor. Ryan lunged forward and grabbed the gun. Drake delivered a powerful upward punch and with an *oomph*, Ryan stumbled backward. Drake swung the gun around and fired.

"No!" The scream shred my throat as I watched Ryan's stunned face slide to the floor.

I scrambled over to him, supporting his head in my lap, wiping the perspiration off his sticky forehead. Hand cradled to his abdomen, Ryan closed his eyes.

"An appropriate ending to your life, Skylar."

I glanced up, my vision blurry, and watched him strike a match against the wall. "Happy burning, witch."

In slow motion, the match fell to the floor. Overwhelming fumes burned my nose, throat, and lungs and I coughed into my arm. The room erupted in flames, licking the walls, and leapt across the carpet.

"Run." Ryan coughed, struggling to pick his head up from my lap. "Run, Sky."

Drake vanished into the smoke.

I propped myself up on my unsteady knees, gripping underneath Ryan's arms. Despite my repeated tugging, he didn't budge.

"Leave... while... you... can..." Ryan said through another round of coughing. "Tell my sister... Sky... tell my sister."

The flames reached within inches of us. I planted my hands on the floor and stood. Lurching to the left, I fell into the wall. The portrait tipped sideways.

"Ebenezer..." I gasped, squinting against the blackened ash of paper floating in the air. "Ebenezer, please..."

As if by magic, he appeared right in front of me. A glimmer at first, then solid, he shouted,

"Go! Now! I'll get Ryan."

Tucking my head and holding my breath, I successfully jumped over the flames and hurriedly escaped through the back door into the alley. I bent over and wheezed in the cool night air. Red lights flashed all around and sirens blared.

"Miss? Are you alright? Miss?"

A firefighter led me to the firetruck and sat me down on the bumper.

"Where are you hurt?"

"Ryan..." I craned my neck to see past the firefighter. "Ryan's in there. Please."

"Miss, Ryan Irwin's safe. Someone pulled him out seconds after you came out. Can you tell me where you're hurt?"

I jumped up and gripped the fireman's yellow jacket. "The detective. Where's the detective? Someone's life is in danger!"

He stuck two fingers between his teeth and emitted an ear-piercing whistle. "Detective! Over here."

Through hoses of spraying water and cops securing the premises, the less-than-thrilled detective made his way over. "Ms. Night, it appears trouble is your middle name."

"Willow Youngblood! She's in danger," I blurted, wild-eyed.

I briefly connected the dots for him, and by the end of it, his nonchalance turned into action.

The detective's phone rang and he held it cell up to his ear. "What's that? Right then."

Stuffing his phone into his jacket pocket, he gave me a pat on the back. "We've got him. Dr. Moore's in custody. A minute longer, and she'd have been dead, Ms. Wren. Get fixed up here, and I expect you to give a statement first thing tomorrow morning."

With a tip of his head he stepped away and disappeared into the crowd of men and women fighting the flames.

Chapter 39

"I can't believe you. Like I'd kill my own sister," Morgana huffed. "Over a house? Please."

My grandmother flitted about the kitchen with a steaming kettle. Filling my tea cup, she set it onto the stovetop and sat opposite of me with Ophelia between us.

"It's not my fault you acted guilty." My body ached from the bruising of the gun and the first-degree burns I'd sustained on my arms and legs.

"What I want to know is how you solved it all," said Ophelia, sipping from her mug, knees drawn up on the chair.

"It was a team effort. At first, I suspected Brooklyn like everybody else. From her attitude at the funeral to her argument with Drake in the alley, things weren't adding up. Of course, it was their argument that changed my perspective a bit. Drake acted weirdly from the beginning. Do you remember him at the funeral? He was constantly on his phone, and he dashed off the second he saw a couple of guys walk in. The detective told me later that they were undercover agents. The Chamberlains are being investigated for tax fraud. Drake didn't seem like he loved Brooklyn, and she was also a puzzle. Anyway, Brooklyn was really on our side. She warned me in the library to be careful. What's so bizarre is that it was Brooklyn who locked me in the cellar *and* was the one arguing with Drake before he attacked Willow. She told me after the fire that she tried stopping him but he overpowered her, knocked her out. When she came to, Willow was already unconscious. She apologized for not sticking around, but she didn't know how to explain everything so she left."

"Why was Brooklyn researching all this in the first place? For what purpose?" Ophelia asked.

"The Irwins are in default on their mortgage," said Morgana. "They've lost a lot of money in bad investments, which wasn't their doing. It was their father's. He was a right nitwit."

"But what was she searching for?" Asked Ophelia.

"Genealogy," I said. "Brooklyn made a comment to me at the funeral. It was something about Hazel and family. She wasn't our biggest fan. Anyway, according to Ryan, she believed they were related to Cleantha and felt like we'd abandoned them centuries ago."

Morgana sprayed her tea across the table. "Horsepuckey."

"True," I said. "But she's not related to us."

Morgana sniffed haughtily. "I should think not."

"She's related to Ebenezer White," I stated.

Ophelia looked shocked. "He's the town founder."

"Right." I informed them of how I found all of that out thanks in part to Willow, Trixie, and Nuri, all of whom I'd already thanked profusely.

We met up the next day after the fire where I got to hug each of them. If it hadn't been for Willow, none of this would have been solved. The only solace I had was that my friends promised to visit once things had settled in New York for Nuri and in Colorado for Trixie and Willow.

"You can imagine their surprise," I added.

"Which is why Drake went mental." Ophelia hopped up and brought over the tray of scones, jellies, and jams from the kitchen counter dropped off by Ely and placed it on the table. "What will happen to the Chamberlain fortune now that we know they're not the rightful heirs?"

"That's for the law to decide. From what Ryan's attorney said, they stand a good chance of getting a sizable sum." I reached for a blueberry scone, slathering it with butter. "What about Dr. Moore?" I eyed my sister. "Will he see jail time?"

Ophelia vigorously nodded. "Oh yeah. He's done for. Medical license will be the first thing to go, although that's the least of his worries. He not only drugged Nuri, but he supplied Drake with enough insulin to kill Great Aunt Hazel. If it hadn't been for his past, Drake wouldn't have bothered him, and Hazel may well still be alive." Her lips quivered into a pout. "Looking forward, the hospital will do background checks on everyone regardless of how desperate we are to fill a spot. That includes me."

I smiled at her. "Does that mean you're staying in Raven's Hollow?"

"Part-time." Ophelia ate a spoonful of strawberry jam. "The rest of my time will be spent in Boston until they can find my replacement."

"Ophelia," I said, "no one can replace you."

Morgana rose from the table and refilled her tea cup. "That's neither here nor there. You're both here now. That's what matters, and neither of you are leaving."

Ophelia rolled her eyes at me and I stifled a giggle. It was great being on better terms with her. I hadn't realized how much I'd missed her over the years.

"Something's on the horizon, but I can't quite see what yet. I mean it," Morgana scolded, sitting down again. "You must develop those abilities, Sky, and fast. Mark my words. A storm's brewing, and we'd best be ready. As for my plans for the town you two keep whispering about, that'll have to wait. First, we secure ourselves from whatever is lurking. Next, the town. Besides, there's no sense in spoiling the fun."

Ophelia raised a brow. "Fun?"

Morgana smugly smiled. "You'll see."

I STOLE UP TO MY ROOM and flopped onto the bed late in the afternoon when Morgana and Ophelia finally left. When I heard the floorboards creak, I grinned.

"Hello, Ebenezer. I suppose I owe you a thanks."

I turned my head to face the door and snickered. He wore jeans this time and a t-shirt with Van Halen on it. "What's with the clothes?"

He looked down at the shirt. "Better get with the times, right?"

I patted the bed and sat, crisscrossing my legs. He sat in front of me, trying the same, but his legs didn't fold as well, and he gave up and laid them out straight beside me.

"You could have died," he said, his voice thick and heavy.

I patted his knee. "I didn't. You were there."

His palm covered my hand. "Don't take risks like that. I couldn't bear to lose you again."

My pulse quickened. "Eb, I'm not Clea."

A faint smile tugged at his lips. "Then how do you know my nickname?"

I froze.

"Clea was the only one who called me that." He leaned forward, his nose inches from mine. "I expect great things from you, Skylar, and I plan on sticking around to see it."

He kissed the tip of my nose, and in a blink he vanished. In his place sat a woman of remarkable stature, the spitting image of me. Her keen eyes smiled deep into mine. A flood of warmth and love emitted from her.

"Cl-Clea?" I gasped, hand to my mouth.

The woman grinned. "You've had an adventurous few days, Skylar of the Night, but there's still so much to learn, child. The winds of change are turning, and soon you'll be in a battle for Raven's Hollow and all the souls within. Pay attention to your lessons. There's no time to waste. Let's get started."

TO BE CONTINUED...

GET THE FIRST CHAPTER of Good Ghost, Dead Host here!

SUBSCRIBE FOR ALL THE latest news here!

Don't miss out!

Visit the website below and you can sign up to receive emails whenever K.D. Upton publishes a new book. There's no charge and no obligation.

https://books2read.com/r/B-A-UAPH-XWDVC

BOOKS 2 READ

Connecting independent readers to independent writers.

Also by K.D. Upton

The Daisy Day Mysteries
Mystery of the Charred Bones
Murder in the Orkneys

The Kaitlynn Dahl Mysteries
The Kaitlynn Dahl Mysteries e-book Bundle
Snapshot to a Killer
Graded for Murder
Key to Murder

The Protectorate: A Supernatural Suspense
The Protectorate
The Guardians

The Skylar Night Ghost Mysteries
Ominous Visions, Grave Decisions

Watch for more at https://kduptonauthor.com.

About the Author

K.D. Upton gained a broad perspective of life from living in multiple places as a child. She combines childhood experiences, her work in the healthcare field, and love of history to produce compelling works of fiction in the Mystery/Detective and Thriller/Suspense genres.

Read more at https://kduptonauthor.com.

www.ingramcontent.com/pod-product-compliance
Lightning Source LLC
Chambersburg PA
CBHW051339020726
47501CB00007B/2179